SPELLBINDER

i

BY THE SAME AUTHOR

FICTION

CRADLE OF SECRETS (As Emma Lorant)
LULLABY OF FEAR (As Emma Lorant)
BABY ROULETTE (As Emma Lorant)
THE GIRL FROM THE LAND OF SMILES
THOU SHALT NOT KILL

THE DOHLEN INHERITANCE trilogy:

THE DOHLEN INHERITANCE
HOBGOBLIN GOLD
LADYBIRD FLY

NON-FICTION

A VOICE AT TWILIGHT (*ODD FELLOWS Social Concern Book Award 1989*)
THE GROCKLES' GUIDE (with Jeremy Warburg)
SNACK YOURSELF SLIM (with Richard J Warburg)

KNITTING BOOKS
(As Tessa Lorant)

THE BATSFORD BOOK OF HAND AND MACHINE KNITTING
THE BATSFORD BOOK OF HAND AND MACHINE KNITTED LACES
YARNS FOR TEXTILE CRAFTS
EARNING AND SAVING WITH A KNITTING MACHINE
CHOOSING AND BUYING A KNITTING MACHINE
YARNS FOR THE KNITTER
THE GOOD YARN GUIDE
THE HERITAGE OF KNITTING SERIES
TESSA LORANT'S COLLECTION OF KNITTED LACE EDGINGS
KNITTED QUILTS AND FLOUNCES
KNITTED LACE COLLARS
KNITTED SHAWLS AND WRAPS
THE SECRETS OF SUCCESSFUL IRISH CROCHET LACE
KNITTED LACE DOILIES

SPELLBINDER

TESSA LORANT WARBURG

THE THORN PRESS

ISBN 978-0-906374-31-3

For my son Richard,

who always encourages me.

NEEDHAM, MASSACHUSETTS, USA.

Friday, June 12th.

He opens the letter, takes out the photograph. The ranch-style he bought his mother in Needham, skirted by woods.

'Come visit with me soon, son. The house is looking great.
You're all I have, Dwight, honey.
Your loving Mom.'

The trees pictured around the house remind him of his childhood, of Vermont. He really should drive out today to visit with Mom. Heck, he hasn't been out in quite a while.

A quiet Friday afternoon in early summer. No sign yet of the heat to come, a gentle breeze. Something – some vague but persistent whisper, a voice in his ear – prompts him to leave the city early. He smiles, anticipating Mom's pleasure, and drives along the freeway, humming in tune with Schubert.

A sudden, explosive sound. Gunshot! cracks across his mind, trembles his hands so he almost loses the steering. He sees the windshield split into long spikes. The glass mists up, dark grey at first, then a bright tinge of red. The colour intensifies, drips down. His hands sweat runnels on the steering wheel.

Dwight brakes, breathes in hard, knows his life depends on feeling his way. Blinking, refocusing, he sees no sign of cracks or colour. A car passes him, backfiring from a faulty exhaust.

The lilting of *The Trout* on his CD player lulls him a little, but he remains disturbed. He stabs his foot on the accelerator, exits the freeway. He drives along the familiar route, takes a left into Pine Avenue, turns into his mother's drive and skids to a violent stop. The front door is wide open. He hurls himself into the house, into the kitchen.

Mom's body flaccid, one limp hand twitching, dangling over the dresser. Her right arm, stretched out and motionless, is pointing towards the dangling phone. He sees blood down her front – a crimson lava flow.

At first he doesn't understand. Bringing up blood? A haemorrhage? Lung cancer? And then he sees her neck. Her throat is cut, wide open, slit. Three parallel gashes cut from ear to ear.

He trembles, shakes, stumbles against her. The body moves, the head lolls back, the widened slashes spurt blood. Bright scarlet, a rush of red he tries in vain to stem. He pukes, sinks to his knees, forces himself upright, then backs away.

He stumbles to the sink, runs the faucet, spreads his hands under it. It takes forever to get them clean. He turns again, reluctantly.

Bristles of hair across her forehead, pupils glazed open, stare at him. Her mouth, a round of surprise, cigarette sticking to silent lips.

He hears her say his name, calling him, yet knows that is the past. Her eyes, still blue, beam their dead stare through his. Tears gather, he turns away, turns back, hand hovering over eyelids.

Can't bring himself to touch her, can't bear to see her stare. He grabs the oilcloth from the kitchen table, clattering dishes, splintering glass. He drapes it over her – a shroud to hide her body, to diminish his pain.

He cradles the receiver, breathes deep, taps in 911. He needs their help.

CHAPTER 1

For a moment Dwight thinks he's lost her. His heart flutters fear. He gulps for air then stands quite still, squinting and straining to spot her in the dappled light of the West Sussex woodlands.

'You're all I have, Dwight, honey.'
'Sure, Mom.'

Dread clutches at him, then he breathes out. Overprotective again, he scolds himself. But Sheba is the only being he dares to love. He can't face losing her.

'Sheba!' he calls. His voice, urgent and pressing, sounds thin. He takes a deep breath in and tries again. 'Heel, babe, heel!' he hollers. A whole lot better, he tells himself; at least she'll hear that.

Nothing but the rustling of dead leaves, a squirrel scuttling in the high branches of the oaks above him. He peers round, panning the brushwood to his left, then eases a little as his feet pick up the vibrations of Sheba's paws pounding through undergrowth. Affection releases coiled muscles in his neck. He can already sense Sheba's love, feel her wet snout nuzzle into his body, see her gentle eyes melt at him. His fond thoughts are shattered by a sudden explosive crack.

Blasts of backfire pop his ears, panic him.

Gunshot? Dwight's mind fires at him, then floods with relief as he recognises the snapping of dead wood under foot. Why hadn't he kept Sheba on the leash? This is their first walk in the woods around his new home. He had no right to let his bitch loose in unfamiliar territory.

'Heel!' he calls again, insistent, loud.

The dog is coming back to him. Sharp hearing, intensified to supplement his poor eyesight, picks out the sounds of ripping. Dwight shudders. The image of barbed wire tearing at Sheba's glossy black coat makes him sweat.

She must be retrieving, he comforts himself. He senses, even before he can spot her, that she will have some sort of booty in her jaws, rushing straight back to bring it to him. She'll want to share it with him, want to enjoy his pleasure at her skill.

Unseasonably strong sunlight cuts through still bare branches touched with that soft green patina promising bursting leaf buds. Dwight tries to make out the body of his bitch among the camouflage of dark shadows and bare earth. The sun is bothering his eyes again. Not much, not yet, it's only just April. He relaxes. Sheba is by him now, whatever was in her flews spread at his feet while she stands back and pants.

The carcass is curved round Pop's wide shoulders.
'Pop's bringing home a deer, Mom!'

'Stay!'

Sheba stands, obedient, wagging her tail.

'Good dog,' Dwight whispers into her ear. 'Good girl.'

The tail swishes harder. The Labrador nudges up to Dwight as he squats back on his heels to get a better look at what she's brought. A small rabbit, he guesses, perhaps a baby bunny too terrified to run. He'll put it somewhere safe from Sheba, give it a chance to get away. He laughs out loud at his panic and leans closer, his short sight forcing him to bend right down, almost touching his bitch. When he's level with her eyes he pulls back, horrified.

Bright scarlet streaming down, a rush of red he tries in vain to stem.

Sheba's muzzle is oozing treacly wet – and dark. The dreadful scene still vivid in his mind brings back the cloying smell of recently

4

spilled blood. His pulse pounds, deadening his ear-drums, his senses. What blood is this? That harsh metallic odour transports him into the past, brings back his grief, makes him heave.

Pull yourself together, his mind hisses at him. Sheba isn't a killer, she's a hunting animal practising her ancient skills. 'Delivering to hand' he's been informed. Part of the deal of owning a retriever.

'All domestic dogs are descended from the wolf, of course,' Mrs Whirral preached at Dwight the time he'd gone to inspect Sheba at that lady's small kennels not far from Petersfield. 'But proper breeding, and proper training after that' – the breeder's severe voice brings back a vision of the schoolmarm in the little Vermont town where he was raised – 'assures you that you won't have any problems.'

Well, putting the best face on it to get a sale isn't confined to the US of A, Dwight grins to himself. He's hired Jock McClough to train his Labrador, right from the start. Jock is doing a great job with Sheba. The problem sure isn't lack of professional dog handling.

Sheba nuzzles up to Dwight. He lurches backwards trying to avoid the blood on her nose.

'We're culling deer, Mom.
Pop needs me along to help him skin his catch.'

Dwight puts his left hand out to save himself. It lands on something squelchy. So she's brought back a kill. Excited by the freedom of the woods Sheba must have hunted, brought back a kill. He feels his fingers tacky, wet.

He runs the faucet, spreads his hands under it.
It takes forever to get them clean.

The memory gets the better of him. He leans into the bushes and is sick. Even so, he knows Sheba is rooting for him. Whatever she's done her motives are loving – he just knows it. It's up to him to sort out what she's brought back.

He draws out his handkerchief, wipes his mouth, then scrapes the blood from his hand on a clump of grass. He holds his fingers close up to his myopic eyes: pretty clean. But they still reek.

5

Time to take a look at the mess on the path. He crouches, shifts Sheba to one side and puts a hand on her rear quarters. 'Sit, kiddo, sit.' He takes out his glasses, puts them on and forces himself to look at the bundle of fur.

A wild rabbit, a coney. Its white rump stands out from the tangled mass of grey streaked with dark maroon. He frowns. Dark maroon. Old blood, not new. Coagulated blood, not the runny liquid he's trying to forget. Sheba hasn't killed, she's simply retrieved for him the way she's supposed to.

Delighted, Dwight puts his hand on his dog's head and fondles her ears. She's about to get closer to him, but he commands her to stay. He's not going to risk blood on himself.

He trembles, shakes, stumbles against her.
The body moves, the head lolls back, the widened gashes spurt blood.
He pukes, sinks to his knees.

Slowly, gingerly Dwight uses his shooting stick to poke at the rabbit. It's oddly thin. He has to bend down again to find out why. It's slit all along its length from spine to belly. The full gaping slashes make the animal's body seem very long. Done with a knife, and with a hunter's hand. Three wide deep gashes along the animal's trunk.

There's more. The ears are practically cut off as well. Pink eyes glaze at him, staring, wide.

Her eyes are fixed, unseeing, dead.

Pink eyes – the rabbit bulges pink eyes at him. Mirrored by his own defect, feeling utterly despondent, Dwight turns back to the rabbit's body. It lies inert, exposed and vulnerable; just like himself, Dwight can't help thinking.

He listens intently: no threatening sound. But something's wrong. What kind of hunter slices up a rabbit for the hell of it? And was it alive or dead when it was slashed? Dwight stoops down again to see if there are further clues. Sheba moves up but, instead of stopping her with his hands, he remembers to use Jock's commands.

'Sit, Sheba! Stay.'

6

The rabbit's body isn't drained. Unlikely to have been cut while alive – something to be thankful for. So how did it die? A hole through one shoulder suggests it was shot.

No problem there. But the maiming of something already dead points to destructive psychotic behaviour. There's danger here – tangible, frightening. He straightens up, eager to get the hell out of the place. The *Financial Times* in his coat pocket catches at him.

He grabs the oilcloth from the kitchen table, clattering dishes, splintering glass.
He drapes it over her. Her eyes no longer stare.

Dwight fingers the newspaper, pulls it out. No way he can leave the rabbit lying there. Some other innocent passer-by will be sickened by it. He ought to bury it, maybe take the body with him, get rid of it back home. He feels involved, responsible even, annoyed. He sure hasn't taken the trouble to leave the US of A and move to rural England for this! Violent death is something he thought he'd left behind in Boston.

Dwight wraps the body up and wedges the package under his arm, trusting the thick wadding of pink paper to protect his clothes.

'Heel, Sheba!'

He's about to turn for home when he realises he's allowed the Labrador to wander off again, perhaps back to where she'd come from. He must learn to follow Jock's instructions, sound in charge when he issues commands. He should have put her on the leash when he had the chance. Nervous again he senses the dog is going to lead him into real trouble. Why doesn't he have Sheba trained to defend?

'She isn't a guard dog, of course,' he hears Jock say. 'If you want a dog with a gentle nature you're going to have to do without the aggression.'

The phone still swinging, off the hook.
She had no time to call for help.

Dwight is aware that the rabbit slasher – slashers? – might still be nearby. Lurking behind briars, hiding behind brushwood. He peers all round again, then grins. No real cover yet, too early in the season. Even if he can't see movement he sure can hear it.

'Sheba!' he calls. 'Stay, girl, stay.'

But the dog has gone. Not far, he's sure, but undergrowth has given way to wild rhododendrons. Last season's leaves, dark, dense, dispirited, are hiding Sheba from him. He has to find her, make a move to go back home.

He catches sight of her sitting motionless in a small clearing beyond the gloomy bushes.

At first he wonders why she's waiting there, stock still. Then he takes it on board. He's given her the command to stay. This time he sounded in control and she's obeyed him. He goes nearer and makes out a sort of platform built from fallen branches heavily laced together with twining vines. Children playing houses, he smiles to himself, a warm feeling stealing over him. It reminds him of the Vermont woods in spring.

Getting closer, he can see bunches of wilting flowers laid on the ground. He leans down. Wood anemones, a few scattered primroses, lungwort, a violet or two. Beyond the flowers several branches are plunged into the platform, catkins dangling. He smiles again. Handfuls of dead bracken fronds, stuffed into the crevices, make quite an efficient-looking level surface. A table to play having a meal on.

His look travels up and the smile freezes. A grey furry shape is lying across the platform.

Her body flaccid, one limp hand dangling over the dresser top.

A second body of a rabbit. He leans on his shooting stick and takes a moment to steady himself.

Her throat is cut, wide open, slit.
Three wide, parallel gashes cut deep from ear to ear.

The rabbit, gashed like the first, is laid out deliberately. The platform is an altar, the rabbit a sacrifice. This must be where Sheba found the first one.

Cold sweat forms on Dwight's scalp. This kind of set-up points

8

to a ritual, maybe a grotesque game. Teenagers copying horror stories seen on TV, perhaps.

He's about to unwrap and dump the rabbit he's carrying back on to the table where it came from when he hears the popping sound of twigs crackling underfoot. Someone – something – is close by, watching him. Dwight feels the urge to run.

Fear holds him pinioned. Poor sight has strengthened his other senses. He picks up a faint odour mixed with the smell of trampled earth, but all he can see is a vague shape looming over the rhododendrons. A tall slender light-coloured form which shimmers for a few seconds above the dusky green.

Dwight catches a brief sense of strong athletic movement. Pale, agile, lithe. He can't tell more and isn't staying to find out.

CHAPTER 2

It isn't so much the tree root as the bulky Balmorals which trip Dwight up. He needs boots for his woodland walks, but these are new, and far too heavy for his liking.

He's fallen on a bed of dead leaves and withered bracken. Helpless without his glasses he uses skilled fingers to brush through the debris, adept at feeling for the steel of his rims, the wedge of a thick lens. He finds them quickly. He's unhurt, but aware that someone is nearby, has watched him trying to run and seen him fall.

About to put his glasses back on Dwight feels himself jostled by a large brown shape. A four-legged animal. A young deer, perhaps, or a... The shape slinks past him, pads to his right, and begins to snuffle.

'Heel, boy!' A clipped curt sound, a low male voice. The animal turns circle, then darts past him silently, a streak of silver-brown.

'Damned hound,' the voice clips on. 'May I?'

Dwight clutches his glasses and, helped by strong hands, levers to his feet.

'Gee, thanks, I...'

'Yours, I think.' The tones are blunt and icy. The *Financial Times* parcel is offered to him.

'I guess...'

The thrust into his hands is firm and sure. Before Dwight can say anything more the figure, much taller than Dwight, strides off.

Dwight puts his smudged glasses on and stares after him. He can just make out beige cords, a shooting jacket.

Pop's rifle is still smoking. He bags the kill in his left hand.

He thinks he can see a rifle tucked under the man's arm, and the slinking brown beast plodding beside him, walking to heel. A poacher, maybe, and a poacher's dog. Some sort of hunting breed he hasn't come across before. These two weren't after him at all. Probably looking for deer, or maybe hare. The faint whiff of strong tobacco lingers for a moment, then Dwight is on his own.

All on his lonesome. Pungent odour of pines, the sigh of a spring breeze.

Nothing but the sound of the wind rattling last year's leaves, the chattering of woodland birds. He panicked, and all because of some other innocent walker. The man even tried to help. He must have appeared ridiculous, brandishing his shooting stick, plunging through undergrowth, falling down.

'Here, Sheba!' he calls, still holding the parcel. He relaxes as his dog comes back to him.

'Good girl.' He turns away from the direction taken by the stranger and moves through the tanglewood. The choking grasping brambles infuriate him. He brushes them aside with his stick, loses his fear, begins to push through.

The motor roars into action, the car tears away.

'Move it!' he shouts at his dog, forgetting the commands Jock taught him. Why did the stranger help, then appear so abrupt? Is he responsible for the rabbits? Unlikely, but he can sense a strangeness in the woods. Something odd sure is going on.

Sheba trots at his side, then runs ahead just out of reach. He still hasn't put her on the leash: too keen to get himself away to take the time to do so. No choice but to go after her.

What at first looks like a deer run is actually a little woodland track winding through to another clearing – maybe a proper path.

11

Unhooking the larger gripping thorns from his deerstalker he looks at the rough-chopped bramble shoots. Made by a blunt instrument, leaving long, slanting edges, some stained and old, some new. This track is used; not often, but every now and again. He pulls his hat down over his white hair and shoulders on.

At last a glint of light ahead, making his eyes water. Dwight drops the sunshades over his glasses and sees a small clearing. And beyond that, squat and solitary, backlit against a bright blue sky, a tiny cottage snuggles into the folds of mossy banks. Whoever lives here must be his nearest neighbour across the woods. Smoke is coming out the chimney. Someone is home.

Their cabin in deep forest.
Mom's flowers colour the front yard, hold back dark evergreens brooding out the light.

Dwight stares at the cottage. 'Tudor' it signals. Been here a long time. It belongs, tranquil and grown into the scene, the gold of Tenby daffodils speckling the gentle green around it. A simple stone-built cottage, reflecting sunlight, uncluttered by improvements. There are two flower beds of mingled pinks and mauves. Neatly cut grass stretches out, edged by espaliered fruit trees. Enchanting, a magic setting. The rabbit in the newspaper slips his mind.

He hears the thumping of Sheba's tail, then sees her prance forward, eager for fresh experience. Someone is there – a figure seated on a low stone wall sheltered beneath a hedge. Dwight, even with his glasses on, hasn't noticed her because she's camouflaged by long strawberry blonde hair which, to his eyes, blends with the russet of a beech hedge in winter leaf behind her.

Long grey hair is spread around her shoulders.
'This how you found her, bud?'

The figure is brushing the glistening mass. There is no face, her head is bent forward and the hair completely covers everything down to her shoulders. Dwight can't judge her age exactly, but fluid sinuous movements and twined slender legs suggest she's young.

'Sheba!' he calls. His voice sounds shrill. He tones it down. He doesn't intend to frighten the girl behind her living yashmak. After all, he and Sheba have obviously wandered on to private property. 'Heel, girl. Heel,' he repeats. Sheba promptly sits instead, panting, waiting.

The hairbrush, he notices unhappily, has stopped, frozen in mid-air. He feels the eyes behind the sheet of hair take him in. Then her head lifts up, unhurried, deliberate. The red-blonde curtain parts to reveal what he's sure are the unlined, almost blank, features of a young girl. He steps nearer, adjusting his glasses.

Jade green eyes brush over him. He stands, speechless at the girl's beauty. He sees her pupils widen. He's startled her, he should say something to explain his being there. But she relaxes the arm holding the brush as Sheba snuffles up to her, wagging friendship. The girl cups the hair on either side of her ears and tosses it back. She looks down at the dog.

Dwight takes his chance. 'I sure am sorry to impose.' He smiles, lifting the deerstalker in old-fashioned courtesy. He keeps his eyes lowered. Experience has taught him to allow the white of his hair to sink in before looking directly at strangers. His heavy sunshades often make people uneasy, but they hide the pink eyes until the white hair has taken effect.

He's older now, almost forty. The contrast between his features and the premature white is beginning to fade. To a young girl it might even seem quite natural.

'Sheba tends to get carried away with enthusiasm,' he says.

He risks looking up. Her lashes flutter, almost a smile. Dwight does his best to tone down his racing pulse. Even if she doesn't think him old she'll think him odd. He's resigned to that.

'That's quite all right.' Her voice is loud, almost the sound of an alarm. 'I expect she's surprised to find open space after all that prickly scrub.' The girl bends towards Sheba, but Dwight can sense her tension.

He steps closer, holding out the white leather leash. The scent of freshly-washed hair, mixed with a very personal odour, overwhelms him. The blonde begins to brush again, long strands flowing around her. He stops short, spellbound. He can't remember having seen

13

such lovely hair in all the years he's been working with top fashion models.

'Are you lost?' The hint of nervousness makes her voice high.

He sees her arms cross protectively and makes himself look away. He's embarrassing her. 'Not exactly.' He nods at Sheba. 'We haven't been in this neck of the woods before. We've always walked straight ahead down the wide track, past Oak Court, then on towards Lodsworth.'

'And your Labrador nosed out the footpath to our garden.' The girl's teeth flash white against the dark background, a hand stretches out and ruffles the dog's head.

Dwight hopes no blood has stained beyond the snout, and that Sheba has licked that clean by now. 'Right,' he agrees, clicking the leash into her collar. He puts the newspaper bundle by his side to do so. 'I live nearby,' he goes on, picking it up and pulling Sheba away, determined to get across his bona fide.

'You live near here?' she says. 'You sound like an American.' Her voice is louder, demanding an explanation.

'Guilty,' he agrees. 'But I've just opened an office in this country.'

'In Midhurst?'

'In London,' he says. 'Albemarle Street.'

He feels her eyes on the parcel. Perhaps she expects all Americans to carry a firearm hidden in newspaper. He's too old a hand at making young girls feel comfortable to give up now. 'Recently settled in West Sussex, I should add.'

He notices her gaze still directed at the newspaper, now somewhat damp. Best to try to account for it. 'Sheba's been displaying her hereditary skills.' He points at the package. 'I've had to cover for her.'

'Someone's been shooting rabbits and you're taking home a free meal.' She laughs her relief. And she seems to relax, whether because he's a neighbour or because he's explained the parcel, now clearly oozing reddish stain, isn't clear.

For a moment he feels she must have solved the mystery. Sheba simply retrieved one of the rabbits left from a shoot – ridiculous, he knows quite well it was slashed. But at least he's pretty clear that rabbits are often killed locally – shot or snared, for food or because they're pests.

14

'And you're from…?'

'I'm a Yankee. From Boston, now transferring my business to the UK.' He sees her hair move sideways, as though she doesn't believe him. 'I'm one of many searching for a gentler pace of life. I enjoy the peace and quiet of your lovely countryside.'

She isn't quite won over yet. 'You have more space in your part of the world than we do here.'

'There are other advantages. History, antiques…'

'And you've picked West Sussex?' Her head jerks up in challenge. 'So where have you settled?'

'Leggatt Hill,' he answered, readily enough. 'By way of Smithbrook.' He speaks softly, drinking in her long slender legs. 'Not far. Sheba and I moved there about two weeks ago.'

CHAPTER 3

'Good afternoon.' Fruity penetrating tones ring out across the grass. Dwight looks towards the cottage. His presence has been spotted – and calls for action.

A small dumpy woman marches her short legs across the lawn. An equally small stubby terrier is puttering beside her, barking at Sheba.

'I don't believe we've met.' The tones, mature and determined, are clipped into a message of dismissal. She stops to watch as the two dogs come together and start to sniff each other. 'And I don't think Raffy has come across your bitch before.' The voice softens at the reference to Sheba.

'I sure am sorry, ma'am.' Dwight tightens the leash, pulls Sheba towards him and doffs his hat. Waste of time. The lady is concentrating on the dogs.

The Labrador resists his orders. She has no intention of leaving the Jack Russell without investigating further. Dwight feels his glasses precarious on his nose and pushes them back. The lady of the cottage would have noticed his dark sunshades but there isn't a darn thing he can do about that.

'I'm Dwight Delaney, and this is Sheba.' He widens his mouth into what he hopes is a winsome smile. The owner of the Jack Russell is still concentrating on Sheba. 'I've recently purchased The Woolhouse. Somewhere about a mile across the woods. I...'

'Of course.' Relief registers in her voice, the round face swivels a brief smile at him. 'Myra Stanhope told me last week that someone

16

has just moved in. She's a near neighbour of yours.' She turns full face towards him. 'You've bumped into each other, I dare say?'

'I guess not. I'm only here weekends.' All the same, he seems to have passed a crucial test, though he's none too sure how. The house, maybe. The agent had called it a well-known local gem, a piece of English history.

'Ah, yes.' She looks him over from deerstalker to Balmorals. 'I'm so glad that neglected old house will have a new lease of life.'

So that's it. He knows the locals are hoping the old place will be restored to something like its former glory. Word must have gotten around. But the easy way she now accepts him is a surprise. On account he's taken on a local property?

Heck, he's also become a landowner. The Woolhouse has a good three hundred acres of farmland attached. Tiny by US standards, and anyways leased out, but expensive enough. That's what they all maintained back home. The law of property is paramount in the UK. Owning your country pile is what counts. Hasn't Harry – old buddy-buddy – always told him?

'You can forget those fairytale notions about 'gentlemen', pal,' Harry laid down the law only last week, grinning at Dwight. 'They get right down to business just like you and me.'

Nevertheless, Dwight shifts uneasily in his heavy walking shoes. He likes to think his clothes pass muster. Harris tweed, Harry insisted, convinced he's the one to tell Dwight what to wear: plus fours and spats. Sounds weird to Dwight, but Harry's been living in London for two years now. He reckons to know the score.

'My tailor swears blind his "gentlemen can't manage without their plus fours, sir,"' Harry passed on to him, making a mess of mimicking a Lambeth accent. Then his mouth widened to show gold, his hand touching his bare forehead to an imaginary forelock. 'Beats the hell outa me.'

Dwight finds tweed uncomfortable, scratchy on his delicate skin. But the woollen fabric does keep him warm, not always easy in the dank climate of his adopted country.

Sheba strains at the leash and Dwight tries to jerk her to his command, the way Jock instructed him. 'We didn't mean to trespass, ma'am. Sheba...'

17

'Trespass? What nonsense, of course not.'

The Sussex dumpling appears friendly, easy to get to know. Where is all that British reserve he's heard so much about? But he notices the decisive speech, and her sharp quick head movements. He can tell she's assessing his white hair, wondering about his sunshades. She says nothing further. Looks like he measures up. Except she's staring at the newspaper under his arm, seems to focus on it.

'We were just about to have tea. Why don't you join us? I'm sure we can find a biscuit or two for Sheba.'

The bitch is almost choking. 'Sit, Sheba.' Dwight pushes a finger into the space between her hip and her belly, so forcing her back on her haunches, just the way Jock taught him.

'Do let her off the lead.'

The Labrador shudders, caught between the terrier and obeying her master. Dwight is only too glad to let her go.

Her body twitches. A last long shudder.

He watches as it slithers off the dresser, slumps down, then bunches on the floor.

The parcel under his arm feels heavy. He has to put it down, his sweating palms simply can't hold it any longer. But where? And how is he going to stop the dogs exposing what's inside?

Peripheral vision catches the lady's dress bulge out. Pregnant? He's sure she's too old for that.

'Here we are,' she trumpets, taking her hands out of two large pockets, deflating her shape. 'Dog biscuits for good dogs.' She holds up two bone-shaped delights.

The dogs rush forward, close together. 'Just make sure you keep your bitch in when she's on heat. Raffy considers himself quite the local Casanova.'

Dwight laughs. Then he takes in the long stare, the turning away. He recognises the signs. His problem has sunk in.

'They won't play with me, Mom.'
'Don't heed them, Dwight honey. They'll soon tire of teasing you.'
He cowers in corners, alone at playtime.

Seems his albinism doesn't worry her. Her gaze is steady as she looks past him at the wretched package now on the grass. He guesses she thinks he has something to hide. The fact that it's true doesn't help.

'I'm Valerie Brooke,' she announces, crisp and clear. 'And you've already met my daughter Emily.'

'Tickled pink Sheba had the intelligence to locate such gracious neighbours.' He's amazed. He finds it hard to believe that the tall graceful young girl is the daughter of this short chunky woman. But he'll worry about that later. The concentration on his package makes him quite nervous. Is she about to demand to see what's inside?

'What's that you got there, honey? Looks kinda dirty. Didn't I say not to bring garbage into the house?'

'American atrocities in local beauty spot' Dwight can already read in the local paper. How will he explain what he's doing with the body of a slashed rabbit? Will they believe that he's only tried to avoid someone else coming across it? Put that way it sounds plumb crazy. He'll have to brazen it out. 'I guess Sheba's been making a raid on the local rabbits.' Same story he's used on the girl. He flashes more teeth, glad his inappropriate sense of guilt is hidden behind his glasses, and points to the *Financial Times*.

'Who did this to you, Mom?' he cries.
Fixed eyes stare, the jaw drops down. She looks astounded at what's happened.
'Mom?'
There is no answer.

'The evidence is buried in my newspaper,' he adds, laughing heartily and tapping the parcel with his stick. He draws it away, realising the point will tear the covering. Sudden hot perspiration turns chill, it's all he can do to control a shiver. He reaches towards Sheba and fondles her head. She responds, as always, by nudging her wet nose against his hand.

'So I see.' Valerie smiles indulgently, evidently unfased by the

19

misdeeds of dogs, or perhaps simply used to them. Just like her daughter she seems to find his explanation entirely reasonable. More than that, Dwight has a curious hunch that both mother and daughter are, in some mysterious way, waiting for a humdrum explanation. Were they expecting him to mention something else? Do they know about the altar?

At any rate they accept what he's told them, no doubt sensing the ring of truth. Nor do they seem to worry about his stopping by, unannounced. Are outsiders expected to visit with new neighbours? Should he have dropped in on Myra Stanhope?

'But we'd have met anyway. Emily and I are often busy in the woods. Gathering firewood, walking Raffy.' The terrier is wuff-wuffing, his short legs planted apart. 'He needs his walks. And occasionally we also pick up game the sportsmen leave behind!' She blinks at the newspaper. 'You wouldn't have been able to avoid us.' An almost carefree note now in her voice.

Dwight becomes aware that part of her bulk is a rug she's carrying, some sort of plaid, in the same kind of colouring as her dress. His colour blindness makes it hard to distinguish patterns.

Valerie spreads the rug on the grass and sits on it, patting it invitingly. Raffy and Sheba promptly make their move on to it.

Dwight's eyes are on the small building behind her. 'What a honey of a cottage. You folks been here long?'

'Since the late nineties.' Prompt, almost smug, as though waiting for him to bring it up. 'I've lived here over twenty-five years.' She pushes the dogs gently but firmly off the rug. 'I found Bramblings when prices were still reasonable, snapped it up. A proper gamekeeper's cottage. Stone built, with a fine Tudor fireplace in the centre.'

'Real Tudor?' His instincts were on the ball. 'Say, that's mighty uncommon.' Dwight is impressed. Her name is Emily, and she lives in a Tudor cottage, he almost croons to himself. A fragile nymph living in fairyland.

'Primitive, of course. We haven't been able to afford improvements. It hasn't changed that much since it was built, though we've added basic plumbing.' Her grin is elfin, puckish. 'We don't have electricity, and we pump water from our own well.'

'That a fact?' He doesn't much care for the idea of Emily pumping water. 'How in this world d'you manage?' He sees the girl tiring with the strain, winces. Maybe Valerie... No way. Sure to be a husband and father around. This is no place for women on their own.

'We're used to it. Calor gas for cooking. A bicycle gets us to the village.'

'You don't have a car?'

Valerie laughs, digging more biscuits out of her dress and feeding the dogs. 'We make do with one bike between us.'

'I hardly see your father any more.'
'Sure, Mom.'

Doesn't sound as though there's a man around.

'I hear you've had The Woolhouse done up very handsomely.'

Real country, the grapevine busy. 'In keeping with its period,' Dwight hurries to agree, 'but adding a few modern amenities.'

'I rather think it needed that.' Her face loses years as she drops her guard. He sees her as she must have been when young: freckled, slim, her eyes enormous in a tiny face. 'Last time I visited old Miss Nelson it was falling down around her. She wouldn't have central heating, of course. Said it would ruin the panelling. Last of a splendid line. Left it to her nephew, I hear. Sounds as though he wasn't interested in the place himself.'

'I guess not.' Dwight begins to relax. The nephew was keen to sell. Dwight is still glowing from the bargain. 'Lucky for me. I've put in humidifiers and air conditioning to make sure there isn't any problem about the woodwork. And to preserve the furniture, of course.'

'You like antiques?'

'To go with the house.'

'How very wise.' Valerie's eyes round into understanding. She looks, Dwight thinks, just like a little owl waiting to pounce on prey.

Emily's red-gold strands are drying in the warm spring sunshine. She stands up, stretches her long limbs and smooths down her skirt. She's kicked off her shoes, her feet almost floating over the newly-cut turf. Dwight's heart begins to beat fast as he swallows her with his eyes. Belly muscles coil tight as he sees her taking in his gaze, her own coolly assessing his. The green irises darken as she looks, unhurried, at his glasses. He can feel his blood drain from his head, making him sway. Will she now ask an awkward question, make some personal remark?

'Pink eyes, pink eyes,' the playground circle chants.
He runs, trips up, holds his breath. The school bell rings deliverance..

'I'll just fetch the tea things, Mummy.' Emily lifts her arms, flicks her hair with her hands.

She isn't repelled, she's encouraging him to stay. Gratitude brings the blood back to his face. It flames into smiles.

'Assam or Earl Grey, Mr Delaney?'

An irritating background hum has turned into a buzz, and then a choking sound. Disappointed, Dwight sees a car has driven up. A blood-red dented MG's wheels are churning turf at the top of the lawn about a hundred yards away.

'It's Alan.'

Emily, not waiting for Dwight's answer, sprints towards the car. A young guy, white shirt sticking to his back, shiny face ruddy, levers out. A head of straight black hair spikes at all angles.

'We're going out to dinner,' he calls. 'You'll have to puts on something ritzy.' He frowns at the faded cotton dress and, putting his hand on Emily's arm, steers her towards her mother. 'Hello, Mrs Brooke.' A flat noncommittal tone of voice.

He turns to squint at Dwight. A startled cough as he takes in the spats and plus fours, then he shifts back to Emily.

'Hello, Alan,' Valerie matches his lack of enthusiasm. 'Mr Delaney, this is Alan Penn-Winton, one of Emily's friends...'

'I think we could say fiancé, Mrs Brooke.'

'One of Emily's friends,' Valerie insists, not bothering to change her tone. 'This is Dwight Delaney, Alan. He's settling in this area.'

'Thought he must be the first of your summer invasion.' Alan shrugs clear disinterest but looks at Dwight and opens his eyes in a sort of condescending acknowledgement.

'What's wrong with that kid?'
'Lay off, Hank. Earl's kid ain't got no pigment in his skin, is all.'

22

Dwight moves the deerstalker slightly, drawing attention to his hair. He sees the white, as usual, signal age – and lack of competition.

Alan stares past him to the cottage beyond. 'How d'ye do.' He swivels, polished leather shoes cutting into the soft grass. 'The pater's waiting, Em. We're meeting at the Angel. Do hurry up and change.'

'I don't believe I heard you ask her if she wants to go, Alan.' Valerie, sitting on the rug, now hugs thick legs. There is defiance in her attitude, perhaps more than that. A call to battle, almost.

'You're not on the blower, Mrs Brooke,' Alan complains, hanging his head but flashing irritation. 'How could I?'

Already on the defensive, Dwight notes with amusement.

'Emily's just about to get the tea things.' Valerie, clearly aware of winning the first round, motions to her daughter. 'Use your mobile to ring your father. Tell him you're having tea with us. We've already invited Mr Delaney.' She turns her body away from him.

Alan scowls, scuffs the lawn, gets ready to follow Emily.

'I don't suppose you've heard, Alan. Mr Delaney's just moved into The Woolhouse. He's our new neighbour.'

He stops short. 'You've rented that tumbledown old barn of a place?'

'I purchased it about four months back and had it done up.' Dumbass. 'Moved in roughly two weeks ago.'

'So you're the mystery owner.' Alan sways back and forth. 'Going to take a bit of doing to get it round.'

Dwight sees his standing has changed – what was it Harry insisted? 'Get yourself one of those gentleman's country residences they're so set on and they'll take notice. They won't accept you, sure. But they'll take notice.'

'Of course the place has death-watch beetle. You know about that, I take it?'

'I guess not.' He's had a thorough survey done. A small amount of wood worm that's been dealt with.

'Just thought I'd warn you.'

'That's very courteous of you.' So what else is new? Dwight is used to envy. A regular home from home.

'My father's head of Chambers,' Alan announces, eyes searching

Dwight. 'Breams Buildings.' The earlier mumble has become clear and plummy. Watching for reactions.

Dwight studiously keeps them nil.

'In the City,' Alan prods on.

Dwight nods his understanding.

'I'm reading law at Jesus,' is volunteered, chin pushed out. 'Oxford.' He gives the word emphasis.

Dwight's vague smile is meant to head Alan off without antagonising him, but he finds it hard to conceal his disinterest.

Clearly unsatisfactory. The eyes spark anger.

'Ivy League,' Dwight murmurs, unwilling to sound impressed but not sure what else to say.

'An American.' Alan's announcement suggests he hadn't noticed the accent earlier on, that the phrase explains not only nationality but background. 'Harvard?'

'Business School,' Dwight admits. 'I'm president of *Models International*.' He doesn't really feel like playing Alan's game, but straightens up all the same. 'Based in Mayfair.' He looks Alan up and down as he feels Valerie's eyes on him.

Alan stares back as Dwight, grimaces at Valerie. She's intent on Alan, eyes slatted into a smirk at his embarrassment.

'Mayfair? Which part of Mayfair?' The bluster looks manufactured.

'Well,' Dwight drawls his vowels, enjoying it, 'there's the house in Burk – in Berkeley Square.' He pauses for several seconds. 'And my office is uptown, Albemarle Street.' He pronounces it Albeemarle.

'Girl trade,' Alan snorts, face flushed crimson.

Jeez. Dwight, incensed, tries to stop giving himself away. Trying to make him out a white slaver, or what?

'Cigarette?' Valerie distracts Alan, grinning at this attack and holding out a squashed, clearly almost empty, packet of Players' Silk Cut.

He turns from Dwight to her. She's not smiling but shaking the packet. A lone cigarette pops up as she offers it.

'You know I don't smoke those.'

'They're all I have to offer.'

'Actually, I've brought you some. Got them on the way back from Paris last week-end.' He fishes two packets of Gauloises out of his trouser pocket and hands them to her. Was it French cigarette

24

smoke he noticed in the woods, Dwight wonders? He doesn't think so. He's too used to telling odours apart to get it wrong. But it was tobacco smoke, no question.

'My special brand,' Valerie murmurs, half-shutting her eyes and, unsmiling, taking them.

'I guess you have a different name for it,' Dwight says, thinking of Emily. Which emphasis is more insulting, that on the word 'girl' or that on the word 'trade'?

Another of Harry's little gems is 'They'll allow the profit so long as it ain't gotten by trade'.

'It's a model agency.' Dwight decides to spell out for Valerie. 'We supply fashion models for events like the Motor Show, and the Boat Show at Earl's Court.'

No sign of interest or understanding from Alan. Stiff upper lip, in his case pretty well pursed. Perhaps young guys in his position have never heard of such commercial events. Sure they have, where else would they find their yachts?

'Or for top photographers,' Dwight goes on, then realises that this, too, can be misinterpreted. 'People whose work is used by *Vogue*, or *Harpers & Queen*.' The syllables take on more Yankee twang as he is bent on diffusing the charged atmosphere.

Valerie doesn't say anything at all. She puffs on her cigarette and inhales, eyes closed in blissful satisfaction. It's the chinking of teacups which interrupts the silence.

'I've made a pot of both.' Emily is carrying a tray with two teapots, what smells like freshly-baked bread, a butter-dish and a jar of home-labelled preserve. She's still wearing the cotton dress. 'I hope you like bramble jelly. We always have it, and this is all that's left of last year's vintage.'

'One of her best,' Valerie cues in. 'Emkins is the one who makes all our jellies and jams. And our very own whole wheat bread, of course. It's easier to bake it ourselves than to go cycling down to the village.' She takes one last drag at her cigarette, nicotined fingers oblivious to the short butt, stubs it out on the lawn beside her, swings her legs to one side and makes room for the tray. Emily sets it down beside her mother. 'Milk and sugar, Mr Delaney?'

'Dwight,' he says, smiling and wondering if this is for real.

What's with bramble jelly? Harry was entirely silent on that little joker. That's one piece of anglo lore he'll ladle out to old buddy-buddy next time they meet. 'I know it's terribly ignorant,' he goes on, unable to resist it, 'but what in the world is bramble jelly?'

'Stupid of me.' Valerie laughs. 'Of course you wouldn't have come across it.' She holds the jam jar up against the sunlight. 'Just look at that: pure garnet.'

A deep translucent glow radiates outwards from the glass. What looks like a solid mass of black now lightens towards the edges, flaming dark purple red. Dwight's reflections on country teas taken on cottage garden lawns shatter back to the caked blood around the rabbits' gashes.

He stares at the counter top, runnels of blood glisten the pale surface, trickling down.

'Mom!' he sobs.

His eyes blink as he remembers earlier sights. The brown bracken wedged between the dead branches resembled the wicker tray. How is he going to swallow tea, let alone eat bread and jam?

'The jelly's made from the fruit of those fearsome thorny brambles that hem us in so protectively,' Valerie explains.

Quite suddenly he registers something that's been bothering him all along. A fairy tale – *Sleeping Beauty* – that's what the set-up reminds him of. Emily, guarded by wild thorns, deep in the Sussex woods, a princess waiting to be rescued by the...

'That's what we call the wild blackberries round here,' Valerie's strong emphatic voice brings him back to the factual world. 'The cottage is called Bramblings,' she adds almost as an afterthought, and laughs. 'Sounds appropriate, though actually that's the name of a small woodland bird which overwinters here.' She smiles at the jam jar as she lights another cigarette. 'Our native blackberries ripen in September. We gather them and simmer them with our own cooking apples, then use the juice to make bramble jelly.'

'It looks delicious.' Dwight glances at the newspaper parcel he's deposited by the stone wall. If it's seeping more blood it's doing so discreetly. 'A little milk will be just fine.'

26

Emily squats by the tray, taking the tea-filled cups from her mother and passing them around. Her hands, Dwight notices, though long-fingered and delicate, are spoiled by rough red skin and unkempt nails. Juliette can see to that, his mind clicks over, and then he remembers he hasn't signed Emily up – yet.

'I've put in your usual two,' Emily turns to Alan, handing him a cup. 'It'll soon be time for strawberry jam,' she adds. 'Now that's a really beautiful colour.'

Alan and Emily. He watches Alan's eyes drink in the girl's supple movements and feels something more than the usual wistful tug of jealousy. Alan is young, and strong, and well-connected, and – well, English. And Emily seems to like him.

As if some sort of magnet were attracting guests to the tea-party, another visitor appears. Another dog, this time a spaniel. Rather a beautiful golden cocker spaniel. He frisks, delicately and none too quickly, across the top of the lawn.

'You expecting Sophie?' Valerie turns to her daughter. 'There's Tatman.'

A sudden chorus of barks erupts as the three dogs begin to adjust to each other's presence.

'Anne's sent Tatman round for me to take him for a walk. She said she might.'

'I thought the new groom – Nina, did you say her name is? – takes him when she's exercising the horses.'

'Apparently she isn't keen on doing that.'

Valerie's lips tighten. 'Looks as though you may have to wait a bit longer than you think, Alan. Emily's got her chores to do.'

'I'll go with her,' he says immediately. 'Or better still, we'll drive to Lodsworth and the dogs can run after us. I'll let the pater know we'll be along a little later.'

CHAPTER 4

It's almost as though he can't stay away, as though some spell were pulling him towards the cottage. Emily's image is forever in Dwight's mind, the green eyes wide, staring at him. Is she repelled, like most folks he meets, or might she – eventually – be attracted? She doesn't flinch at his appearance, doesn't cringe away.

> *'What's wrong with the kid, Sadie?'*
> *'He's OK, Earl.'*
> *'He got white hair, and his eyes look pink.'*
> *'Just got no pigment in his skin. Ain't nothing special.'*

Absurd, Dwight tries to tell himself. He knows Emily is bound to think of him as some kind of cripple. No way he can make out with her. All the same, he'll head for Bramblings every time he gets a chance.

Keen both on Sheba's company and a good invigorating walk, Dwight rushes for the kennel door at the weekends, morning or afternoon and, occasionally, both. Each time he talks to his bitch before drawing back the bolt.

'Just give her time to get over her excitement at seeing you,' Jock instructed him. 'She's got nothing to do but look forward to that.'

He tries walking her in different directions but Sheba heads straight for the lane to Bramblings. 'This way, babe,' he calls after her, sounding ineffectual even to himself. He goes ahead for several yards. There's never any sign Sheba is trying to catch up with him.

'Stay in the back yard, honey.'
He has to go, has to feed Owlet. Mom mustn't know about him yet.
He snatches small pieces of raw meat from the refrigerator, smuggles some scraps of cloth for roughage, sneaks out in back.

Dwight turns to follow his dog. 'Sheba! Heel!' he shouts out. Not masterful enough. Maybe he actually invited the dog to go to Bramblings by thinking about it non-stop. She'll be on heat some time soon. He'll have to keep her in then, or mate her before Raffy gets a chance to get at her. That little whippersnapper is well named.

Dwight walks slowly along the wide sandy track. Lofty oaks, planted at least forty years before, are coming into harvestable timber. Valerie's neighbour, Tom Butler, has begun felling at the far end. Dense woodland suddenly gives way to bright skies, huge tree trunks lie fallen, denuded of branches stacked in great mounds ready for burning. The undergrowth is cleared to bare earth, the soft leaf mould soil already drying out, an intense woodland scent rising from it. Dwight drinks in the aroma, the sweet breeze on his face, the dapple of light playing hide-and-seek with clouds scampering across a scarcely-veiled sky, and savours the quiet.

Saturday afternoon and no one else about, just the hum of bees hunting nectar in the almost-hot of the afternoon, the flies droning. Not so much droning as burring, it dawns on him. Not the normal drowsy tone of sun-warmed insects but an angry competitive buzzing. Even before he comes across it, he can already nose what he will find. Another mangled corpse.

The acrid pungent smell of death rushes at him from her body.
'Mom!'
Tears run unchecked.

Suddenly the quiet and the fact that he's on his own appear sinister. The sky seems to become grey, brooding instead of skittering little clouds, dropping a lid on to the woods, boxing him in. The cut trees are behind him now. He's coming into hazel brushwood interlaced with bramble thickets which have taken over bare soil while saplings planted a mere five years ago are growing a slow yield.

Sheba is sitting, stock still, right in the centre of the path ahead of him, sniffing the air. Not a smell she's keen to follow, he realises. Too cloying, too rank. 'Walk, girl.' His tremolo infuriates him and has no impact on the animal. She stands up but doesn't move.

'Get along there, Sheba. Heel!' He remembers the command, swishes his stick at yet another bramble shoot about to tear his tweed, then hugs his coat around himself to blend with the surroundings. The flecks of beige and bracken, umber and russet are a perfect cover in the spring woodlands.

'That's what the tartans were for, buddy,' he hears Harry's New York twang in his head. 'Hiding the hoods in the heather.'

Maybe that's what Harris tweed is for as well. He feels safe, confident enough to push ahead. He bends his stick against the grasping thorns and listens to the cacophonous cooing of woodpigeons. It has a soothing, almost hypnotic effect. He saunters on as if in a dream.

Soft stirrings of dark trees, intense odour of pines.
'Owlet,' he calls. 'Where are you?'
He waits for the fluttering of wings, the squawk of recognition.
Only the rippling trees, a scurrying vole. No Owlet to greet him.

Glancing along the path, catching a scattering or two of pale yellow promising primroses, Dwight's eye is caught by something globular. The feeling of safety is dispelled. He should have known, the buzzing has reaches a frenzy now and, as he pushes the brambles away he reels from the fetid smell of decaying flesh.

'Just something which has died of natural causes,' he mutters to Sheba. 'Nothing to do with us. Leave it alone!' He puts his glasses on. Something with quills: a baby porcupine? No wonder Sheba is being careful.

He can't bring to mind what shape the animal should have, but not this. The brown body is hard to distinguish from the surrounding earth and twigs, and some of last year's leaves are still about. But the shape is bunched, not simply lying limp.

Bristles of hair across her forehead, eyes open, stare at him. Her mouth, small round of surprise, is silent.
'Dwight, honey...' he hears her say. Yet knows that is the past.

A closer look shows the creature was hacked into several pieces, tumbled about and heaped into a pile. Large chunks of spine-covered substance have spilled over each other, darkly oozing. The smell of rotting meat discourages more detailed investigation.

Just something that has died Dwight tries to tell himself again. Everything must die. Maybe killed by a predator, and left. But he can't kid himself, no way. Done with an axe. An inexperienced woodcutter, he tries on for size, someone who doesn't know that woodland creatures are part of the landscape, someone who thinks it's a dangerous animal. He knows that's crap.

Fine, try another line. Woodcutters stripping trees of branches, the porcupine gets in the way by accident...

Half a mile from the place where they're cutting down trees? Hacked into several pieces and carefully piled up? This time the animal's remains are piled atop a sort of mound of twigs – a funeral pyre. The hacking was deliberate. He has no idea why, but he knows how and when. Sometime on Friday evening, most likely after the woodcutters finished work for the week. He hasn't been this way since last weekend.

Her body covered in oilcloth.
'Did you find her like this, bud?'
'No, officer. I did that. I had to cover her.'

'Walk, Sheba,' Dwight thunders. He isn't prepared to hide this deed. He'll not only mention it to Valerie, he'll ask to go into local characters, possible motivations – background she'd know about but an area new to him. Find out if anything like this has happened before. He knows the signs. It isn't safe for any of them.

Does that explain why mother and daughter eyed his parcel so suspiciously that first day? Incidents like this have been happening and are worrying them? Quite likely they'd think he might turn out to be the guilty party. A newcomer – a stranger, a foreigner – and an albino. Well, could be. It sure seems to him Emily and Valerie have come across stuff like this before he'd even arrived. A hell of a sight more to it than he can work out right now.

The bitch shudders, muscles rippling under her black coat, then bounds off along the trail, clearly as glad to leave as he is. Dwight peers into the tangled brushwood. The little path to Bramblings is nearby, but even after a couple more visits he isn't too clear exactly where. He puts his glasses back in his pocket, happy to rely on Sheba to find the way. Maybe not call on the Brookes after all. Putting off what he might have to face eventually. But not now, not yet. He'll leave it up to destiny.

Sheba is way ahead, but he hears her bark mingled with Raffy's. Emily walking the terrier! Dwight's feet frisk speed as he hurries towards the racket. The figure coming towards him is too squat. Valerie. He slows, aware he has a perfect chance to point the latest finding out to her.

'I said you wouldn't be able to avoid us,' Valerie greets him. Raffy scampers up and jumps him with dirty paws.

'All right, boy, all right,' Dwight imitates Sheba's trainer, the accomplished Jock. Raffy sure hasn't been trained by anyone. 'Down, boy. Down.'

The little dog stops and looks at him, surprised. Valerie picks up a stick and heaves it as far as she can. Raffy, barking joyfully again, brings it back all too quickly.

'He quite wears me out. I'll be glad when he gets a bit older.'

'He's overexcited,' Dwight finds himself saying. 'He needs to have a little discipline.'

'I always think a happy childhood is such a wonderful backing for later life.' Valerie tries to wrest the stick from Raffy's jaws but he growls and holds on.

"That won't do at all," Jock instructed Dwight when he made the same mistake with Sheba. "Yer got to show 'em who's top dog. Otherwise they reckon it's 'em. They be pack animals, remember, with a strict hierarchy. Jest make sure Sheba knows you're the leader of her pack.'

'I'll just walk back with you a little ways.' Dwight watches as Sheba races Raffy for the stick.

'Splendid. The woods are so wonderful in spring. Have you seen the primroses?'

'They're beautiful.'

'And we have kingcups by the stream. We don't broadcast that, people might come and pick. Visitors often have no idea how to preserve the countryside.' Valerie stops and points right. 'I know you wouldn't think of picking rare wildflowers. I'll show you where they are.'

They're walking side by side, nearing the place. Not that Dwight can see at all well without his glasses, but he can hear and smell. He knows he should be telling Valerie about the chopped-up body, warn her there's something wrong. It's his duty, for Emily's sake. Valerie has no husband to look after her, and Emily no father. Dwight can sense danger in the neighbourhood, palpable, ominous.

Her ring finger is almost severed, just hanging by a thread.
'Why d'you wear his ring, Mom? You say you're glad Pop's gone.'
The thin gold band winks at him from the floor.

These two women are living in an isolated cottage, at least half a mile from their nearest neighbour, without a telephone. What in hell is holding him back? 'You're not worried about living in these parts on your own?'

'Worried?'

'You're quite cloistered here. You don't even have a phone.'

'You mean worried am I worried about being attacked?'

'I guess it happens even in West Sussex.'

Valerie laughs. 'I'm not remotely frightened, if that's what you mean. I don't even bother to lock my doors.' She laughs again. 'My front door isn't even fitted with a lock, though I do have the ancient inside bolts.' The chuckle rings out, as though she dares roving thieves to hear what she has to say. 'Anything I have people are welcome to. But I don't think they'll bother with my little bits and pieces. There's really nothing worth stealing. Not even a television. Just an old battery radio.'

'Can we get a TV, Mom?'
'We can't afford it, Dwight.'
'Everyone has TV!'
'We have each other, honey.'

'Hear no evil, see no evil, speak no evil, is that what you mean?' Dwight stands aside to let her go ahead. The overhanging branches makes it hard to walk abreast. Is he chickening out, like he always has? Ignoring the threat to the personal safety of two women living alone? Which, he rationalises to himself, they've probably done for years before he happened along. He isn't sure what else he can do right now. Valerie will simply laugh again if he mentions a dead porcupine. But he has to try. 'There's something I think you should see.'

'You sound rather grave.' She holds another stick for Raffy, about to throw.

'It's kinda weird, and quite disturbing.' The carcass has to be very near them, but he can't quite locate it. He puts his glasses on, the light moist damp of sweat now making his clothes cling to him. He can feel his face blaze into fire.

'Perhaps if you could tell me what you're looking for?'

'The body of a small porcupine...'

'There are no porcupines in our woods. They're not a native species.'

'It's a baby chipmunk, Mom! A real hummer.'

'Don't bother me with nonsense, Dwight. Give me a hand to get the clearing done.'

'I saw it,' he insists, annoyed at her smug attitude. 'A small rounded body with quills...'

'A hedgehog, you mean. They're quite common little creatures around here, and quite harmless. Wonderful for the garden; they live on a diet of earthworms and slugs.'

'A hedgehog?'

'Roughly a foot long, at the outside. Small brown-grey bodies with spiny hairs. Their worst crime is eating pheasants' eggs in a dry season.'

'Sure thing, a hedgehog.'

'They're not dangerous,' Valerie goes on. 'You'll...'

'It's hacked to pieces.'

She stops. It's sudden enough for him to have to pull himself up to avoid bumping into her. She recovers, picks up yet another stick

34

and calls to Raffy.

Suddenly they're right by it, the little mound lying by the side. Dwight points. 'There it is. All chopped up. Who'd do a thing like that?'

'That is rather odd.' Valerie uses the stick still in her hand to pull the pieces apart. 'It really is a hedgehog.'

'Sure, sure. The point is it's hacked into little pieces.'

'That's why you started thinking about our living out here alone?'

'And placed on a sort of small bonfire, as though ready to burn the whole thing. I guess that seems even worse than hacking it into pieces.'

'People do take their frustrations out on some types of animal. Hedgehogs are not well liked, snakes are another target. It's ghastly, but it's true. I think it's a sort of safety valve.'

'The type of twisted mind that can do this can be quite dangerous, you know.'

'Dangerous?'

'Likely to do something worse. Attack someone's pet, for example.'

'It sounds as though you have some experiences to go on.'

Owlet isn't in his usual place. A hunk of meat, flies on it.
He's never left food before.

'My early years were spent in Vermont.' It all rushes back at him: the pungent odour of pines, the breeze on his young face.

'That's a beautiful state.'

'You know it?'

'I have a very dear friend, Loretta. She's been to New England and often goes skiing in Vermont. She invited me one year.'

'So you've been to the States?'

'One holiday. A long time ago, before Emily was born.'

'But your friend lives there?'

'No, not any more. She moved to Scotland; the Highlands. The nearest place she can find like it in the British Isles. Would it surprise you to hear that Emily was born there?'

'In Scotland? It sure would.'

'By accident. I was visiting Loretta and Emily decided to arrive early. So she was born there. Two months premature, I'm afraid.'

'Your husband's from Scotland?'

'You think I couldn't stand it up there and rushed back to the South? No, Reginald Brooke is very English, his parents come from quite near here, from Hampshire. We were divorced for completely different reasons.'

'I didn't mean to pry...'

'A long time ago now. Nearly seventeen years.'

'Where's Pop, Mom?'
'In the woods, I guess.'

'Emily can only have been a few months old. Does she often see her father?'

Valerie smiles wryly. 'Not really. By the time Emily was born he'd changed from the man I'd married.' Her voice is harsh, over bright. 'I certainly didn't want what he'd become as an example for Emkins.' She swishes the surrounding greenery with the stick, swiping off catkins hanging from an innocent hazel bush. 'Do tell me about your corner of Vermont.'

He isn't about to come clean about his family, how Pop left Mom, how... 'There's not that much to tell. We lived in a little wooden house – a log cabin – in the forest. My father was a ranger at the time. I guess you call it gamekeeper, though it's a different kind of job.'

'I think I've seen a ranger in action. They use a high platform in the woods to keep a look-out for fires and other problems.'

'Not just one platform. Several in strategic places.'

'So you've lived in woodland before.'

Lank dark evergreens brooding out the light.

'Forest, yes, ma'am. Mostly evergreens, darker than anything you have here.'

'No wonder you love our woods. How old were you when you left?'

'Just on nine when my Mom and I moved to Needham. That's a suburb of Boston. They have some light woodlands there. It kind of made us feel at home.'

'Your parents are divorced, I take it.'

'My father disappeared. We never knew what happened to him. Things started going wrong on the job. He tried to cope, but he just couldn't seem to make hack it.'

'Fires, you mean? He didn't spot them in time?'

'Smoke. I can smell smoke,' his Mom calls to him, shrill and insistent. 'Hold my hand, Dwight. This is a big one. We have to run like hell.'

'That's what it ended up with.' The fire that threatened to come right up to them, with the truck gone, and Earl Delaney nowhere near. Will he ever be likely to forget the terror? 'But unpleasant things were happening before then,' Dwight explains to Valerie. 'That's why I'm worried about you and Emily.'

He sees his Owlet strung up between two trees.
Wings broken, dangling by his side, his body turning slowly as it swings.
His beak is smashed.

'I had a pet owl, a little owl. You have some in these woods. Found him as a chick. He'd fallen out of his nest and had a broken wing. My father said it would be useless to look after him, the wing would never mend. But leastways I wanted to give it a try.'

'How old were you then?'

'Six – maybe seven. I didn't know how to get the wing to set properly, so he couldn't fly too well. I named him Owlet – he became a real favourite of mine.'

He loves his Owlet, keeps him a secret.
'Your Mom'll raise hell if she finds out,' Pop tells him.

Dwight grins. 'At first I even stole for him. I'd feed him raw meat and a few shreds of cloth. They need the roughage, you see. In the wild they eat the whole prey, fur and all.'

'I know,' Valerie agrees.

'He was a great guy. Even my mother liked him in the end. I had him for at least two years. Every morning I'd be up early and hang out with him. Until he didn't show when I called.' He pauses, even now that memory is worse than that of the fire which burned their forest home. 'I walked further and further into the trees, calling him. I couldn't find him. Eventually I had to leave for school. My mother promised to look out for him. But he hadn't shown when I came back that afternoon.'

He finds a wooden clothes peg on the ground. Has Mom been here?

'My mother thought maybe he'd finally taken off. He was a wild bird, after all.' He sighs as he remembers. 'I didn't go for that. He wasn't strong enough to hunt, not fast enough to swoop on prey.'

'Of course.'

'I searched the forest for him.' Dwight's voice drops low. 'And then I found him. Not a pretty sight.' He looks at Valerie, wondering why he's telling her all this. To convince her she's in danger – she and Emily are in danger. 'He was strung up by the neck, both his wings broken, pegged on some rope between two branches. His legs were all mangled.'

'I see.' Valerie's eyes avoid his.

'That was the worst of it as far as wildlife was concerned. And it started just like this, small animals maimed, or slashed, or hacked into pieces and found deep among the trees.'

'Did you find out who was responsible?'

'We never did. But it ended up with the fire, and my father gone forever. I guess you need to be careful, maybe.'

They're still standing by the hedgehog. The mound of twigs is just beside the track, not really hidden. Dwight catches sight of something coloured. Flowers again. Somehow that makes it worse. Kinda celebrating the ghastly deed. 'This is what really freaks me out.' He threads his way through. 'Come look.'

Valerie follows and they see the pyre from the other side. Facing them is a sort of shrine, or altar. There are primroses and wood anemones, but this time also some daisies from a nearby field, and even dandelions. Early buds of uncultivated rhododendron, mauve tips showing against the dark twigs, form a canopy over the other floral offerings. The whole thing looks innocent until the eye travelled upwards.

Valerie gasps, recovers. 'It's only children playing,' she laughs. 'They're playing funerals.'

'I guess those aren't the sort of childhood games one wishes to encourage.' Dwight is tiring of her insistence on a harmless interpretation. 'I don't think that's so, Valerie. This is the second time I've come across a set-up like this, and I know there's something odd going on. Odd and sinister – sick, even.'

'Whatever do you mean?'

'That first day I came over.'

'About a fortnight ago.'

'Two weeks, right. I had a rabbit wrapped in my *Financial Times*.'

'Yes, you told us. You said Sheba retrieved it for you.'

'That was perfectly true, but not the whole truth, I'm afraid.'

'Which is?'

His beloved Owlet – murdered, hanged.
He vows to take revenge.

'Sheba did bring a rabbit to me. I couldn't work out where she'd retrieved it from. First off I thought she'd killed it. And then I looked at it real good. The animal was slit all along its body, from spine to belly, its ears nearly cut off. A deliberate methodical mutilation.'

'It does sound odd.' Her eyes shift away again.

'But that isn't all.'

'You mean you found it still alive...'

'No, no. Sheba brought it to me. I was so upset I forgot to put her on the leash, and she went off again. I shouted for her to stay. When I found her she was sitting by a sort of platform, with another rabbit lying across it. Slit exactly the same way as the first – real horrifying. The worst part was these floral offerings.'

Is Valerie dodging his eye? She looks evasive. 'It can still be children playing. People forget that children don't always play the way adults expect them to.'

'Children who slit dead rabbits? Right through their fur, down to the bone? What with? You need a pretty good cutting tool for that.

And know-how.'

Valerie doesn't answer, she just throws the stick for Raffy. 'Go, boy, go!'

'That's what I think is really dangerous. Cruel youths cutting up rabbits – dead or alive – is one thing, louts chopping hedgehogs to pieces is another. But shrines built to display these mutilated corpses? That shows some sort of psychopathic personality at work.'

'I really think you're exaggerating, Dwight. Not very pleasant games, I do agree. But nothing incredibly dreadful. You said it yourself, the animals were dead before they were maimed. No harm done.'

'The rabbits were already dead, I'm pretty sure. Especially as you and Emily mentioned the hunters often miss game killed on a shoot. We don't know about the hedgehog.'

Valerie looks towards the pile but makes no sign to investigate it further.

'And it certainly isn't children.' Dwight allows his feelings to show in clipped syllables and loud consonants. 'Anyways, not young children.'

'How d'you know that?'

'I thought I saw someone near the rabbits. A lightish blur of head against the dark background of the rhododendron leaves. Whoever it was is tall and fair. I sensed someone watching me, looking to see what I would do.'

'Just a local walking their dog,' Valerie laughs.

'Sure made me nervous. I turned to leave and tripped, and lost my glasses. Next thing I knew a huge dog was on top of me. Reckoned it might attack me, but its owner called it off. Came over to give me a hand up.'

'Probably a lurcher. They're very popular round here.'

'That a special kind of dog?'

'Lurchers originated in Ireland and parts of the UK. They're usually quite sensitive, and very devoted to their owners.'

'As soon as I was back on my feet the man took off, refused to speak to me.'

'British reticence,' Valerie assures him. 'Probably nothing to do with the whole thing. There can be any number of ordinary explanations.'

Too eager to dismiss the whole affair, Dwight decides. She's holding something back. And then he shrugs. He's done all he can for the time being.

CHAPTER 5

'Sophie and her parents are taking the boat out this afternoon, Mummy. They've asked me to go with them. You don't mind, do you?'

Emily, her hair twined into one long sinuous plait, is wearing faded jeans and what looks like a man's shirt under an open wind cheater. She trundles the bike she and her mother share across the lawn.

Valerie straightens up and leans on her hoe, kicking the weeds aside. Brown corduroys, evidently acquired in a jumble sale with shoes to match, merge into earthiness between the bare rose bushes. Dwight busies himself, raking weeds into a pile, watching as Emily passes by him to pet Raffy and Sheba.

'Hello, Dwight.' Her eyes, half-shut, dark-ringed – grooming that fat old Myra's mare – centre on the dogs. 'I didn't expect you here so early in the day.'

'Mom! I came early to see you...' Tears gather, his voice breaks.

He turns away, turns back, hand hovering over the eyelids. Can't bring himself to touch her.

Dwight stands tall and makes as if to move towards Emily. She doesn't draw back, just looks beyond him, then leans down, her arm brushing his, and pats Raffy's head. Sheba looks soulful and Emily leans even closer to Dwight to get at the Labrador. The girl fondles the dog, and Dwight catches an intoxicating whiff, a curiously pervasive, very personal smell. It reminds him of – something he can't pin-point. Body chemistry, he guesses, working on him.

Emily takes her coat off. Dwight watches her stoop while she holds the bike, smiles briefly and pets Sheba again. He wishes he could turn himself into animal form just to be stroked by those long firm fingers. A hint of horse smell, mixed with Emily's personal odour, now wafts over. It makes him giddy, then he catches yet another aroma. That odd hint of something he can't place but which he's come across before. What is it?

Overwhelmed with longing to touch the girl, unable to do so, he squats down to scoop up weeds, looks up from this vantage point. This time he can see her thighs. He closes his eyes and drifts into a dream. A flutter of sunlight fondles his back into a fantasy of sensual warmth.

'Of course not, Emkins. What a splendid idea,' he hears Valerie agree to the outing.

'I should really help you prepare for the Mastertons.' The glorious eyes have crinkled a little. 'They're coming next weekend, aren't they?'

Emily's slender fingers are not only rough, but becoming chafed with the horsy chores the girl undertakes. Simply, he guesses, to earn a little money for some clothes.

'We have to watch the pennies, Dwight. Your father left us.'
'He might have been killed in the fire, Mom!'

He feels fury rise within him against Emily's father. I'd like to get hold of that son of a bitch, he tells himself. All the hard work Emily has to put in on top of her school work. Childhood slipping away from her, too much responsibility heaped on such young shoulders. He longs to do something – anything – to make her life easier. He'll work it out.

He bends down to collect as much vegetation as he can. Rose thorns catch at his tweed. He brushes them aside, hardly aware they've pierced his delicate skin and that blood is trickling down his fingers. It's the stickiness which makes him pull out his handkerchief to wipe it off.

Bright scarlet streaming down, a crimson lava flow.
Whoever did this can't have gotten far.
He heads out of the house, scans the road, sees a car just ahead
accelerating off. He'll chase the bastard!

He feels irritation with Valerie turn to anger. What right does she have to direct Emily's life to this extent? Allowing her to ruin her hands, to become exhausted with the chores she undertakes, to accept charity?

'You can use the break,' he hears the mother's voice floating into his consciousness. 'Don't burn your hands on the ropes.'

She sounds altogether brighter than Dwight knows she feels. Sciatica, she winced when her left leg seemed to stiffen up as she was leaning over. That's when he offered to help her with the gardening.

'Don't worry, Mummy. I know my way around a boat!' Emily's frown furrows disappear into smoothness. 'I'll have to rush. They said they'd wait ten minutes.'

Swinging her leg over the barred bicycle Valerie has, as she boasted to Dwight, rescued from a junk heap, Emily speeds up the lawn and on to the drive leading to the lanes. Dwight watches, savouring the split-second movements of her limbs, treasuring them in his mind, caressing her mentally until she is, all too soon, out of sight behind the tall beech hedge.

He'd stayed with Valerie, announcing his willingness to gather up the weeds, because he'd hoped Emily would be back quite soon. Not that he checked with Valerie, he kinda skittered round the subject. But he had the distinct impression Valerie knew why he'd come. She's had plenty of practice, he tells himself, despondent.

Valerie gazes after her daughter for a short time, then fishes a cigarette out of her pocket. 'Let's have a break.' She lowers herself on to the front porch step, lights up, begins to inhale deeply. The acrid smell of smouldering Gauloises once again revives the fleeting memory of another smell Dwight can't pin-point.

'I'll just puts these weeds in the garbage.'

'Compost heap. You'll see it round the back. My dear old Jem – he does the heavy gardening – makes a neat box for me.'

He crunches the pebbled path towards the back. Warm slants of sun play dark and light across the vegetable patch. He rocks the

43

ancient wheelbarrow across tilled earth towards a neat box filled almost to overflowing. More careful of his hands now, he's about to heave a sheaf of weeds on to the rest when his eye is caught by colour. Wildflowers: cowslips and bluebells, lady's smock – all intertwined with wild rhododendron – form some sort of floral bouquet. He covers it, spreading the weeds across, then pivots the empty barrow back towards the front.

Valerie is where he's left her. The two dogs have joined her, dozing at her feet, catching brief glints of sun and warmth.

'Is flower arranging a hobby of yours?'

At first she stares, round eyes, then slides them into laughter. 'The flowers on the compost heap! That's Em, she gathers the plentiful ones and brings them in. They only last a day or two.'

Emily? He shudders, in spite of feeling the heat of his exertions. He has to find out… 'Amazing she has the energy.'

'It's part of what we do to earn our crust. The visitors go mad about bouquets of wild flowers, and she only picks the common ones. Our season starts around Easter.' She waves Dwight to sit next to her. 'The first batch usually arrives on Maundy Thursday. This year we're starting a little later. I had to have a leak in the roof repaired. A couple with one little girl of eight are coming next Friday evening.'

She sighs as she looks at the tidied rose beds. Old Jem, Dwight knows, does the digging and the mowing. At least Emily is spared that. 'I guess you're none too keen.'

'It's our way of life.' Valerie's smoke rings loop up in the still air as she pokes her fingers through them, showing off her control. 'It's not too bad in a good summer.' The last ring writhes along the window ledge.

Dwight remembers what she's told him. She lets out the house while she and Emily camp in the wooden garden shed with its make-shift bunk beds. A Calor gas stove does the double duty of providing warmth and a flame to cook on. 'It means we can go on living in this marvellous setting,' she explains. 'The council did offer us accommodation, but I turned that down flat. I prefer to make my own way.'

Valerie told him of the long, often wet, summers she and Emily have endured in that cramped space when Emily was a small child. Crouched over the Calor gas rings to keep them warm, too poor to buy much food, they'd whiled away long hours by telling each other

44

stories. Now, at least, Emily has her jobs and suitable school friends to relax with. In those days she attended the village school.

'Village school kids aren't suitable friends?'

'It's not that there's anything wrong with them.' Another smoke ring curls up, floats away. 'Just not quite the right background.'

'Background?'

'He's your son, too, Earl.'
'Nothing like his problem among my folks.'

'Her own kind. Her father's people are Navy.'

'Jack Tar, right?'

'We don't really use that expression any more. Her grandfather is an admiral.'

If admirals aren't sailors, what the hell are they? The famous British snobbery rearing its head, he guesses. No lesser ranks for Emily.

'And Em's out a lot now.' Valerie finishes the cigarette, shivering slightly as a cloud slides over the sun. She lights up again. 'She seems to have acquired quite a clientèle for exercising dogs and horses. I believe there's even competition.' She smiles as she thinks of her popular daughter. 'They all adore her, owners and animals. She's a real country person.'

Country person? She's a humdinger, and that's a fact. 'It's just not good enough,' Dwight says, no longer able to contain himself. 'That husband of yours should be horse-whipped! It's his duty to make sure Emily doesn't have to work while she's in school.'

'Ex-husband,' Valerie reminds him. 'I try not to feel bitter about Reginald. Wouldn't help Emily if I said anything to make her think badly of her father, so if I mention him at all I point out his virtues, nothing else.' Another puff, a deep one. 'She thinks very highly of him.'

'He visits with you?'

'Why not come along of me, son? We'll make a campfire, roast our catch.'

'No,' Valerie says, her mouth tight. 'That wouldn't really do.'

'Wouldn't do? You mean you don't allow it?'

45

'I thought it best not to meet after the split-up.' The lips press shut and Valerie turns away her head.

Reginald's family, Dwight gleaned from one or two comments Valerie let slip, is deeply ashamed of their son's behaviour towards Valerie and Emily. They'd insisted on paying for Emily's schooling at nearby Grove House Chapter. Originally set up for the daughters of impecunious clergy, it's now a much sought-after private school for girls, only six miles away from Bramblings. Emily attends as a day girl. Old Admiral Brooke was a governor there. After his death they'd co-opted Reginald – because he's a Brooke, and because he lives in the area.

'And Emily's father is also in the Service, right?'

'The Navy, d'you mean? Left before Em was born.' Valerie leans back against the door.

'So what's he doing now?'

'I'm not quite sure. He used to be the PT master at Cranford. That's a boys' prep school.' Valerie smiles at him. 'He coached the boys at fives.'

'That's some sort of sport?'

'It's a court game with walls.'

'Like squash?'

'No bat,' she says. 'You use a gloved hand instead. Keen players end up with very large, strong right hand.' She smiles, amused. 'I don't think you know it in the States, it's mostly played at English public schools. This prep school took it up to help get the boys into the right schools.'

'I guess we call it handball. Public schools, that's private, right? So Emily goes to public school?'

'Not exactly.' He can see Valerie trying to work out how to explain the complications of the British educational system. She inhales for inspiration. 'Grove House Chapter is an independent school.'

'That makes real sense.' Dwight laughs. 'OK, whatever it is, it's six miles from here. That mean Emily bikes over?'

'Usually Anne Pontings gives her a lift. She takes Sophie, you see.'

'That's the folks she's boating with today? Lucky break.'

Valerie puffs another smoke ring, large and solitary. It wavers slowly past them. 'Actually, it was I who suggested that school for

46

Sophie. Exactly right for her.'

Snobbish enough? Or willing to take a wealthy girl not too good at academic work?

'Em walks Tatman whenever Anne, or the new groom, can't get round to it.'

'They need a groom?'

'The Pontings run several horses. Hunters for themselves and a mount for Sophie. They've just employed a girl called Nina to groom for them. Em and Sophie used to exercise the horses after school, but it got too much for them.'

'So how did you cope, when Emily was small?'

'I remember it all so vividly, Dwight. As though it were yesterday. We had some wonderful times together, in spite of everything.' Valerie's eyes soften as she burbles about her daughter. 'She's such a child of nature. "Aren't we lucky, Mummy," she used to say to me, "to have all these riches on our doorstep." She's always collecting nature's largesse: mushrooms, wild berries, posies of wildflowers.'

'The huckleberries are ripening now.' Mom smiles at him. 'Let's go pick some.'

It irritates Dwight. Valerie insists on her self-respect at Emily's expense – a young defenceless child abandoned to the whims of a woman without the father of her child.

Bunches of bluebells, lungwort and sweet honeysuckle perfumed the small cabin, Valerie babbles on, unaware of Dwight's reactions. Mother and daughter, she tells him, always gathered wild strawberries, profuse on their drive, and on the railway banks a few miles away. Their pungent flavour exceeds anything the large cultivated ones can offer. Wild raspberries, growing in the woods, add their potent tang. September brings luscious blackberries for apple pies and bramble jelly. They foraged daily for mushrooms in the fields and chanterelles in the light beech woods, steeping the bright orange fungi in milk to make them tender enough to cook. Protein in plenty to keep them healthy.

'An offering fit for a queen and her princess,' Emily proudly claimed, Valerie tells Dwight.

The paying guests, then as now, all fell in love with Bramblings, and even more with Emily. Bored with the hustle of city life they delight in the fresh produce grown by Valerie and picked and brought to them by the artless young girl. They bask in the tranquillity of the Sussex woods, the absence of the telephone, the novelty of paraffin lamps. They don't have to clean them! The succession of summer visitors produces sufficient funds to buy food and fuel for the cold dark unproductive months of winter. Reginald's basic contribution barely covers the repairs and the rates.

'How are we going to manage without Pop, Mom?'
'I don't know, honey. We'll get by.'

There must have been quite some bust-up if Reginald Brooke can't even call and meet his daughter at her home.

'Sometimes I wonder whether it's my fault we ended up like this,' Valerie drifts on. 'Maybe I invited Reginald's irresponsibility by insisting on that one last trip to Scotland.' She holds the glowing butt to a new cigarette. 'I wasn't young, you know. Thirty-seven. In those days that was considered a risky age for a first pregnancy. Maybe I should have foreseen that there'd be problems, that I'd give birth prematurely, and that I'd have to stay in Scotland two months instead of the planned two weeks.' She smiles at Dwight. 'My last fling at freedom. I just wanted to visit Loretta one more time before immersing myself in motherhood. Once I'd taken it on it was going to be the most important thing in my life, of course.'

'You're all I have, Dwight. You know that, don't you, honey?'

The only thing in her life, except for the inverted snobbery of living in an unconverted gamekeeper's cottage in the woods, Dwight thinks grimly.

When she got back from the Highlands, Valerie goes on, Reginald had changed. He wasn't interested in the baby, hardly came home. After three months he told her about Pam Downs – that he was going to leave her for Pam. As far as Valerie was concerned that was betrayal. She'd take her chances on her own, and protect Emily

48

from Reginald's influence.

'You think he's been a bad influence on Emily?' Dwight asks with interest.

'Where you going, Earl?'
Pop slams the door as he runs out.
He tries to follow, but Mom grabs his arm.
'You're staying here,' she says. 'He'll never bother looking after you the way I do.'

'Reginald decided to breed lurchers. I hear there's something unsavoury going on with his dogs, rumours of badger baiting. Quite horrible.' Valerie looks steely. 'I got in touch with my solicitor. Suggested it might be best if Reginald signed Bramblings over to me .'

'And did he?'

'I thought it only fair. I had a little money saved, you see. Paid the deposit. But I stopped work after we married, so Reginald paid the monthly mortgage fees. Which means the cottage was registered in his name.'

'Presumably he has to let you live here.'

'Yes. But Reginald's got a second family, so I have to pay half the mortgage. That's why things are so tight.'

'D'you allow access?'

'I hardly see him now. Your Pop sleeps rough, just like the bum he is.'

'Not here. He sees Emily at the school. Apparently he never misses a Governors' meeting in case he misses her.'

'Surely you can take him to court to help out a little more?'

'I've no idea,' Valerie says with great dignity. 'We can manage as we are, and that's all I'm interested in.'

'We'll get by on our own, Dwight.'

So like his own childhood. He slept on the living room couch, while the roomers took up the bedrooms. Mom always working in the kitchen, baking cookies.

49

'What about your attorney? I guess you do have one?' Dwight looks at Valerie suddenly, suspiciously.

'Solicitor, Dwight,' Valerie corrects him, then goes on hurriedly. 'I already mentioned him. The best. Gilbert Sunnington, in Chichester. Heart of gold. Agrees Reginald behaved like a cad.'

Cad. Dwight almost explodes but manages to restrain himself. Reginald is a gentleman – a cad who leaves his wife and daughter living on a pittance while he sets up another family. But he's still a gentleman.

'It's quite funny,' Valerie goes on. Gilbert thought she shouldn't go on living in the cottage, tried to persuade her that he had the solution to her problems. 'You can always sell, you know,' he told her. 'I can get you half the profit. That property has gone up out of all proportion. Especially as you haven't made any improvements – people have gone mad over that sort of thing. Get yourself a nice little flat in Midhurst or Petersfield.'

'I make good money now, Mom. You can be much more comfortable in Boston.'

'This is my home, Dwight, honey.'

'I told Gilbert right away, without even bothering to think, that I've no intention of losing my home as well as my husband. 'I'm the one who found Bramblings, I paid the deposit, I pay half the mortgage. Emily shall be brought up there.'

'It's a hefty premium...'

'I've managed so far,' Valerie boasts to Dwight, smiling broadly, puffing one smoke ring after another. 'Emily has her country cottage home, even if I can't provide a father to go with it.'

'One up on Reginald,' Dwight agrees.

'And eventually Emily will inherit Bramblings,' Valerie smirks. 'I shall be leaving her a Rembrandt – a little masterpiece.'

The patronising smile on Gilbert's face when she told him what she intended to do only added to her determination. The years proved her right. Property prices escalated ever upwards, beyond all expectations. The little keeper's cottage in the woods has become the envy of the toilers in the city.

'You can sell for a really good profit now,' Gilbert harangued her time and again. 'Get rid of this noose around your neck and buy a nice little modern house. Think how comfortable you'd be.'

'A house now,' she grins at Dwight, a victorious flash in her eyes. 'Gilbert promoted me to a house, not just a flat.'

'You wouldn't have to struggle...'

'That isn't all there is to life, Dwight. This is my home. I love it, Emily loves it, and this is where we stay.'

'This is our home, and a fine one at that.'
'Sure, Mom.'

But there is a price to pay, and a high one at that. Dwight wonders if Valerie realises that Emily herself has paid a large part of it.

Dare he say what he really thinks? No way. He'd never see the pair of them again. 'I have to hand it to you,' he says, however, standing up. 'You sure do a good job looking after the cottage.'

Dwight and Valerie drift indoors and sit in front of the dying log fire. The great Tudor chimney, its mellow bricks streaked black from centuries of fires, takes up half the room. Little alcoves are built in on either side, great wrought-iron firedogs stand at the left. Valerie is using bellows to bring fire life back into splendid logs straddling a huge mound of ash.

'The secret of these fires is only to clean them out once a year,' Valerie instructs Dwight. 'We're just about to do it, before the season starts. Though it always means the fires don't draw properly until some ash has built up again.'

'You're taking a bit of a chance renting out to complete strangers, aren't you?'

'Still worried about our safety?' Valerie works the bellows vigorously. 'You get a feel for the right people,' she shrugs. 'I always puts my ads either in the personal column of the *Times*, or in *The Lady*. Those are the best. I've never had any problems.'

CHAPTER 6

Bosham lies quiet, basking in welcome sunshine, calm waters lapping against the tall grey walls of houses built on the waterfront. None of the hustle of Chichester Harbour. Here it's almost silent.

Dwight is standing forward on First Lady, the brim of his straw hat projecting over his glasses. His trim figure sways with the boat, his feet practised in retaining their hold. What interests him is Maidenhair Fern just a few lengths away. Two girls are stretched out on the forward deck – both slender and young, but one a short brunette and the other a much taller strawberry blonde. They're lying on their fronts, elbows akimbo, heads turned towards each other, bikini top straps undone. The blonde has to be Emily – those long, lissom limbs, that incredible hair. She mentioned joining some friends on a boat last Saturday. This must be it – Charles Pontings' pride and joy.

Charles and Anne Pontings, Valerie told Dwight, are the owners of Oak Court, the rambling manor house along the road to Lodsworth, ten minutes walk from Bramblings. Their daughter Sophie is Emily's best friend. The parents often invite her to join them on their boat, or at their parties. Charles is something or other in the City, Valerie closed her eyes at Dwight. Her air of dismissal implied that a career in money is suspect.

'A stockbroker?'

'I suppose so,' Valerie agreed. 'Something incredibly boring, but they're very well off.' She stops for a moment to consider. 'Well, usually, anyway. There was a rather bad patch about twelve years ago...'

'The early nineties...'

'Well, yes, I think that's when it was. Not too good now, apparently. It doesn't make sense, house prices have gone up and up. I always says property is the best investment.' She sounds surprised. 'So how did you know about Charles's past?' A flicker of understanding. 'You've already met!'

'Dip in the market,' Dwight shrugs it away. 'I started in business in the early nineties. Had a little trouble financing the show.'

'The bank offered me the full loan for the business, Mom.'
'Keep your nose clean, Dwight. No need to get in debt.'

Valerie isn't here to introduce him, so he'll have to wangle an introduction for himself. He pulls the rudder round and *First Lady* creeps towards the other boat, gently and silently.

'Grub ready yet, Anne?' Charles Pontings' bellow is directed down the hatch, yet the noise quite startles Dwight, busying himself arranging his craft to be in just the right position.

He looks up to see a very broad posterior covered in white shorts blocking the entrance to the cabin. There is a reply from within, but he can't quite make it out. From the satisfied grunt he gathers the answer is yes.

Dwight is startled to see Emily by the hatch, her bikini covered by a long T-shirt. Her legs show up to her thighs. A firm lean body in prime condition. Her skin has tanned a deeper apricot than the last time he saw her, the sinuous plait is fastened into a circlet at the nape of her neck. A burgeoning but understated bust, a long curvaceous neck and the most graceful movements he's ever seen. The thinning T-shirt gives her a look of artless simplicity the most prestigious fashion model might try in vain to copy. Nor is she one of those bony untoned girls. Her muscles moves smoothly and gracefully beneath her tanned unblemished skin.

'Can I help, Anne?'

Determinedly blonde hair, frizzed into equally determined curls, has come up from below. A striped navy-and-white sailor shirt emphasises coarsening red skin around the emerging neck and face, smeared orange lips pull back on large insistent teeth.

'You are a dear.' Two chunky arms are raised, the hands grasping four plates. 'Take the plates, there's a pet,' she wheezes. The effort of cooking and climbing steep steps must have got to her. 'I'll grab the rolls and cutlery and bring them up.'

Emily takes the pile of plates and waits. She balances the whole load with ease. Long sure strides take her to the far side of the deck where she spreads it all out.

It's an almost still day, only a slight sea breeze ruffling the water. Sophie is distributing glasses ready for drinks. Her father is fastening the ropes and lowering anchor.

'Hi there!'

Sophie looks up at Dwight. He sees her eyes mirror a small middle-aged man in dark glasses, white hair almost eclipsed by the expansive straw hat, mouth smiling at her as he stands on the deck of the elegant trimaran alongside. She goes on setting out glasses, ignoring him.

'It's Dwight!' A surprised but friendly shout. 'Hello! I didn't know you sail!'

'Sure thing.' He grins at Emily. 'It's one of my hidden talents.'

'This is my friend Sop – Sophie Pontings,' Emily introduces them. 'The only member of the family you've met so far is Tatman!'

The cocker spaniel, right.

A faint disinterested smile crosses Sophie's freckled face as she turns. Charles Pontings looks up at the first sound of a male voice. He lumbers over, causing the boat to jiggle. The cutlery slides to one side.

'Charles Pontings,' he announces to Dwight, standing as straight as his paunch will allow. 'You know the Brookes?'

'We're neighbours,' Dwight is keen to explain. So far everything is going as he's rehearsed it. 'I'm at The Woolhouse.' Harry's assurances have been vindicated – his house is his introduction to the club.

A pause as Charles takes that in. His brows, bristling over his sun-glasses, disappear below them. 'Of course! Valerie mentioned you'd strayed into her little patch,' he brays. He takes off the dark glasses and examines first Dwight, and then his vessel. 'She yours?' He stretches his neck to try to read the name, but the two boats are too close for that.

'*First Lady*? You bet!' Dwight smooths his right hand over a nearby rail. 'She's some sweet lulu.' Too late he realises he's allowed his enthusiasm to betray him. English decorum decrees he should have sounded less brash. Quite a nice boat would have been more in keeping.

Anne's appearance saves Charles the bother of thinking up a suitable reply. 'My wife Anne,' he says, unenthusiastically.

'Dwight Delaney. Delighted to make your acquaintance, A...' He stops and turns the A into an indecipherable Ah, never can quite tell about using the first name.

'Mr Delaney!' Anne gushes. 'Valerie's told me all about you. Will you join us for lunch?'

Charles scowls at his wife but she doesn't even look at him.

'That will be dandy.' Dwight decides to risk offering a contribution. 'I was just about to fix lunch myself. May I donate a little something?' He turns, lithe in immaculate white dacks, feet dapper in their Churchills, and disappears into his cabin. He resurfaces with a Fortnum and Mason's hamper and a bottle of Veuve Clicquot, beads of moisture trickling down the green glass neck clasped in his fingers.

He smiles at Emily and hands her the bottle across the water separating the two decks. He offers the hamper to Charles.

'Do I smell steak?' he sniffs, turning to Anne.

'The butcher managed the most fabulous Angus.'

'That's real neat.' Dwight whiffs, appreciative. 'Almost like being back home. I was making do with a little Ossetra.'

Charles' eyes hood and his nostrils flare, but he takes the wicker basket without comment.

'How marvellous!' Anne trills. 'We'll have to have the hors d'oeuvre after the main course, but I think we might be able to manage that!'

'I can certainly manage that.' Sophie dips her hand into the basket and draws out a small jar of caviar and slices of brown bread and butter wrapped in cling film.

'So you're a keen sailor, Mr Delaney?' Anne asks.

'Dwight. It's relaxing after a hard week's slaving in the city. But I'm no expert. I just fool around.'

'You're in the City?' Charles looks up, interested for the first time.

'I'm with Stoare Vantile...'

Dwight laughs. 'I should have said in town. I run a model agency in Mayfair,' he admits, nervously. He's not too sure about that, remembering Alan Penn-Winton's response – girl trade – and talking rapidly to make sure they don't get the wrong impression. 'As a matter of fact, I'm looking for new talent for the East Coast Boat Show right now.'

'You're at the Boat Show?'

'Harry Solferino's a buddy of mine.'

'You mean Solferino Trust?'

'That's the guy, crazy about boats. He's just taken over Janner's Yard. Personally picked this little lady out for me.' He looks back at *First Lady*. 'He wants her on his stand, together with the best fashion model I can come up with!' Dwight smiles around. 'Harry's a great believer in the selling power of human beauty.' He turns his head towards Emily and is struck again by her uncanny loveliness. That casual air, those long, smooth limbs, that gorgeous hair...

'Gee! Look at that Ferrari, Mom. Look at her lines!'
'Don't touch, Dwight, honey.'

So near and yet so far. Should he give it a try? Most girls would do anything for a chance to model.

'You know Harry Solferino well?'

There is a note of reverence in Charles Pontings' voice. Dwight knows that Harry's name counts in the financial world – 'I'm the greatest!' Harry is forever insisting – but he's always assumed that to be Harry's usual exaggeration.

'He's on my board of directors,' Dwight says, now understanding the implications as far as Charles is concerned. Job hunting, of course. But Dwight is much more concerned with his own brain wave about the modelling.

'Appearances are so deceiving, honey.'

'Have you ever considered modelling?' He turns to Emily, forcing his voice low key. It sounds husky and he clears his throat. 'I guess you have what it takes.'

She giggles, amused but nervous. 'I've shown horses at gymkhanas.' The giggle turns into an impish grin. 'If you think that counts!'

'Not a bad start, I'd say,' Dwight tells her. He guesses the judges found it hard to concentrate on the horses. 'You know about boats. Why not have a try?'

The grin has gone. 'I don't think...' But her eyes belie her.

'Go on, Emily. You'd be a real knockout. Lay 'em out cold,' Charles, gulping champagne, leers at her. So he's been sniffing round.

'I'm sure Valerie will think it a good opportunity, Emily.' Anne glances at the girl, takes in her figure, her hair. 'Why not discuss it with her?'

'Your Mom'll raise hell if she finds out.'

Dwight sees Anne compare blonde and brunette, an expression of sad resignation. Sophie's close neat cap of shining brown and enormous chocolate eyes gives her a coltish gamin attraction – the pull of youth. Gangly arms and legs, though glowing with health, lack that indefinable quality which Emily carries within herself.

Emily frowns, examines her worn shoes, the colour heightening on her cheeks.

'It's a wonderful idea, Em,' Sophie encourages her. 'Give it a whirl. I would!'

'To the pure all things are pure,' Mom repeats.

Inspiration strikes Dwight. Harry will kill him, but he'll learn to live with that. Harry is no kind of dummy, he'll get the point. He'll even come to see the freckles as an attraction – Sophie will be the perfect foil for Emily's beauty. Dwight doubts anyone else will have such youth, such innocence on their stand.

'You come too,' he nods at Sophie. 'I bet Harry'll be real bucked to have a pair of beauties.'

The immediate change in Emily's eyes is all he needs for self congratulation.

CHAPTER 7

Dwight has to sell two ideas to Valerie: Emily working as a model and that she'll be doing it at the Boat Show. Neither will be easy, but peanuts compared to selling her Harry Solferino.

'I'm not quite sure how this friend of yours fits in,' Valerie objects the moment Dwight raises the subject.

'My company provides models for special occasions. Harry is a client – a long-standing client and an old buddy of mine. He has a prime stand at the Show. He's quite big in boats.'

'A boat broker?'

Telling Valerie precisely what Harry does will be counterproductive. 'That's one of his businesses. He runs a number of them.' Dwight bares teeth in what he hopes is a disarming smile.

'He's a tycoon?'

'Guess so; a VIP in the business world. You can be sure he won't hold back on expenses. He'll put the girls up at Hintlesham Hall,' Dwight says nonchalantly. 'They'll enjoy that.'

'You mean he has a house there?'

Dwight doesn't follow that right away, then gets her meaning. 'House? No, no, Harry's not a country type. He's gets his kicks from heavy exhaust fumes! Hintlesham's a quite superior hotel outside Ipswich.'

'A stately home turned commercial, you mean.'

'I guess. All the girls have to do is put on some gear I'll arrange

58

through the agency. And learn to sweet-talk people looking at the boats.'

'What sort of gear?'

He has to reassure her he isn't thinking of skimpy swim wear. 'Wide-bottomed trousers and...'

'A proper sailor look?'

Wide-bottomed trousers on women aren't quite the navy style, but he lets it go. 'That's the idea. With a hat...'

'And Anne is allowing Sophie to do it?'

Seems that matters. 'I got the idea Charles Pontings is quite keen.'

'Is Anne going up to Ipswich with Sophie?'

'She'll drive up to London with Charles every day and take the train. Then she'll look in on the pair of them.'

'And what about the evenings, Dwight?'

'The Pontings have offered to take care of that. They'll pick the girls up after the Show, have dinner with them at the Hall, tuck them up for the night.'

'So they can come home every night, actually?'

'Not a good idea, Valerie. The trips will be very tiring, and they'll have to make a real early start.' He puts on his professional air. 'They need their beauty sleep!'

Valerie earths up potatoes with a great show of soil, bent on finishing the row. The whole project should seem quite innocent to her and he'll offer Emily – both girls – professional models' rates. Sure bet Emily hasn't passed on that piece of information.

'There won't be time for them to get in trouble, Valerie. Juliette will be staying at the same hotel and standing guard.'

'Juliette?'

'One of my best tutors. Very capable and the new recruits really take to her. The girls'll need a few tips on how to put their make-up on.'

'You need to know how to protect your skin, Dwight, learn to handle your disability.'

'Make-up? You're going to cover Emily's glowing skin with disgusting make-up?'

59

'Just a touch or two of colour, eye-shadow, lipstick.' He stands erect to show what a straight guy he is. 'Learning the right way to talk to clients is important, too,' he hurries on, eyes smiling away difficulties.

'I'm not really sure, Dwight. Emily's never been away from home before, let alone without me.'

'Ipswich is just a small country town.' Time to raise how much Emily will make. Even folks like the Pontings count their bucks. Just a question of getting round to it diplomatically. 'They'll be doing a professional job. No kinda picnic, I can tell you! They'll have to get up real early, around six, make their way to the sea front...'

'That's nothing, Dwight. Emily is used to getting up at dawn.'

'Sure, but these Shows are hard work, and it'll be new to her.'

'How are they going to get to the actual Show?'

For a moment Dwight thinks he's blown it. If he offers to pick the girls up she could put the wrong angle on that. He sees the way out: 'Marjorie Jennings will pick them up on her way. She's my training manageress and a real tartar. She'll explain any snags the girls might come across and how to deal with them.'

'I thought you mentioned someone called Juliette will brief them?' Valerie's suspicions turn her round face to oval.

'Juliette's the expert on make-up, Marjorie will make sure they're properly briefed on where to stand and how to show off the boats.' He sees Valerie look uncomfortable and rushes on. 'Not that that's a problem, no way. But they'll need to come up a couple of days before the Show so she can rehearse them. All Harry really needs the girls to do is look decorative, smile at customers.'

'Do your best to get face, honey.'

'Make encouraging noises, offer them a drink, that kinda stuff. They won't have problems.'

'A drink? You mean an alcoholic drink?'

Are the Brookes teetotallers? No way. 'A glass of sherry, I guess. Rye or bourbon for some of Harry's pals.'

'And someone else will be there all the time?'

'No white slave trade,' he grins at her, 'I categorically give you my word on that!'

She laughs at last and he sees he's there. One more sweep along the potato row and she's through. Just a little oiling of the wheels...

'Naturally they'll receive the normal rate for the job.' She seems busy cleaning her rake, but she's listening. 'You can probably dispense with the paying guests for the rest of the season. Have the whole place to yourselves all summer.'

'They're all booked, I'm afraid.'

'There's plenty of time; unbook them.'

'Some of them haven't confirmed yet, actually.'

'So grab your chance. It'll do you both a power of good.'

'The roof does need doing, it's always leaking. It really will be wonderful to be able to afford to have a proper job done.'

'A new truck? We need to take care of the roof, Earl!'

Roof? What the hell has the roof to do with it? Dwight feels himself warm with fury. Why is she assuming Emily's earnings are hers? He hasn't set this up so that Valerie can pay her bills. But he has set it up. If he's honest, he's set it up so he can see something of Emily away from her mother.

'Bright sun's too much for you, honey. Your skin can't take it.'
'We'll be under the trees, Mom!'
'Risking your health for those silly games your father plays.'

More than that, he has to admit. He's set it up to help the girl finish with all those exhausting chores, ruining her youth, her looks. Show her what life outside West Sussex can offer, what he can offer. Valerie is keeping an unjust stranglehold on her daughter.

'I suppose it will show Emily just how lucky she is, living out here. She'll find it hard to cope with Ipswich air!'

She'll gulp it down and ask for more, Dwight guesses. 'It sure will,' he says demurely.

'They always say children get restless at Emily's age, want to do exactly the opposite to their parents' wishes.'

'They need to find their own feet, I guess.'

61

'She thinks the world of her father.' Valerie returns to a subject that appears to bother her a good deal. She sounds bleak.

He looks forward to weekends with Pop. Taking the boat out, fishing on the lake.

'You said she doesn't see that much of him,' Dwight reminds her.

'She doesn't. Three or four times a year.'

Maybe, Dwight thinks, Valerie is worried that the guy will hear of Emily's job and start hanging out in Ipswich. 'Does he have business interests near Ipswich?'

'What? Oh no, nothing like that.' Valerie laughs. 'I'm not expecting Reginald to kidnap her! He's somewhere on the south coast, I hear, running a kennels or some such thing. Never bothers to keep in touch, let alone send her a little something.'

'So she doesn't really know him?'

'They get together at Emily's school, before the Governors' meetings. He's on the board...'

'You mentioned that.'

'... though I've no idea what he can possibly do for the place.'

'And what about her half-siblings?'

Valerie stares at him as though she hasn't understood.

'Her extended family. Didn't you say Emily's father has a couple of kids with the lady he ran off with?'

'I know what sibling means. It's just that I never think of them as anything to do with Emily.'

Half-brothers or sisters. Valerie reckons the girl is all hers, no other relatives at all. Seems to be happy to have it that way. But is Emily?

'Of course she occasionally sees her uncles. Her grandparents are long dead.'

'No cousins?'

'Reginald's brothers never married.'

'What about your own folks, Valerie? Don't you visit with them?'

'I haven't any,' she says. 'My parents died just before I married. That's how I had the cash to put down the deposit for Bramblings.'

That kind of explains why Valerie is so keen to hold on to her

62

home, her daughter. No wonder, there's no one else at all. 'And then you met Reginald,' Dwight prods.

'I became a photographer's assistant. He was one of our clients.'

'So you know a little of what my girls do.'

'Not really. The chap I worked for just took pictures at weddings and family portraits. No fashion photography. I touched up the negs. I was always quite good at art.'

'How did your husband fit the bill?'

'He came in to have a portrait taken for his mother – as a present for her sixtieth birthday. He's her youngest.'

Just one more try, one more attempt to get her keen. 'Why don't you come up with the girls on the first day? I can drive the four of us up, and you can go back with the Pontings the next night.'

Dwight sees Valerie hesitate. Maybe offer to put her up for the whole time ... defeats the whole purpose, he tells himself. Let it ride. 'Why not spend the night as my guest at Hintlesham Hall? Give me a chance to repay all your hospitality.'

'I'll mull it over, Dwight.'

'Sure thing. I don't want to rush you none. But I need to know in a day or two, the Show's in the third week of May. We need to start work on it now.'

'I know you think I'm being over protective.'

'You think I'm a fussy old mother hen.'

That's exactly what he thinks. 'She's your only daughter.'

'It's not that I want to cramp her style, nothing like that. It's just – well, it's rather throwing her in at the deep end.'

'You don't need to worry about Emily. She'll take to the water in no time.'

'She's a quiet country girl, Dwight. She's used to animals and the countryside, not crowds of rich people who can afford expensive boats.'

Nothing like the Pontings, for instance! 'Think it over, Valerie. Just let me know as soon as you can.'

CHAPTER 8

'You've let her get away with it again, Mr Delaney.' Jock McClough's strong army boots and heavy dark-brown waterproof cover him almost like a second skin. 'I can tell right away, you know. She isn't even obeying the heel commands.'

The young guy's mournful look tweaks at Dwight's conscience. Not just a dumbass from the city, he can hear Jock think, but an American at that. Not a hope in hell of learning how to handle a dog properly.

'That's what you pay me for, you know. To get Sheba trained.'

'Sure I know that, Jock. Coupla things been on my mind.'

Jock always brings the bitch round for Dwight on Friday afternoons. No amount of business can keep him from his weekend at The Woolhouse. Since there's no way he can get in touch with Clanesbury's gamekeeper and cancel the appointment he always keeps it. Jock theoretically lives with his parents in Petersfield, but he's hardly ever there. He spends his time in the woods. When he isn't working he studies the local wildlife from his hide. And he's happy to train Sheba for Dwight. The arrangement suits the both of them. Jock enjoys handling a dog well, Dwight needs a trainer for Sheba.

Dwight considers yet again if he should bring up the subject of the mutilated animal bodies he's found in the woods with Jock. They are, after all, on his 'beat'. He had a stint in the police force, he told Dwight at their first meeting. Obvious from the beginning that Jock has all the makings of a good detective.

'So why leave?' Dwight asked at the time, careful before entrusting Sheba to him.

'I likes being outdoors.'

'Didn't you have a beat?'

'Squad car. Couldn't stand that. And all the pen-pushing that goes with it.'

So the indoor job's a soft option.

'I likes to be out and about. All weathers.' He looks Dwight up and down. 'And I likes being in the woods. When Lord Clanesbury advertised for another gamekeeper to look after the Smithbrook Estate, I applied right off.'

'And you got the job,' Dwight prompts, waiting through a silence which wasn't going to end.

'That's right.'

'Clanesbury naturally snapped him up,' Valerie filled Dwight in. 'And made him head gamekeeper within the year. Brilliant at the job, of course.' Her owlish eyes turned on Dwight. 'But he's a bit rigid for my taste. Does everything by the book.'

Dwight is reluctant to broach the subject of the woodland oddities with Jock. He can't rid himself of the feeling that somebody is in great distress, and asking him for help. That isn't in Jock's line. He doesn't suffer weaklings gladly.

'You promised to help me, Earl!'
'I got to run.'

The almost physical sound of an insistent voice, whispering in his ear, is urging Dwight to action. If something really were seriously wrong, he reasons, Jock would be the guy to stop it. Should he confide in him now? He shrugs the tiresome feelings off, unwilling to commit himself with so little to go on.

'I sure am sorry, you guys,' he grins at both dog and man. 'We'll do better this weekend.' He looks at Sheba, glistening with energy, fighting fit. Except he doesn't want her to have to fight.

Jock takes Sheba with him on his shooting expeditions against the magpies and crows which threaten the estate's game-bird nests. 'Them bloody birds is vermin,' Jock has exploded several times. 'If

I don't keep they pests under control we won't have no game-birds left.'

While his dog learns to retrieve Dwight arranges his business activities in London. Once Models International is up and running, he promises himself, he'll take more time with Sheba. He's pretty well given up on finding a human partner. The most he reckons he can hope for is Emily's bright smile.

Jock's determination to get rid of predators is something Dwight prefers not to dwell on. It's countryside peace that he's looking for.

'She needs to be kept up to scratch,' Jock now mutters. 'Otherwise we can't get on.' He runs a grubby hand through a shock of Titian red.

'The trouble is she's in love,' Dwight says, on impulse, then regrets it almost as soon as he's said it.

'She's not on heat...' The guy takes in it's meant to be a joke. 'Oh, yeah,' he says, shifting from one foot to the other.

'With Raffy. From Bramblings.' Is he trying to get a rise out of Jock?

Steady grey eyes look at him. 'Been up there, has she, gov?'

The 'gov' explodes like a rifle shot. So he's right, Jock is one of the hopefuls Emily has under her spell. That explains Valerie's muted reservations about him. No chance for the poor guy, naturally. But he can't blame him for trying. Better make sure Jock knows it isn't he who's getting in his way, or he'll lose the best dog-handler in the whole of Sussex – East and West. And he has plans for Sheba. He wants Jock to train her in tracking. He's determined to get to the bottom of what the hell is going on without alerting any of the locals.

'I guess you know Mrs Brooke. She's being real helpful about introducing me to a couple of her friends. And young Raffy hasn't been slow to get acquainted with Sheba.'

'Daresay,' Jock mumbles, bending down and adjusting the choke collar round Sheba's neck. He puts the connection on top so that, as soon as it's released, gravity opens the collar wide again. 'Just keep her on your left side as you walk, hold the lead across two of your right hand fingers and give a sharp jerk upwards with your left hand if she tries to dawdle or to rush ahead. She knows better'n that.' He demonstrates on the dog who doesn't immediately respond. A more emphatic jerk keeps her in line. 'Sharp, mind!'

'You sure she needs that choke thing?'

'She's got to learn.'

'OK, Jock. You're the boss.' He unties the string Jock uses for a leash and pulls a soft white leather one out of his pocket. 'I bought her this one. Fancy, right?'

'Good sight too fancy, if you asks me.' Jock snorts, but doesn't say anything more against it.

'Why don't we split a couple of beers tonight?' Dwight suggests, just as Jock's turning to leave.

'Meet at the Fox and Hounds you mean?'

Why is he so hesitant? Emily? The local pub is the place everybody meets, as Dwight understands it. Perhaps Jock isn't crazy to be seen palsy-walsying with the stranger from the US. The job is one thing, drinking together quite another. 'Wherever you say.'

Jock looks at him uncertainly, then nods. 'I'll be there around eight. Can't stay too long, got to get back to the hide.'

And he's gone, striding down the path with long sure paces, glancing neither to left nor right. Sure knows where he's going, Dwight reflects, and that he's going to get there. Emily could do a lot worse.

CHAPTER 9

A shy sun is playing hide and seek among the mackerel clouds, the creeping mists of drizzle softening bare branches summering into green. Rain earlier in the day held onto leaves in drops, large globules reflecting gentle light and nodding drips on to Dwight's deerstalker, then sneaking down his back. Dwight turns up the collar of his coat and plods on.

A familiar bark tells him they're near Bramblings. Suddenly, as though she were an apparition, he sees Valerie advance towards him. He turns right round to change direction, polite, to keep her company.

'The odd thing is,' she greets him without preamble, 'that these peculiar things should happen in a neighbourhood like this.'

So the savaging of dead animals has preyed on her, in spite of what she said. Dwight, a little out of breath from walking the two miles from his house at Sheba's pace, hoped for a short break at Bramblings before moving on. He'll be fitter when he walks Sheba every day.

'Sit, Sheba,' he says hopefully as soon as he sees Valerie.

'I'm just off to the millpond,' she breathes at him. She is, clearly, just starting her walk and he changes the command to 'Heel' almost at once. The bitch trots beside him dutifully, used to keeping up Jock's pace.

'OK if I join you?'

'Delighted.' At first Valerie's slower tempo forces Dwight to jerk the choke collar several times to check his bitch.

'Let's go this way; there's something I promised to show you.'

Does she mean that this time she's found a mutilated body?

'The kingcups are out.' She scrambles down the steep slope, then looks back at Dwight. 'Am I going too fast?'

Dwight insists Sheba follow him instead of the other way around. Small pebbles trickle underfoot and cause him problems.

'She's only a puppy,' Valerie protests, clearly unhappy that he has ordered Sheba to adjust her speed to his. 'I always think a loving upbringing matters more than strict control.'

'She'll never learn if I don't stay in command,' Dwight counters, irritated, thinking of Jock. 'I see you've let Raffy go off on his own. Aren't you nervous that something might happen to him?'

'He'll give as good as he gets, I expect!' But she stops and whistles for him. 'I really don't think things are as bad as all that,' Valerie goes on, but hooding her eyes. 'Only a certain type of person lives in this area. Hardly the sort to go slicing up dead rabbits and hacking hedgehogs to pieces.'

'It doesn't just happen, Valerie. Somebody is taking out their frustrations, and they're doing it right here, right in your own back yard.' The constant refrain about the glories of West Sussex is beginning to exasperate him. He knows about that, it's why he's here.

He kicks at what looks like a small spruce branch lying across the path. It reminds of his childhood by the smell of resin. But these are young trees, specifically planted. Quite different from the dense forests he was raised in.

'Don't, Dwight.' Valerie stands stock still. He nearly crashes into her, it's so sudden. She seems to make a habit of changing course. He's taken off his glasses and he simply hasn't been quick enough to grasp what she's doing.

'This is appalling.' Valerie remains motionless, looking at the newly planted saplings. They're Tom Butler's latest project. Dwight follows her gaze. Nothing seems very different from the week before. Undergrowth cut back in a rough sort of way, a few odd branches lying around, chestnut paling enclosing the area to protect the trees from the ravages of deer. And, specifically to protect against hares or rabbits gnawing the bark in winter, the saplings are surrounded by translucent plastic cylinders about four feet high. They looks like serried ranks of phallic symbols, erupted in Sussex woodlands. He puts his glasses on to take another look.

'The saplings, Dwight. Look at what someone's done.'

They looks exactly as such plantations always look.

'Savagely cut level with that plastic stuff.'

Now he can see why he hasn't realised something's wrong right away. His interest in trees isn't keen enough for him to notice anything more than the cylinders. The devastation is extraordinary. Every single sapling, as far as they can see, has been decapitated. The small defenceless tops are scattered by the pull of gravity, strewn higgledy-piggledy on the ground between the planting tubes. That's why he didn't see them, they just seemed part of the general untidiness. In a way, he can't help feeling, it's quite funny. Of course it's necessary, but somehow he hates those plastic totem poles. They wink at him, topless and pointless now.

A desolate playground. Charred upright trunks stand stark and black. They have short stubs for branches, natural ladders for him to climb.

'Won't the trees just grow anyway?' Dwight tries out. Something to say, he knows well enough the trees are ruined as a crop.

Valerie rounds on him. 'You really don't know the first thing about tree management.' Her arms flail about. 'I thought you said your father was a forest ranger.' She scrutinises, rather pedantically Dwight feels, the totem poles. 'They might, if there's sufficient rain. But the whole point is to get trees, not bushes. How are they supposed to grow into long trunks for timber if they're topped like this?'

'So whoever did it knows something about growing trees.'

There is a pause while Valerie digests this piece of deduction. 'Almost anyone knows that.'

'It's a calculated act of sabotage, whichever way you look at it. Seems there's someone with a gripe against Tom Butler, wouldn't you say?'

'Not necessarily. It could have been done by one of those groups who don't like plantations.'

'Deliberate plantings, you mean? What's wrong with those?'

'Too regular, or not the natural species for this area,' she says. 'That line of thinking. But people have to make a living. Tom's planted quite a few of the indigenous trees, too. Up on the ridge he's even planted oak. Well, you know, you walk past all the time.'

They walk on in silence – the whole plantation, not a single sapling missed out as far as Dwight can tell.

'I think I'll call on Anne,' Valerie bursts out. 'Charles said the next odd thing that happens, he wants to know right away. He's going to set up some sort of vigilante group.'

So she's been disturbed enough to discuss things with Anne. 'Charles? Is he home during the day?'

'There are problems with his firm. I think they're laying off staff again.'

Interference from Charles Pontings is exactly what Dwight is trying to avoid. 'I'll come with you,' he volunteers. The time has come to enlist Jock's help. He'll talk to him this evening, at the Fox and Hounds.

Valerie, somewhat out of breath from climbing the steep drive winding up to Oak Court, leads the little deputation towards the front door. They can see Anne through the wrought-iron gate at the side, kneeling in her beloved white garden, secateurs poised above the silver white foliage of anaphalis triplinveris. She's snipping away, but turns at the sound of crunching gravel.

'This is a surprise!'

Dwight gulps for air after the climb, notices Valerie is only slightly winded. He certainly isn't very fit.

'Not a very pleasant one, I'm afraid.' Valerie sounds grim. 'We've just seen the most appalling piece of vandalism you can imagine.'

'Another mutilated animal?'

'Worse, in a way. This time, whoever it is, has gone for something living.'

Anne stops the snipping. 'You mean, this time they actually maimed a live animal...'

'Not an animal. We've just walked past Tom's new softwood

plantation – you know, the one by the bridle path down towards the millpond. I was taking Dwight to show him the kingcups. He hasn't been that way so far.' Valerie pauses dramatically. 'Hacked to pieces.'

'Err, hmm, well not quite hacked, Valerie. All the tops have been cut off, down to those plastic plant guards.'

'All the saplings? Are you sure?'

'We've just come from there.'

'Only the right sort of people live around here,' Anne says, as though echoing Valerie, 'it's never happened before.'

'Why doesn't Gramma like me, Pop?'
'C'mon, Dwight, she's OK.'

That woman's pretty sure I'm responsible, Dwight decides, taking in Anne's hostile state, furious at the idea. She's been thinking that all along, and now she's sure.

'Someone's acting very oddly,' Valerie agrees. 'And the only thing we can be sure of is that it's somebody, or somebodies, human. Animals don't behave in that way!'

'The plastic guards are there to protect against hares,' Dwight reminds them.

The two women stare at Dwight, then turn away.

'Must be someone who's definitely mixed up,' Anne volunteers, as though that solved the mystery, frowning at Dwight.

'Mixed up?'

'Mentally, I mean. Abnormal; you know the sort of thing.' She sweeps her eyes over the white hair, glances towards the pink eyes and then beyond, reddening faintly.

'Psychopathic, yes,' Valerie agrees.

So she did listen!

'Someone who doesn't live here, presumably.' Valerie sighs. 'There are all these tourists now...'

A stranger cut down every single sapling? Dwight doesn't believe even Valerie can kid herself to that extent.

'Well, you know what I mean, Valerie. We can vouch for almost everyone.' Anne turns away from Dwight, shrugging.

72

'How's the new groom working out?' Valerie asks.

Dwight gathers right away that something is going on in the Pontings' household. Hell hath no fury... Anne certainly seemed huffy, bad-tempered, when they arrived. She's much calmer now.

'Nina? She handles the horses well enough.' Anne dismisses the subject quickly, very quickly. 'Eats almost as much as a horse herself,' she adds, forcing a laugh.

'Actually, we came in hopes of catching Charles. Is he at home?'

'Matter of fact he is. They're not as busy at the office as they used to be... Computers taking over, he says.'

'Then we're in luck...'

'Come down to the stables with me.' She puts the garden trug inside the potting shed. 'Charles said he wanted to check on Landrover. He'll be delighted to collect evidence from everyone. Thrilled to get in on a fresh trail.' A look of triumph. 'And this time we know exactly where the crime has been committed!'

Dwight finds himself wondering whether they think the dead rabbits and the hedgehog were imported.

The trio, dogs following, walk Indian file towards the stables set below the house, near the paddock at the back. Anne, in front, pushes tall rank greenery bowed low with the weight of earlier rain to either side, swishing her secateurs. Nobody speaks. Anne opens the top of the stable door and the two women walk up to it and peer into the gloom. Dwight holds back, hoping to catch Charles later.

Landrover hears the familiar creaking and noses up, momentarily covering the age-old sound of two forms clinched together in the hay, heaving and panting. The horse's neighing partly covers Anne's sudden intake of breath. Quickly, inspirationally, she shuts the stable door, pushing Landrover's nose gently out of the way.

'Don't think anyone's there,' she says, abrupt. 'Charles is probably already spying out the land.' She wheels right round and looks at Valerie who has stepped back and turns to signal Dwight not to come further.

There isn't even a change in tone as Valerie smiles at Anne. 'We'll be off then. The dogs have had rather a long walk.'

Dwight is impressed by Valerie's instant manoeuvre.

'Send Charles round to Bramblings when he gets back and we'll sort out what to do.'

'Sounds like the second time around for Charles,' Valerie suggests to Dwight as they're walking back, 'Stoare Vantile let him go before, then took him on again when things were hotting up in the late nineties. Now things have got really tight. Charles is fifty-four. I imagine they're looking for younger blood.'

'I daresay he's squirrelled away his little pile.' Dwight is taken aback by the sure grasp she seems to have on what is going on in the City. 'Something terribly boring' – bullshit! Good on property values, too.

'Lost the lot in the crash.'

How does she know that, he wonders? Wishful thinking, or just exaggeration? For the moment he's more concerned with Anne's reactions.

'Anne thinks I'm a prime suspect,' he tries out on Valerie.

'Not really. She just doesn't like the idea of it being anyone who lives here...'

'I live here!'

'Of course you do, my dear. How silly of me.'

'I still think you ought to take precautions. These things have a habit of escalating into something really dangerous, you know.'

'You sound as though you have personal experience of that. Anyway, what d'you want me to do, Dwight? Carry a gun?'

'Install a telephone,' he answers promptly. 'Let me do it for you, Valerie. You'd be doing me a favour.'

She walks ahead of him without saying anything.

'It'll mean you can call Emily when she's in Ipswich.'

'You're assuming that!'

'I really think it will be good for everyone. Anyway, I was counting on her – I haven't even looked for other girls.'

'All right, Dwight. I promise to think about a telephone connection.' She sighs. 'I don't think you really understand. We're quite a long way from the nearest line.'

'At Oak Court, presumably.'

'That's it exactly. I'd have to pay for BT to bring the line to me before they'll connect us.'

'It's not a problem, Valerie. I said I'd be glad to do it.'

'That doesn't mean I want to take you up on it.'

'As a friend, Valerie. Simply as a friend. No strings ...'

'I'm not doubting your motives.'

'You can pay me out of Emily's fees. Deal?'

'I'll sleep on it,' is the best he can get out of her. 'Now let's do something pleasant, let's go and see those kingcups.'

She thinks there may be something else, she wants to know whether there's another flower-decked altar, Dwight feels convinced. 'That will be nice,' he agrees. He's quite tired by now but even so – he, too, wants to see whether there's anything else. What's more they're company for each other – and protected by two dogs.

More slowly now, both of them tired, they retrace their steps, past the beheaded saplings, down to the mill stream. There are no obvious altars or offerings of picked wildflowers along the way.

They're walking beside the stream: sparkling, laughing water skipping over moss-covered rocks, the sound of rushing water up ahead. Beside the mill the pond stretches round, mirroring the trees, silky smooth. And on the other side, winking bright, the marshy edge is speckled with little yellow globules.

'There they are,' Valerie points towards them. 'Real kingcups. They're getting awfully rare. Isn't that a glorious sight?'

Dwight puts his hand up to shield his eyes from the glare and stares. Right across the pond he can see little chalices reflecting gold into the shadows. They warm his heart numbed with the gloom of further unsavoury happenings. Will they now stop? Has the miscreant had his fill? Kidding himself again, he knows it's only the beginning. He's seen it all before, remembers all too well.

'That is beautiful,' he breathes. 'Let's go a little nearer.' He turns to look at the small round woman with him. 'That is, if you can manage.'

'Of course I can,' she says at once. 'That's what we came for.'

A moorhen, her flotilla of young chicks behind her, scuttles across the water, squawking her disapproval of disturbance. They see the noose right by her.

There's a noose around his neck, drawn tight.
'Owlet,' he whispers to his pet. 'See what I got?'

A thin round piece of wire attached to a long slender bamboo is being drawn away from the water. Dwight begins to sprint as fast as he can towards the further pond side – so near and yet so far. He hears a crashing through the trees and sees the flutter of light-blue material. When he arrives at the actual spot he finds a fishing net lying on the edge, caught up in the kingcups. Small holes, already filling with water, show where gumboots stood. A small child.

Dwight tries to drag the evidence in from the water but, unwilling to ruin his shoes, it eludes him, gliding slowly into the centre of the pond, the pole pointing accusation for a few seconds, then sinking down. Valerie is by Dwight now, staring at the net.

'Tha' be mine,' a treble voice behind them squeaks.

'Peter! What are you doing here?'

'Fishin',' the boy answers, wading his boots towards the sinking net. 'I always fishes 'ere.'

'Why did you run away when you heard us?'

'I dinno 'oo you is,' the child grumbles, water now almost to the top of his boots.

'You'll have to leave it, Peter. It's too far out.'

'I ain't got hanother one.'

This child isn't the culprit who has cut down the trees. He's too small to reach the saplings, unlikely to have the strength to use even good secateurs. And, anyway, where would he get them from?

'I'll get you another fishing net,' Dwight offers. 'Better come back to shore now. We don't want to have to wade in to rescue you.'

The boy looks at Dwight, then at the water trickling into his boots. 'Tha' were yer fault, yer frightened us.'

'Why, Peter? Why are you frightened?' Valerie asks.

'Yer be runnin'.'

'Is that all?'

'Grandad says not to have nothink to do with strangers.'

'Have you seen strangers around here?'

'Dunno.'

'You must know, Peter. Yes or no?'

'Dunno,' he says, edging away. 'Bloke with a great brute of a dog were 'ere. I's to get back now,' he says. 'My Mum'll be waitin'.' He backs determinedly away, then starts running off.

'Old Jem's grandson,' Valerie says. 'A bit rum. He knows

76

practically everyone who lives here. I suppose someone could have driven here to walk their dog.'

'The kid's allowed to fish here?'

'I don't think anyone will take exception to Peter dipping his net into the millpond.'

'So he didn't run because he felt guilty, frightened?'

'He's seen something, yes. But he's too short to have been the one to cut the saplings.'

'I'll call BT when I get back home,' Dwight interrupts, staring at the bamboo now halfway under water. The boy has seen a strange man with a large dog. He himself is a stranger here, and Sheba is quite large. The child will have them all thinking he's the one responsible. He has to find the real culprit, fast. Meanwhile he'd really very much prefer Valerie to have a phone. He turns to her. 'OK?'

'You can send them round to me,' Valerie agrees. 'But I'll decide whether I want to install a phone or not.'

CHAPTER 10

The long balmy evenings of English summertime are a special delight for Dwight. He decides to walk to the Fox and Hounds though the light will have gone by the time he leaves. No problem, Sheba will guide him home. He wouldn't stay late. Just long enough to persuade Jock to train Sheba to track.

The village pub is roughly two miles from The Woolhouse. Dwight walks down a narrow lane cutting through embankments canopied by high trees. The evening has turned sunny, and he's struck at the speed of darkening in the lane, the blotting out of daylight by overhanging greenery and steep banks rising on both sides. He shivers; he should have brought a coat. Rain in the morning has left wet patches underfoot, cold driblets weeping from high branches. Sheba trots to heel at his left. Jock would be proud of them. Dwight increases his pace to test the dog. She dutifully adjusts her gait to his.

A small brick Victorian house smiles rosy-warm welcome. The door is open and he can hear the thump of darts homing in on the board. Jock, right hand poised, is about to throw. Dwight clears his throat and the dart misses. Disappointed 'ah's and 'missed's reverberate round the room.

Jock swivels round. 'You've come, then.' He nods at Dwight, his tone unsmiling.

'Hi there, Jock,' Dwight says, jovial. 'Can I get you another beer?'

'Still got most of a pint.' The gamekeeper turns and aims another dart. The cheers from the watchers tell Dwight it has hit the target. 'I won't be long,' Jock goes on. 'This one's a cert.' He throws the last dart and picks up his drink.

'E's got the double ten,' someone standing next to Dwight breathes. The stench of stale beer is overpowering.

'That's two-one, Bob,' Jock says. He inclines his head at Dwight and marches towards a corner of the room across on the other side. Dwight follows, forgetting to order himself a drink.

'What will you have, sir?' Jock sets down his glass.

'Gee, no, I meant ...'

'I'm afraid they don't run to rye.'

'A small lager will be just fine.'

The room is hushed, as though Dwight were invading territory reserved for others. He can't distinguish much. The bar lights glitter and hurt his eyes. He feels inhibited from wearing his dark glasses. But he can hear well enough, a sort of muted mumbling, words spoken out of the side of the mouth and swallowed more than usual, reach him at intervals.

'... new chap at T'Wool'ouse ...'

'...' er be a bitch'

'... rabbit ... pink...'

'... not that long...'

'... black Lab ...'

'Here we go, then.' Jock sets the half-pint down on the table and slides into the bench opposite Dwight's. 'I see Sheba's on her best behaviour.'

'You'd have been proud of us.' Dwight is eager to report success. 'She's very good at adjusting her speed to mine now.'

'I should think so, too.'

'I expect you all have heard.' Dwight is determined not to lose his chance. 'The whole of Tom Butler's new softwood plantation has been topped.'

'Whatever d'yer mean?' There is no mistaking it, Jock hasn't heard about the outrage and he's startled.

'That new plantation of saplings in those plastic tubes. The one you pass when you take the route through the woods from

79

Smithbrook to Lodsworth. You know, about half way along.'

'That's not on the estate,' Jock says. 'But I know where you mean.' He stares into his beer. 'You're saying someone's deliberately cut the tops off all they new saplings?'

'Right,' Dwight says, 'that's exactly what I'm saying.'

'I hadn't heard.'

'As far as I know it only just happened when I walked past this morning. In fact, from the look of the cuttings, it can't have been much before then.'

Jock pours the remaining beer in his glass down his throat in one go and stands.

'Let me.'

'I think I'd best be getting back,' Jock says. 'Thanks all the same.'

'I'll walk with you,' Dwight insists, taking a gulp from his glass and following the gamekeeper already side-stepping tables towards the door.

'If there's some maniac about topping saplings I'm stopping him,' Jock explodes as he leaves, striding fast and furious towards the little lane and on towards Smithbrook. 'I never heard o' such a thing afore. It's disgraceful.'

'The pits,' Dwight agrees. He keeps up with Jock's stride as best he can. 'Anything unusual going on in your neck of the woods?' The time has come to fill Jock in on what else has been going on, but it does strike Dwight as curious that the young guy is so worked up about Tom Butler's trees. Does he suspect someone he wants to shield? Perhaps Jock already knows about the other incidents. He sure is in a hurry to get away. Anyway, how come Jock hasn't heard about the topping? He's just been in the pub, talking to other locals. Surely some of them know?

'Unusual?' Jock slows to allow Dwight to catch up.

He's a gamekeeper, Dwight remembers. Could be he wouldn't be told of damage in the woods. 'Any tree damage? Any problems with the plants or animals?'

'There be something else, then?'

'Not exactly.' Dwight explains about the rabbits and the hedgehog, though he leaves out the flowers. Why does he do that? Because Jock might consider him a wimp, he guesses. He only wants to confide in Jock because he needs his help to find the miscreant without involving the authorities.

'Too late for that, Mr Delaney,' Jock tells him. 'Damaging crops is a crime. The police will have been called in.'

'It can just be malicious, can't it?' Dwight asks.

'Mr Butler's well liked,' is all Jock has to contribute.

'I thought we might get Sheba on to it,' Dwight suggests. 'You can train her how to track. Matter of fact, I found something that might prove helpful.' He takes a small plastic-wrapped parcel from his trouser pocket and passes it over to Jock. 'It's a matchbox. Nothing special about it, just the ordinary Brymays. But I noticed Sheba snuffling it as we were looking at the devastation, just figured it might come in handy.'

Jock actually stops. He takes the box from Dwight and turns it round and round, looking through the plastic, then makes as though to unwrap it.

'Don't touch it, or you'll get your scent on it.' The box is lying loose, inside the plastic. 'Quite dry, you see. Must have been dropped there just before we got to it ...'

'We?'

'I met Mrs Brooke ...'

'Smokes like a chimney.' Jock laughs. 'Daresay it's hers.'

'No way. She uses a lighter and she had that with her.'

'Well, it's a thought.'

'If the same person is involved with some new damage, Sheba can pick up the scent. Have I got that right?'

'It'll take a bit of time to get her trained.'

'But you can do it.'

'I can do it a'right,' Jock says, overlapping the plastic snugly round the matchbox and pocketing it. 'I'll pick her up tomorrow night.' He turns, jumps over a fence enclosing the Smithbrook estate, leaving Dwight to continue home on his own.

'Wasn't much of a drink, baby cakes,' he confides to Sheba. 'Maybe we'll take another walk.'

There's still enough light to see along the path if he puts his glasses on. Dwight has a hunch: something is happening – right now! He can almost smell it. He trembles.

There it is again. That odd, elusive smell he can't quite identify. He shivers and wishes once more that he hadn't come out without his coat. The skies are clouding up, cutting down brightness. Sheba trots beside him, obedient, going the way he leads. What is he thinking of? Why is he looking for a needle in a woodpile? What purpose can it serve? He can't see much, it's getting chilly, the dog isn't trained, he doesn't even know what he's after.

The acrid suffocating smell of smoke amongst tall trees, tall evergreens. He chokes on it, runs home.

Another happening, another odd, mysterious happening in the quiet woods around him. That's what he's expecting. But can he handle it if he comes across it?

It's as though he has no choice, he's impelled deeper into the woods. Leaf cover, so comforting when the sun shines, begins to blot out what light is left. An evening mist rises into eerie form and embraces him and Sheba in a light soft veil of dimness. A gentle breeze stirs branches overhead. An owl begins to screech, a rustle of fallen leaves betrays a mouse scurrying to find food.

Bramblings is just a sprint away. He isn't all that far from the little track leading to the cottage. Should he call on Valerie? Discuss tactics?

Dwight freezes. He steps aside from the path, behind some rhododendrons, and listens. 'Sit, Sheba,' he commands, guiding her into the shadows. He hears it quite distinctly, the muffled but unmistakable sound of a horse – clipperty, clipperty ... clipperty, clop. Not the right rhythm, the animal is hobbling. A live, maimed animal? He shudders, puts his hand on Sheba. No one likely to ride at this time of night.

A curious, squeaky sound.
The windscreen mists up, dark grey at first, then a bright tinge of red.
Appalled, disturbed, he tries to find his way.

Something terrible – evil – is about to happen: he knows it will. Sweat drenches him as the sound comes nearer, nearer. And then he sees the horse's breath, a funnel of vapour writhing into mist, swirling uncertainly away.

Dwight begins to breathe again. Walking beside the blundering grey, sweat glistening a halo of alabaster around the massive form, are two people. A soft mist shrouds them in a white haze but as he stares, intent on imprinting their features, he's surprised to see two very similar faces. The classic oval shapes, aristocratic noses. One wearing a hard top, eyes straight ahead, virtually disembodied. A double cameo, etched white against the darkening gloom, moving towards him. They're wrapped up in each other, their steps in unison, a melody of eager twittering interspersed with occasional lower rumbling tones accompanying them. And laughter, gay delighted laughter punctuates their conversation like a drum roll.

Not far from where Dwight is hiding he can see the one leading the grey tugging off the riding hat, tossing her hair loose, luxuriant and long. Emily! But who can that be with her?

Her father, something inside his brain clicks at him. Perhaps it's the similarity of the faces, even though veiled, which makes him almost sure Emily is with Reginald Brooke.

The girl, coaxing her charge along the path, stroking the animal's neck, now whispers in his ear just a few yards from Dwight. He notices the form beside Emily brush a white hand across the horse's mane, skirt Emily's left shoulder, then dissolve into the swirling mist without a further word or sound. Has he – it – really been there? Or has he seen refracted spears of light holographed into the haze – a will-o'-the-wisp? Perhaps the sounds he's heard were nightjars telecalling to each other, maybe the laughter the hooting of a predatory owl?

Sheba holds to his command but can't control her tail from brushing at the leaves, panting with the exertion of keeping her master's word. The horse, now passing them, shies away.

'Come along, Landrover,' Emily murmurs, patting the horse's flank but looking round.

The dog's eyes glow reflection of the last beams of light as Emily walks past.

'Sheba!' she calls out, surprised, stopping the horse.

Dwight moves into the path, laughing his relief. 'My goodness,

Emily,' he says, trying to control the tremor in his voice, 'what in the world are you doing out at this time of night?'

'I didn't see you, Dwight.' A strained forced sound, nothing like the happy noises of a few minutes ago. 'Landrover stumbled whilst I was exercising him, and he's slightly lame. I've got to walk him home.'

'You've heard about the saplings?' He adjusts his pace to that of the lamed horse. 'I really don't think you should be about on your own as late as this.'

'Mummy did tell me, yes.'

There is the long interval he has come to know. Has he really heard her chattering to someone? It seems so unlike her usual reticent self.

'I can't stop, Dwight. I can't let Landrover cool down without seeing to his leg.'

'I'll see you back,' Dwight announces. There's no way he's going to allow her to continue alone. He'll make Valerie understand that Emily should be allowed to take the job at the Boat Show. That way she can stop doing all these idiotic – and dangerous – chores. It's ridiculous for the girl to do physical work which will, eventually, ruin her looks. And to add the danger of meeting this vandal stalking the woods is going beyond ordinary common sense. He'll force Valerie to understand.

Then he remembers that Emily wasn't alone. Just who was that with her? Dare he ask? Was it the slasher and does Emily know him?

'Honestly, Dwight. I'm perfectly all right. I've got to take Landrover home first. You'll only have to hang about while I settle him.'

The girl is oddly dismissive, more taciturn than usual, even. He remembers the happy twittering and feels depressed. She is, in his experience so far, not a chatty girl. Dwight has noticed her remarkable reserve before. No question of her joining in the small talk. She simply stays around, demure and silent, while her mother leads the conversation. But just now he's heard her burbling to someone. Did he imagine it? Day-dreamed himself walking next to her? Even seen himself making out! She might just have been talking to the horse.

This is the first time since meeting her that Dwight has found himself alone with Emily. His prodding about the topped saplings brought no response at all. He tries asking about her school days. His questions are politely, firmly, brushed aside and Emily contributes nothing else. She's nervous, holding back.

'Where in the world have you been, Dwight? I've been worried sick about you!'
'Just playing in the woods, Mom.'

'Did I see you with a friend?'

There's something furtive about her attitude. Perhaps his guess about who was with her is way out. Not her father: a boyfriend! She's been meeting someone, now she's worried in case Dwight has seen him, maybe even recognised him. Charles Pontings? Jock?

'A friend? Just Landrover and me.' Emily speaks so softly he can hardly distinguish what she says. It's too dark to see her face, but her voice sounds guilty – a forced nonchalance. 'Oh, listen to that, Dwight. Can you hear the nightingales?'

A blatant lie, then. Should he alert Valerie? He can't even begin to describe the person he's seen, or thinks he's seen. A man, he's pretty sure it was a middle-aged man. He catches the whiff of tobacco smoke on Emily's clothes. And that odd spoor he can't place ... Not necessarily a boyfriend, of course, just someone Emily doesn't want Valerie to know about. Her father would certainly fit that category.

'I heard the horse and stepped aside to let it pass. I saw you quite a long ways off. Surely there was someone walking beside you?'

No reply.

'Of course it's getting dark but I'd bet my bottom dollar he's a relative of yours, he looked so like you.'

'It's very misty; sometimes one can see double in these swirls.'

'I heard you chatting to someone.'

'Talking to Landrover, I expect.' She laughs, a brittle edgy sound, so different from the one he remembers hearing just a few minutes before. 'I do that sometimes. Especially when an animal is hurt, like Landrover. They get worked up, you know. It comforts them if one talks to them.'

85

Such a long speech. They walk in silence while Dwight allows Emily to work out that he knows there was someone. He can feel the girl brooding, grudging at his persistence. 'I know you had company, Emily,' he finally says.

'There's no need to say anything to Mummy,' she blurts out. 'It's not exactly a secret, but I'd just as soon not worry her.' She pulls up the horse in her anxiety. 'You do understand, don't you, Dwight?'

'Can you keep secrets, son?'

'If you say so.' Dwight clears his throat. 'So you see something of your father?'

She tugs at Landrover's reins and the horse nearly blunders into Dwight. 'At the school. He's one of the Governors at the school.'

'Your mother said. I mean apart from that.'

A silence. Dwight is used to that and waits.

'Sometimes I run across him in the woods. If he has time he helps me exercise the animals.'

So it could easily have been Reginald Brooke who was with her, seeing her back. Whether Emily admits it or not, Dwight guesses she was with her father tonight. He wonders how often they meet.

'He breeds lurchers for a hobby. He likes to hunt. They're interests we have in common.'

Taking the boat out, fishing on the lake.
Mom doesn't like his trips with Pop.

The admiration, the excitement in her voice tells Dwight his guess was right on the nail. 'Lurchers?'

'Hounds specially bred for hunting. They're very strong and fast, and almost silent.'

So that's the animal he came across that day he found the rabbits. A lurcher, and maybe Emily's father. 'Sure, Emily. I won't split on you. But it's very late. Shouldn't we at least tell your mother you're OK? Won't she be worrying?'

'Landrover's lame Dwight,' she says as though he's proposing denying the animal help. 'I have to get him home.'

They're at the fork where the drive branches to Bramblings and the path leads on to Oak Court. Emily continues on the path. The horse is more important than her mother? 'If you say so.' He has no right to interfere.

'I'm perfectly all right, Dwight. I know the woods.'

She's now very close to him and makes no move away but brushes against him. That heady smell ... he can make out a mixture of stale smoke mingled with the horse, but there's something else. Suddenly, virtually touching her, he catches her body odour and feels almost delirious with desire. She doesn't worry about being very near him – doesn't notice him at all.

'You can always call on Mummy while I go on to Oak Court,' she suggests.

She trusts him. It's absurd, but it makes his day.

'Remember we're in the shed now.'

The summer visitors have taken over Bramblings. Even if he installed a phone it wouldn't work out. What they really need is a couple of mobiles, to keep in touch with each other. But he knows without asking that Valerie will never even entertain the idea of those.

'I'm not letting you carry on alone,' Dwight perseveres.

They continue in silence to Oak Court.

CHAPTER 11

'Dwight! What a surprise.'

Valerie is standing by the open door of the garden shed, Raffy at her feet. She must have been getting anxious. Looking out for Emily, Dwight guesses.

'I ran into Emily in the woods and decided to escort her back, Valerie.'

'Landrover went lame, Mummy,' Emily says airily. 'That's why I'm late. I told Dwight not to worry. He insisted on seeing me safely to Oak Court and then back here.'

'That was very gentlemanly of you, Dwight.'

'May I visit for just a moment?'

'Of course. Come and have a glass of elderflower champagne.'

It's typical of Valerie to call her concoction champagne. Dwight had some before. A rather syrupy, bubbly drink which she's assured him is as good as that 'ridiculously expensive French rubbish'. Dwight obediently swallowed a small glass before, pretended to appreciate it so as not to hurt Valerie's feelings. He's dismayed to find he'll have to do so yet again. In a good cause, he decides, drinking the fluid without breathing through his nose.

The kerosene lamp glows warm but gives off a most unpleasing odour. Dwight now recognises the smell which eluded him before. The acrid aroma of kerosene oil.

There's a whiff of smoke as the flame burns bright and blackens the glass around it. That's what he'd sniffed on Emily. Because she's the one who cleans the lamps.

'Sorry. These paraffin lamps need fairly constant adjusting.'

Valerie turns the wick lower and the flame comes under control. She leans over the top with a new cigarette end and draws back with satisfaction. Cigarette smoke billows and combines with the smoke from the lamp. Dwight feels a cough rising in his throat and sips the disdained elderflower. At least it might soothe his gullet.

'I have a proposition to make to you, Valerie.'

She laughs. 'I don't suppose you mean quite that. A suggestion, perhaps?'

'A suggestion, right. You know what I mean.' It's not his business. But he can't – he damn well won't – allow the delicate Emily to be exposed to such a life. Why, she's virtually imprisoned with her mother in a hut and forced to carry out unsuitable physical chores far beyond her capacities. Tired out, the poor child is unable to attend to schoolwork properly. No wonder she looks for her father's company.

'I think you should think very seriously about Emily taking on the modelling for the Boat Show,' he urges Valerie again. 'If you agree I'd be glad to pay you in advance ...'

'That's ridiculous, Dwight.'

'Give me a break, here. I'm thinking of the weird happenings in the woods. I guess I don't feel comfortable with Emily roaming the woods on her own at this point.'

'She's always with the animals.'

'You saying that Landrover can protect her?' He can't help the anger in his normally controlled voice. What in hell is the woman thinking of, exposing her only daughter – beautiful, delicate, enchanting – to these grotesque outrages? It puts him in mind of – what? His mother's renters taking over their house, leaving him to sleep in the TV room, he guesses. Yet Valerie is making every kind of sacrifice so the girl can live in a fairy-tale cottage in a fancy setting.

'We have a fine home, Dwight, honey. It's worth making sacrifices for.'

The similarities are remarkable. Valerie keeps her daughter from

89

her father, just like his Mom kept him from Pop. Hiding her among the brambles, like Sleeping Beauty in the fairy tale. He sees himself as the prince who defies all the evil surrounding his sleeping princess, sees himself as her saviour. Knows very well that the tale will not end with his marrying her, but tells himself that he's only interested in Emily's escape from drudgery.

He clears his throat. 'Maybe you really should consider the house the council offered you.'

Valerie jerks her head up at him, eyes slit.

'I'm talking a few weeks, until we clear up what's going on. Emily could be in real danger, Valerie.'

'I know you mean well, Dwight. It's very good of you to take such an interest in us. But we've chosen to live the life we lead, and I don't want it any other way.'

We? Does Emily have a choice? 'Maybe if your solicitor wrote to your ex-husband ...'

Does he spot a reaction from Emily, or imagine it? The girl leaves the room and disappears into the section they use for sleeping.

'We don't need charity.'

So what are they getting when the neighbours rally round with second-hand clothing, offers of holidays, use of their telephone, use of their cars? 'Sure thing, Valerie. I've offered Emily a job of work. She's need to start training, and I don't expect her to do it for nothing, is all.'

'Training?'

Can he spare Juliette to come down and give Emily some tips on looking after herself? Manicure, hair, that kinda stuff. A day or two will do it. 'Think maybe I'll bring down one of my behind-the-scenes ladies next weekend. Emily can get a few pointers from her to get started. She needs to look after her hands, Valerie. Grooming horses won't help her hold the line.'

The silence swirls around the room with the smoke-rings. Glowering, he guesses, though there's no telling in the murky little place.

Her cigarette tip starts bobbing up and down, glowing bright in the cramped little shed, drawing zigzags, ambivalent. He's had his say, can hardly wait to escape from the mixture of fumes threatening

90

him — and, worse, Emily — with cancer from passive smoking. He'll assume consent.

'Great. How about £150 a week while she's learning the ropes, and I'll deduct that from the final fee?'

The cigarette tip comes to rest. 'That sounds quite fair.'

'Here we go.' Dwight places two twenties by the lamp hoping they won't go up in smoke as soon as his back's turned. 'That's all I'm carrying. I'll bring the rest next weekend.' He stands to leave, turns towards the rear section. ''Night, Emily.' There is no answer.

'She'll have gone to check the chickens.' Valerie's voice holds the usual pride in her daughter's skill. 'She makes sure everything's secure against marauding foxes. Real devils. I'll say goodbye to her for you.'

It's almost ten. Dwight, tired, strides out for his comfortable house. Take a shower, he promises himself, settle down with a drink. He keeps Sheba on the leash by his side, insisting she obey Jock's inculcated commands. They walk fast, sure of their way. Dwight avoids the overgrown track from Bramblings to The Woolhouse and chooses the easier path he walked with Emily a short while back. The rain clouds have cleared and a shy fitful moon shines enough reflected light to illuminate the way. Besides, Dwight is accustomed to steering by his other senses. He takes great gulps of sweet woodland air to clear his lungs. The smell of smoke clings to him, filling his tubes.

He brushes that aside. He feels great, he's just done a good deed for the sake of it, no selfish motives. He goes for Emily's beauty, sure, would love to court her. She wouldn't want to know, that isn't hard to tell. She walked beside him just tolerating his presence, reluctant even to exchange a couple of words. If the truth be told, she'd have preferred to be on her own with Landrover. She walked close to him, right. Close enough to bring his feelings into play, to make his body ache, to make him unwish his inheritance for the millionth time. He can tell it was reward for the secret she wanted him to keep. No further come-ons. He isn't about to try to make a play for her and ruin it all.

Stepping along, lost in his memories, he notices a yellowish orange glow wink at him from the more wooded area to his right.

Someone with a large torch? Too big for that – a large lantern? The sapling-cutter intent on more destruction?

He takes on board that he smells fresh smoke, not leftovers from Valerie's cigarettes or the kerosene lamp.

His Mom calls to him, shrill and insistent: 'Smoke, I can smell smoke!'

A forest fire! A touch dramatic for a woodland fire, but real all the same. He hurries on, the yellow showing the way, the smoke getting nearer. He's near home and, without thinking, rushes towards rather than away from the fire. He's seen wide shovels standing against trees. For smothering flames Jock told him.

No way he can do it. Flames crackle on the high ledge above his path. He hasn't a hope in hell of putting out leaping flare-ups which are, by now, high in the trees. He taps 999 on his mobile, alerts the fire brigade.

Taking the leash off Sheba he thunders: 'Home, Sheba. Fast!' and lumbers after her as quickly as he can.

Out of breath, fumbling the key, finally indoors, he reckons there isn't anything further he can do. No way he can get in touch with Valerie or Jock, and he's utterly exhausted.

Fire engines blaze past his house and on into the woodland lanes within minutes. Cars, presumably driven by neighbours, roar past. It dawns on him that his house is, among others, under threat.

CHAPTER 12

The fire has made Dwight really nervous about leaving his country house vacant during the week. He can't stop himself thinking back to his mother's place in Needham. Set in surrounding woodlands, she chose it to remind both of them of the woods they loved.

An ordinary unpretentious home – nothing to mark it out. But the bad luck which drove her from Vermont when Dwight was only nine seemed to have come back a couple of years ago.

Mom's colonial. The door wide open, smoke billowing out, flames high above. He'd hurled himself towards the figure in the front yard, cradled her in his arms.

Mom's heater started it. The spreading flames gutted the entire house. Her own fault, the fire department told her. She'd forgotten to switch off the kerosene heater she insisted on using. Even later, after Mom moved to the new house he bought for her a couple of blocks away, things didn't improve. First there was the burglary, then her health began to falter. It frightened him, a sort of slipping away before his eyes. He visited with her as often as he could.

And that last time, now over a year ago, that's when he found her body. Her throat was slit from ear to ear. Not once but three times. Three long gashes. Dwight felt – feels – helpless, impotent. And her murder hasn't been solved. Grief still depresses him, devastates him. He can't put the tragedy out of his mind.

Is a similar fate dogging him? Has bad luck pursued him across the Atlantic? He swots the thought away, slanging himself. But if whoever is responsible for all these odd happenings in the woods were to realise The Woolhouse is empty during the week ...

A loud knocking on the back door brings him out of his fears. He isn't expecting anyone. He goes to the upstairs hall window to check who's there, then remembers – Jock, of course! Come to pick up Sheba for the week.

'I thought we'd agreed you'd not have her in the house?' Jock greets him. He strides past Dwight without invitation and goes through into the living room. 'I looked for 'er in the kennel. She weren't there. I reckoned yer wouldn't be out for a walk at this time o' night, so I knows she 'as to be indoors.'

Jock always comes to pick the bitch up from her kennel sometime on Sunday evenings – whenever it suits him. Right for the both of them. Right for all three.

'I'm not happy leaving her out on her own,' Dwight apologises, following Jock.

Jock grins. 'Daresay she can give a good account of 'erself.' He squats where the dog sprawls in front of a dying fire and ruffles her head. 'What'll yer want me to do? All right to leave 'er in the kennel on Friday night, then?'

'If you've got time for a little talk, Jock.'

'Time to be getting back.'

Jock seems intent on never spending more than a few minutes with Dwight. Does his albinism make Jock nervous? The contrast between the gamekeeper's robust youth and health and Dwight's delicate body, with its evident physical shortcomings, is downright disconcerting – but just a fact. Jock is used to hard facts. More likely he doesn't want to be seen associating with a foreigner – that is, anyone from outside 'these parts', as he refers to the area.

What the hell is he doing in a place as backward-looking as this, Dwight asks himself. He hasn't a hope of fitting in.

'I won't keep you long.' Dwight tries hard not to envy Jock's easy stride, his casual assumption of success in whatever he undertakes. 'Just kinda wondered if you'd have the time to come by the house occasionally, take a look round.'

Jock looks up, Dwight stares back without wavering and Jock

94

relaxes. 'If yer wants I can sleep 'ere every now and again. That bit of a room off the kitchen. I can bed down in that.'

'Doesn't have a bed in it ...'

'I'll bring my sleeping bag. It's what I use most times, so that's not exactly going to be an 'ardship.' His eyes slit. 'Won't be interfering none with your being 'ere, only be staying when you're not about.'

'You bet.'

'And I'll keep Sheba in the kennel. If you want a proper working dog you got to treat 'er like one. Bringing 'er indoors makes 'er into a softie – a pet.'

'You're the boss, Jock.' Pointless thing to say. Time he treated Jock the way he's hired him – fair and square. As usual the gamekeeper's right: the dog, though quiet and obedient, has no place in the house.

'Yer might've 'ad a point about they matches,' Jock mutters, addressing the dog rather than Dwight. 'That fire were started on purpose. Don't look right. The fire chief found traces of paraffin.'

'Trailed along the ground?'

A sharp glance. 'That's be the way 'un looks.'

Dwight hasn't considered how the fire might have started. And he's shirked introducing himself to his near neighbours, aware some might assume him to be the arsonist – because he's the outsider.

'Nothing like that wrong with my folks.'

He assumes the locals think these odd happenings only started when he came to live in their patch. Nonsense, but kinda understandable. Valerie had mentioned that there'd been cause for concern for quite some time. At a lower level, maybe, but definitely there. And he's been proved right about the woodland vandal carrying matches.

'Is there much damage?' Dwight, due at an important meeting in London on the morning after the fire, felt it wrong to intrude at Bramblings late that night.

'Not too bad, considerin'. Bit o' luck yer was walkin' that way at the time. Another half hour and the whole bloomin' lot would 'ave got out o' control.'

He has his alibi down pat. Jock knows where he was until he

95

left the pub, the Brookes will vouch for him after that. 'I just knew something was about to happen.'

'What d'you mean, you knew?'

He should drive out today. A quiet Friday afternoon in early summer. It's time to leave for Mom's right now!

'I had this strong feeling that night. That's why I walked back with you through the woods, even though I find it difficult in the dark.'

'Yer get used to 'un.'

'I guess. We all have to learn. So you'll teach Sheba to track?'

''Spect so.' He stands, the worn piece of string slung through Sheba's collar. 'Heel, girl.'

Sheba waits, silent, obedient, to follow Jock's lead. She doesn't even glance back at Dwight.

CHAPTER 13

The Bentley purrs through the narrow lanes. Harry Solferino sits in the passenger seat glaring through the windscreen.

'Jeez, Dwight, where in hell are we?'

'Almost there, bud. The Woolhouse is just down this lane and round the corner. More or less on its own. My nearest neighbour's about five hundred yards along.'

'That's good? Aint you fuck...' Harry turns round and winks at Juliette Bourgine in the back. 'Aint you bored to death?'

'Bored, Harry?' Dwight takes in the squat figure and wonders again how come they're good pals. Short swarthy and ugly, not even young, Harry has all the vitality of his Italian heritage. And plenty of business acumen besides. An A1 wheeler-dealer who's recently bought into yacht broking.

'Now that's a new market I can appreciate,' he'd mumbled, mouth full as he scanned the leisure section of *The Mail on Sunday*. It seems to suit him. Anything that makes a profit suits him. Recession, boom, makes no difference to Harry. Whatever he touches turns to gold. And he touches plenty.

'So where's the little girl?'

'I told you, pal. They live in an old keeper's cottage about three miles from here.'

'Finders keepers!' Harry roars gleefully. 'What do they get to keep?'

It startles Dwight; Harry seems to have got it in one. 'Gamekeeper's place, guy who sees to the deer and other game on an estate. The Brookes' cottage was built in Tudor times. No doubt to protect the king's game.'

'How sweet,' Juliette says.

'Three miles,' Harry repeats. 'As the helicopter flies or as the local traffic creeps?'

Dwight pumps hard on the brakes, still unused to allowing for unseen traffic round the blind bends. Doesn't like to honk his horn too much, but his Bentley can't pass another car in these lanes without finding one of the rare passing places. He's getting better at it. Still finds himself backing more often than he enjoys. He suspects the locals of bullying him. Besides, driving isn't one of his greatest skills.

'Sorry. We'll have to back a little.'

'Sure, sure. I always drive backwards myself.'

'You'll enjoy the house, Harry. And the woods.'

'Mainly the broad, eh, Dwight?'

Dwight winces. 'C'mon Harry, give me a break.'

'Sure, sure. Sorry, Julie. I forget you're there, you're so f... — damned quiet.'

'It sounds like a sort of fairytale,' Juliette says. 'When are we going to meet them?'

'Lunch first, I think.'

'Never mind the lunch, bud, bring on the rye.'

'There's plenty at the house. And Mrs Dean has left a meal for us. All laid on.'

'Complete with touching forelock and blazing fire,' Harry puts in.

'A blazing fire, sure thing.' Dwight swings into his driveway, twirls the Bentley round the substantial turning circle and stops by his front door.

Polished oak welcomes them: gleaming, inviting.

Harry stays in the passenger seat, looking round. Dwight's 'country funk hole', as he terms it, is impressive. The large long house spreads sideways, facing south. Sandstone walls glow warm in gentle May sunshine. Ten windows, set in two rows one above the other, suggest a good array of rooms. A chimney stack curls smoke into the sky. Perky spring flowers wink in a soft breeze, the sweet scent of apple blossom wafts over a garden wall and mingles with the heady perfume of late narcissi. 'Not a bad spread.'

'It's beautiful, Dwight,' Juliette breathes, almost husky with emotion, stepping out and going over to the wall. 'Look at those flowers.'

Dwight glances over the frontage before opening the door. No sign of damage, all seems tranquil and in good repair. 'Drinks, lunch and then the walk to Bramblings.' He beams his relief at them.

'Walk? D'you mean we gonna have to foot it?' Harry demands.

'I told you, Harry.'

'Just kidding, buddy boy. The little lady sounds worth stepping out for.'

It is, Dwight thinks, rather more than the ordinary rags to riches story. But he doesn't doubt that Emily will strike it rich.

Dwight shepherds his small party through the woods to Bramblings. Juliette is cajoled into wearing Cuban heels rather than the stilettos she 'feels most comfortable in' and Harry, expensively wrapped in camelhair and sporting a trilby, makes play by using his gold-headed umbrella to push brambles aside.

Dwight chooses the easy path. Suggestions for suitable clothing haven't persuaded Juliette to wear anything practical. The sheerest denier, topped by a pencil slim skirt – 'I've been very good Dwight. I've gone all tailored' – and a magnificent blouse which, though wool, isn't designed to keep her warm.

'I'll lead with Sheba.' Dwight strides ahead, proud of the myriad emerging leaf buds showing brilliant greens. 'Harry, you go last. I'll keep the brambles from catching on Julie's clothes.'

The kidding is becoming fewer. Harry begins to puff and Dwight shudders at the thought of elderflower 'champagne' proffered to his friend. Why didn't he think to bring a flask, if not the Bentley? Already regretting his impetuosity he realises he's showing off, that's what it comes down to. What if the Brookes aren't in?

'We're almost there.'

'Big deal. Are these US miles?'

'It's only another five hundred yards.'

'Gimme a break, Dwight. Aint nothing here but ...'

The little cottage appears, as suddenly as it appeared to Dwight that first time, now over a month ago. Harry stops in mid-sentence. The sun shines bright and clear, illuminating the white stone with a compelling glow. The trim lawn gentles down towards the front door standing open in welcome. Harry's smile broadens and he started hurrying towards the enchanting cottage.

'Hold your horses, Harry.'

'This ain't it?'

'Sure it is. It's just they're not living there at the moment.'

'You brought us all this way just to see some empty pile o' stones?'

A young woman, mousy haired and somewhat thickset, comes out of the door followed by a cat. She looks at the trio curiously, but gives no sign of recognition.

'That ain't her?'

'I've told you, Harry. She's a strawberry blonde. And no, it's not her. She and her mother are in that small building over on the right.'

'What building? I don't see nothin'.'

'The wooden shed.'

Harry stops dead and looks at the grey-brown slats, the whole structure crumbling into holes, on their right. It doesn't really deserve the label of building. It's simply an old tumble-down garden shed. Shadowed by some myrobalan plums lanking long branches overhead, it looks forlorn and somehow desolate. The open door shows no sign of Emily, Valerie or the attendant smoke. Not even a barking Raffy appears to welcome them.

Out in the woods. Gathering firewood, Dwight wonders, or bagging game? He walks uncertainly over to the door and knocks. Got to get them that mobile, he thinks. Then realises that it would be useless – no electricity to charge it up, maybe no signal either.

No answer. He's about to turn and sweet talk Harry into walking back when Valerie comes out. She peers at him as though she doesn't recognise him, a look of frowning distrust.

Instantly he fears the worst. It's happened ... Someone has attacked Emily!

'Dwight. I'd no idea.' She takes in the trio and stops short. Raffy is at her feet and begins to bark: short, snapping, unfriendly barks. He threatens to approach Dwight's little retinue now nervously backing its retreat.

'Gently does it, Raffy,' Dwight says, calm and forceful, aping Jock. The dog stops his noise and turns his attention to Sheba. 'I've just brought my friends round to say hello to you both,' Dwight explains, as casually as he can manage. 'You're not on the phone and we thought, such a lovely day for a walk...'

'Of course.' Valerie pulls her cardigan more closely around her and looks beyond them to the top of the lawn.

'This is Julie – Juliette – the young lady I told you about. And my friend Harry Solferino.'

She doesn't even look at them. 'I'm sorry Dwight. Usually I'd be delighted. But I'm afraid Emily's ill. As a matter of fact I thought you were the doctor.'

'Doctor?' This has to be serious. His heart flaps, he feels faint. 'I'm terribly sorry, Valerie. We shouldn't be intruding.' She said ill, he tries to calm himself, just a disease, not an attack. 'Emily's sick?'

'She's finding it hard to breathe.'

He sees the house in flames, too late to save it.
Mom's gulping air, out of breath. He'll find a real good place for her.

'Perhaps there's something we can do.' He smiles to cover his fear for Emily. 'Pick up some groceries from Midhurst, or even further off? Get medication from the pharmacy?'

Spluttering from the top of the lawn interrupts him. An old VW Beetle chokes to a stop. A tall lean man gets out almost before the engine dies and starts walking towards the cottage, evidently missing Valerie hidden behind the visitors.

'We're in here, Doctor Pringle.' Her voice rings loud. 'For the summer, you know. The paying guests have the cottage,' she adds, more subdued.

'Of course.' The doctor turns towards them without any sign of hesitation. 'Now then.' He looks at his Gladstone bag as though that entitles him to enter otherwise forbidden territory. 'Mrs Pontings was really quite insistent that I come at once.'

'Emily can't breathe properly.'

He increases his pace. Doctor and mother disappear into the shed, then Valerie comes out again. She looks harassed, but in full

101

control.

'If you can hang on for just a minute, Dwight. Anne's gone off for the day, and Charles ... Well, you know ...'

'Of course we'll wait.'

Harry is scrutinising the cottage. Beady eyes turn to Juliette as he asks her to stand in front of it.

'Pretty as a picture,' he enthuses. 'C'mon, Julie, let's shoot some pics.'

'For chrissake, Harry.'

The doctor is already walking back to his car. Valerie patters along beside him. 'I've rung for the ambulance, Mrs Brooke,' he's saying as he folds himself into the driving seat. 'It's best to be on the safe side, and you're so far off the beaten track and without a telephone.' He stops, shutting the Beetle's door and talking through the window. 'There's nothing to worry about, it's just a precautionary measure.'

Valerie watches him start the engine without contributing anything further, no doubt bewildered by what's happening. But she manages to go up to Dwight as soon as the car has gone. 'He says it's pneumonia,' she explains to him. 'He says he's given her antibiotics, but that it will be best to take her into Chichester Hospital as a precautionary measure.'

Dwight knows what the doctor means and what he's doing. 'He tell you to keep her quiet and give her plenty of fluids?' he checks anxiously. Only some country quack.

'Yes. Yes, he did.'

It isn't the time to say I told you so, but Dwight fumes the reasons for Emily's illness to himself. Too much work, too much stress, not enough decent food to eat. The girl's resistance is low – so she succumbed. He knows very well how it feels, pneumonia is one of the diseases he's well acquainted with. And he understands the doctor isn't simply careful, he wants to be able to offer oxygen, good food and proper conditions for Emily to revive. So much the better.

'We'll get back and pick up the Bentley, Valerie. Then we'll pick you up from the hospital after you've settled Emily in.' The woman looks exhausted, might as well feed her. 'We'll take you out to dinner and then home. After that we'll make ourselves scarce.'

'Oh, Dwight, that is good of you.' She flashes a smile, then dashes inside the shed without another backward glance.

He'll have to explain it all to Harry, Dwight realises, but he can't let the woman take the ambulance ride to Chichester and then come back on public transport. Bus to Midhurst, then to Lodsworth, and then walk the three miles up to Bramblings. She'll end up with pneumonia herself.

And Harry? Maybe sell it to him on the basis that he'll show him Chichester Marina and take him out for a slap-up lunch. Take him to the Yacht Club or the Spinnaker Restaurant, or go into Chichester itself.

'OK, you guys,' he turns to his visitors. 'Back the way we came.'

'Don't we even get a glimpse?'

'No, Harry, you don't. The girl's sick, real sick. What d'you wanna do – kill her off?'

Harry pushes his trilby back on his forehead, exposing shiny pink scalp. He lifts the hat, then pushes it back down on his head again, flicking up the brim and adjusting it.

'OK, Dwight. It's your show. All I wanna say is I get to see her before she comes on my stand.'

Dwight glances towards the shed but Valerie has gone. 'Sure thing.' If she survives, if Valerie is willing: if, if, if.

'Is she going to die, Dwight?'

'Let's not get this out of proportion, Julie. It's just some sort of pneumonia, probably brought on by hard physical chores, and living in that appalling shed. It's been damn wet, and my guess is the roof leaks.'

Juliette is beginning to get worked up. 'This is just awful. Can't the council do something for them?'

'Matter of fact they offered the mother a council house, long ago.'

'A what?'

Council houses, Dwight grins to himself, are not part of Harry's deals. 'Housing the local authority rents out to people at a very reasonable rate. Valerie turned it down flat. She wants to live here, and the only way she can do it is to let out the cottage during the summer months. She and the girl sleep in the shed when they have roomers.'

'But that's really dreadful.' Julie looks truly horrified.

'Valerie reckons it's the right thing to do.'

I can get a good price for my cookies,' Mom tells him. 'I'm not having you going short of anything.'
'I'll get a job...'
'You finish school, Dwight. That's your job for now.'

There's a nagging suspicion he can't quite put his finger on, but Dwight has the feeling that he's missing something along the way. Why hasn't Valerie come down with pneumonia? Is she tougher? She looks it, but actually she's smaller, older – and she smokes.

The fact is that Valerie enjoys their situation and Emily – well, likely Emily resents giving up her home to other people. Could be she's fed up with the damned chores, finding the unending work irksome. Her shy timid bearing Dwight sees as a cover for her real feelings. Best she can figure out is to arrange to meet her father behind Valerie's back.

Dwight thinks back to the Needham homestead his mother was so proud of. She didn't rent it out, but she did take in roomers, and there'd been precious little time, or privacy, for him.

He, too, couldn't wait to get away and sort out his own life. Emily is biding her time. The pneumonia is, perhaps, one way of getting the hell out in the meantime.

'So now we have to chase off to some other godforsaken place.'

'You'll like Chichester better than The Woolhouse, Harry. I'll take you both out to a slam-bang joint.'

'They cook Italian?'

'Can't promise that. But I do know a place where they serve Manhattans.'

'On the rocks?'

'If I have to get the ice cubes out of their freezer myself.'

'Great,' Harry's eyes are narrowed but not slit. 'So now we get to do the round without even a drink half-way.'

'Good for your figure, pal.'

Rather more sedately than earlier on they set off down the track and walk, almost in silence, through the woods decked to perfection.

'It's really beautiful, Dwight,' Julie breathes at him, her heels digging into the soft soil and slowing her down.

An insistent cawing noise is getting more and more raucous as they amble along.

'What's that racket?' Harry demands crossly. 'A nightingale?'

'It's a crow or a magpie calling for a mate.'

A shot rings out, and then another. Dwight turns to see Harry duck, then, somewhat shamefaced, straighten up.

'Don't tell me the birds around here shoot.'

'The locals keep crow populations down by trapping a caller bird and setting it in a pair's territory,' Dwight explains pedantically, regurgitating one of Jock's lessons.

'They trap live birds?'

'They catch one so that the resident pair thinks there's an intruder. They have to keep the corvids from eating partridge and pheasant eggs.'

'The what?'

'Corvids, crow family.' Smug but satisfying.

'It sounds awful, Dwight.' Julie has stopped to listen to the squawking. 'It sounds as though it's in pain.'

'Not in pain. Just calling for a mate. Country ways aren't always gentle.'

'You mean the bird in the cage stirs up the other males?'

'Not exactly that, the caged bird excites the pair whose territory it's in. They charge in to attack the intruder and the guy who set the trap shoots at them.'

'Real cute,' Harry says quietly. 'You really got something going for you here, bud.'

'Estate management.' Dwight assumes a lofty air. 'They have to protect their property, like anybody else.'

'So's they can practise their shooting skills,' Harry grunts.

'It's their living, Harry.'

'If this is the peace of the countryside, gimme the city any day.'

'You got it,' Dwight laughs.

'At least I knows my way around a city.'

Dwight looks about him. Does Harry have a point, is he kidding himself? Has he merely exchanged one form of violence for another? Walking with his philistine companions he still relishes the glorious dapple of sunlight glancing off shiny green, the sea of bluebells spread out below the ridge shimmering azure. It's worth its weight in kingcups.

'How much further, Dwight? We taking the scenic route?'

'We're almost back.'

'I guess you're lost, bud. We bin twice the distance we came to start with.'

'Just round the corner, Harry. Honest.'

They're coming to the felled trees, much of the timber already taken off with the site almost cleared now. Dwight, remembering the hedgehog, sweeps his gaze across it,. All in apple pie order. His eye is caught by what looks like a collection of stones in the near corner, to the left. Might have been there when they went past before, he was too eager to get to Bramblings to notice. But it sure wasn't there last week. Another shrine?

A feeling of dejection grabs hold as he watches Sheba trotting off. He hasn't even the heart to call her. No colour – no flowers – he prays. All he can see are flecks of green at odd angles. Spikes – of holly? – spearing over the rim. His breath turns to gasps: a funeral wreath, a prickly funeral wreath.

'There's something I got to see.' Oblivious of his guests Dwight strides across to check it out. This time the structure is reminiscent of some sort of primitive stone monument. A jagged curved outline girdled by boulders roughly set into a ring, with what looks, from a few feet away, like an empty centre. Only he knows it isn't even before he gets there. He'll find a bigger animal – a deer perhaps, its head hacked off, lying in a pit.

As he comes up to it he sees the stones circle a kind of scooped-out shell filled with coils of green plastic netting.

'C'mon, Dwight. Stop pissing around.'

'You got to see this, Harry. It's unbelievable.' Dwight stops and gapes into the hole. It seems to be alive, heaving and twisting. He stands, hypnotised, as he makes out the writhing of an intertwined collection of reptiles. A snake pit. But it's worse than that. The animals are held tight, twisted into the plastic netting, unable to escape. That's what the stones are for. Not as a decoration, but to weigh the netting down, hold it in place.

'That sure is weird.' Harry is by him watching the grotesque coils of undulating threshing animals. 'They rattlers?'

Juliette has followed Harry and, seeing a head emerge from the mass of squirming forms, shrieks out a horrified 'Snakes!' She turns to Harry and clutches him. 'They'll kill us!'

He disentangles himself, holding her away. 'They can't hurt you none, Julie. They're all tied up.'

'They aren't snakes,' Dwight hisses, infuriated. 'They're only slow worms. Completely harmless, Julie. Don't make such a danged fuss.' He feels ashamed of sounding off. Thanks the lord Emily's going to be in hospital, at least for a short time.

He'll have to cut them loose. What with? He doesn't carry a knife. Only scissors can possibly get through that mess. He can't face freeing the wriggling shapes with his bare hands. They might be harmless, still can't bear the thought of touching them. He isn't even sure they can be untwined, some heads are poked through the plastic, others are threshing, caught in loose folds.

'Most of them are dead.' Harry pokes at them with his umbrella.

'Better help the rest out of their misery then,' Dwight says to Harry. 'You wait down there, Julie.'

Quickly, methodically, Harry uses the top of his stick to finish off what turns out to be only three live glass snakes.

'There's something real weird going on around here,' Dwight explains to his friends. 'It's kinda freaky.'

'So what's the deal?' Harry asks.

'First off I comes across some dead rabbits, all sliced up.'

'So what?'

'Laid on a kind of altar, flowers and stuff all round.'

'Big deal!'

'Then there's a hedgehog, axed to pieces. Flowers again, now this. You can see the wreaths, holly and rhododendron. More ghoulish, this time. Whoever it was snared the live animals intended them to die.'

'You think there's a criminal about?' Julie asks, holding her breath and looking round.

'Not a criminal. Someone disturbed, mentally sick, I guess. A psychopath.'

The Woolhouse chimneys rise to greet them behind the privet

hedge looming up ahead.

'That it?' Harry asks carefully.

'That's it.'

'We allowed something strong – some of that malt you said you had – before we set off again?'

Dwight is already at the bar getting ice-cubes and slicing up the lemon. He takes his Glenlivet and a bottle of Gordons from the cooler, brings out a large Slimline tonic, and turns, his hands shaking, arranging glasses.

'All set.' He forces his voice into heartiness. 'Gin and tonic, right Julie?'

'Is it Slimline?'

'I haven't forgotten you've got a figure to look after.'

'Make it a big one.'

CHAPTER 14

'What about your friends, Dwight? Are they waiting in the car?'

'I've left them at the marina. Harry wants to set up an office there. He'll be quite happy casing the place – and then they'll find a bar. Julie knows how to keep him company.' Dwight smiles paternally at Valerie. 'How's the patient?'

'Fast asleep. I think the antibiotics worked right away.'

'Good.' She thinks the ball game's over, Dwight realises. A couple of shots of penicillin and she reckons the girl will be back to normal. 'Lucky I caught up with you out here,' he says. 'Guess I could have missed you.'

'Just came out to have a smoke while I was waiting.'

There's a faraway dreamy tone to Valerie's voice. Is she fantasising some sort of glorious outcome from the situation? The hand of destiny bringing Emily to hospital for a specific reason? Dwight feels irritation constrict his throat, choking off a reply. He's offered her a ride home. Is she really so wedded to hardship that she hasn't even thought about the practicalities of getting back?

'It's quiet here, the sun is shining, and they've planted a soothing arrangement of annuals. It helps to calm one down.'

Back to nature. And not so much dreamy as impassive. Maybe she's coming down with pneumonia herself. 'I don't think you need worry, Valerie. I'm sure Emily will be just fine.'

'I'm not a bit worried about that. I know she's on the mend. Settled in splendidly, her breathing's already easier. It isn't that at all.'

He notices a distinct gleam in her eyes. Hooded, but Dwight can swear he can see a look of, well, triumph. Cold steely triumph.

'The most extraordinary thing's happened.'

'Another monstrosity in the woods, d'you mean?' She must have heard about the slow worms. Dwight looks at Valerie's closed cold face. Whatever he caught before has gone. Just pissed off, probably. 'Or something worse?'

'Something really odd. As I was sitting here, treasuring the fact that Em's all right, I felt a shadow on my back, the warmth had gone and it felt quite chilly. I looked up and saw someone standing between me and the sunshine. Guess who?'

Again that look – he'd have to describe it as vindictive. 'I don't have any idea, Valerie.' Jock McClough? Got wind of Emily's illness and came running? 'Someone I know? Charles?'

She turns, blue eyes unblinking, circular. He's again reminded of an owl ready for the kill. 'Nothing whatever to do with the Pontings,' she says. 'Alan Penn-Winton.'

Dwight has no idea who she's talking about.

'You remember: the young man with that noisy red car.'

'The budding attorney,' he recollects now, without much pleasure.

'Barrister,' Valerie says judiciously, dismissing this. 'He's was just standing there, sort of aimless and shambling. None of that pugnacity he usually goes in for. In fact he seemed – well, strange. Had a leaden look in his eyes, and trouble focusing on me. His hair was all dishevelled – standing up in little spikes, as though it hadn't been combed for ages. Not a bit like his normal self.'

As Dwight remembers it Alan's hair stuck out in odd clumps that time he met him – on that first visit to Bramblings. Eons ago. 'Maybe he's had pneumonia too? The bacterial form is catching.' An idea strikes Dwight. 'Might have been he who infected Emily.'

'You don't get it, Dwight. Of course he's a patient here, I'm not denying that. But not because of pneumonia.'

'What's wrong with that kid?'

Dwight feels irritable. For some reason Valerie seems to hold it against Alan that he has a problem which needs to be taken care of in a hospital. Annoyance, even hostility, makes Dwight feel hot.

'He was wearing his rowing blazer, and some casual-looking light-blue trousers under it. First I thought it an odd combination for someone normally so formal, and then I grasped what was going on. The hospital garb was underneath the blazer.'

Dwight still has no idea what on earth she's so excited about. What is a rowing blazer, anyway? He simply waits, coursing blood reddening his face to a deep crimson.

'Don't you see?' she brays, clearly exasperated herself. 'Look!' She points to a sign above a door leading to another wing of the hospital.

Dwight dutifully puts his glasses on. Psychiatric Department.

'He's in the psychiatric department! He's here because he's got some sort of mental illness!'

'I sure am sorry to hear that.' Dwight, still bewildered by her violent reactions, waits again.

'Not really all there, you know. Only sort of realised who I am. There was this dull fixed stare he turned on me, but he didn't really recognise me.'

'I guess they give them drugs.'

'I know all that! You still haven't got my point.' The irises, sharpening to slits, peck at Dwight's face. 'He's mental, Dwight. Mad, out of his mind. I don't know what's the matter with him exactly, but it has to be something quite drastic for them to keep him in. They hardly ever do, these days.' She flourishes her cigarette. 'I always knew something was wrong. He'd disappear for weeks on end and never explain why. Just some nonsense about having to go to Paris to see his ailing grandmother. Never did believe a word of that. So now we know.'

'Know what?'

She inhales several times, allowing for a dramatic pause, then intensifies the smoke rings. 'He's obviously been in and out of psychiatric care for years.'

Lay off, Hank, ain't nothin' special. Earl's kid ain't gets no pigment in his skin, is all.'

'I'm not clear why that's a crime, Valerie.' The Pink Rabbit,

Dwight suddenly hears in his mind. That's what they called him at the local. That's why Jock is reluctant to be seen with him. So does Valerie hold the damned albinism against him?

'Of course being ill isn't a crime, Dwight. I never suggested anything of the sort. Not at all.'

She's worked out that he can put himself in Alan's place.

'All I know is that he's very keen on Emily, but even so he disappears for weeks on end. This explains why. And it explains a whole lot of other things which have been bothering me.'

Her lips purse into a thin red line as she turns to accompany Dwight out of the hospital grounds. He steers her towards the Bentley and settles her in the passenger seat.

'The safety belt, Valerie.' She fumbles with it, unable to fasten it. He has to do it for her. 'Explains what?'

'You still haven't rumbled it, have you?' Her voice rises thick and throaty, almost a croak. 'Now we know who's been committing all these detestable outrages in the woods. It's Alan. He's crazy.' She positively sparkles, sitting forward, clenching the ashtray open. 'And dangerous, I imagine.' A virtuous smug intonation. She's tried and convicted Alan before he's even been accused. 'Psychopathic. You were quite right, Dwight. You saw it right away. You warned me.'

Most of the glass snakes were dead when Dwight and his party came across the latest outrage. Dwight tells himself that it would have been possible for Alan to arrange that delightful scenario before being admitted to the psychiatric department. 'That's possible, Valerie, sure thing. But I guess we can't just assume it, you know. It doesn't necessarily follow.'

'Doesn't follow? Of course it follows. Really, Dwight. You're just like all the rest. So slow.' She pulls the pack of Players out of her bag and lights another one.

Dwight feels anger choking him. She hasn't bothered to ask whether he minds her lighting up. The exhaled smoke is watering his eyes, blurring his vision. He opens his window wide only to find the noxious fumes of exhaust gas caught in the narrow Chichester streets and billowing in. Equally nauseating. Why didn't he order an air conditioner for the Bentley? Why the hell isn't it standard, anyway?

'It's perfectly obvious. He's completely smitten with Emily, and she won't commit herself, one way or another. So he takes it out on dead animals and trees.'

Rush-hour is crowding the streets. Dwight concentrates his eyes on the traffic, but feels Valerie's look of contempt. She thinks him slow – and stupid.

'Emily has shoals of admirers, as I'm sure you've already noticed.'

'Sure I know that. She's very beautiful, and a real cutie-pie at that,' Dwight agrees.

'Yes, well.' Valerie sounds startled, but recovers herself. 'As I was saying, she's driving Alan wild.' He hears her puff at the cigarette even more rapidly than usual. 'The question is, will he stop with the wild life, or will he start attacking her?' Smoke fogs the car. 'I don't think it's safe for him to be around.'

'Your pop isn't safe with a gun, Dwight, honey.'
'He only shoots at deer, Mom!'

'Seems he isn't, Valerie. Seems he's being treated in hospital.'

'At the moment, yes. But for how long? I'll have to talk to Gilbert. We've got to stop him before he assaults Emily.'

Suddenly Valerie's gesticulating wildly, the glowing butt swooping across the windscreen, ash trickling everywhere.

'Watch out, Valerie! I do think ...'

'Stop, Dwight! This is it. I get out here! Gilbert's office is round the corner. You're driving past!'

The traffic is now heavy and Dwight is easing the car sedately along the crowded street. But there's no sensible way he can stop right then and there. Before he can slow further she's opened the passenger door. He lurches to a sudden halt, deaf to the hooting motorists behind.

'I know you mean well.' Valerie's oblivious to the chaos she's causing. 'But it's my job to protect Emily before something happens to her. A telephone's not much good once a crime has been committed.' She has no trouble undoing the seat belt.

Dwight hears the door slam shut as he puts his foot back on the accelerator. The Bentley purrs forward along the cobbled streets, smoothing them out. He noses his way to the marina and wrestles with parking spaces meant for smaller cars. The place is stacked with Landrovers, and the larger Mercedes and Volvos. He wonders whether it's inverted snobbery which makes the bureaucratic powers in charge ensure only the smaller cars can be accommodated easily. With some surprise he finds himself right next to Charles Pontings' metallic blue BMW.

CHAPTER 15

Red hot and sweaty Dwight walks along the jetty, relishing the cool sea air, sauntering past the Boat Club. Julie and Harry must be somewhere around, sipping gin fizzes.

'Hi. How come you're on your own?' Dwight looks in vain along the road. Harry's disembodied voice, but no Harry.

'Up here, old man.' Charles Pontings' voice.

The elevated Boat Club terrace stretches towards the marina. Dwight puts his glasses on and follows the sound with his eyes. Charles Pontings, Harry and Juliette are sitting at a table with a huge umbrella shading it, drinks set out in front of them.

'Just tell them you're my guest.' Charles, standing up, waves down jovially. 'They'll let you in.'

Dwight hasn't bothered to become a club member as yet. He goes to the imposing entrance door. How in the world has Harry gotten past the rules?

'With Mr Pontings? No problem at all, sir. Up the stairs and to the left,' the doorman bows Dwight through.

'The marina's really beautiful,' Juliette is gushing as Dwight arrives. 'And look at that boutique. Watch the customers crowding in.'

Juliette's dream to own a fashion boutique isn't a secret. She tells everyone who'll listen. Dwight has promised to set her up as soon as she's trained a replacement as good as herself. 'So how's Diana coming along?'

115

'I don't think that's going to work out, Dwight.'

'Then you'll have to find someone else if you want that store.'

'Some solid boats here, buddy.' Harry is examining several of the finer craft anchored towards the end of the marina. The telescope on a leather halter round his neck is brand new. His short chunky form, huddled in his camel hair coat, stands out, incongruous, among the expensively casual tall men sauntering drinks to waiting friends.

'I tried to put you wise earlier, Harry. Plenty of business potential round here.'

'That's exactly what I've been telling him.' Charles is standing, on his way to the bar to replenish drinks.

'Where these guys from?' Harry asks Dwight as soon as Charles is out of earshot.

'Round here, I guess. Families set up in country houses. Stockbroker belt, they call it.'

'They work in the City and live here?'

'You bet. Midhurst, Haslemere, Winchester ... the countryside around. Commute into downtown London.'

'That a fact? Maybe I should open an office here.'

Dwight laughs. 'Maybe you should at that, Harry, though it looks like you already have. Part of the clubhouse crowd.'

Harry grins. 'Isn't a problem. We got talking in the store, buying this little souvenir.' He flourishes the binoculars. 'I mentioned Solferino Trust and your friend here checked us in.' He cackles, strong teeth crunching the ice left in his glass. 'Turns out he knows the name.'

Charles touting for work. Neat. Dwight reckoned he'd be a fast worker, but this is real speed.

'So where's the mother, Dwight? You hiding her someplace?'

'Taken off to meet with her lawyer.'

'You mean we don't even get to catch up with her?'

'Not this time round.'

'A bitter lemon for you, Dwight. And a rye on the rocks for Harry, snowball for Julie.' Charles Pontings sits down heavily, his breath pure whisky. 'Hear there's been some sort of crisis with Emily.'

'Pneumonia, yes. She's been taken to hospital.'

116

'Valerie drives that girl too hard. Insists on keeping up that dilapidated old cottage when she hasn't got a bean. Ridiculous.'

'You know many of these guys?' Harry asks, eyeing several newcomers.

'Guys? Oh, club members. Of course, same crowd as at the polo meets.' Charles glances at Harry, who doesn't react. 'And the golf course.'

'You been retired?' Smoke from Harry's glowing Havana blows straight into Pontings' eyes.

Charles snorts, his face darkening to purple, but manages to grunt what turns out to be a yes.

'Might be in the market for a job, then.'

Another snort agrees he might.

'I've been waiting for hours.' A tall young woman has come up to Charles and is standing by his side. The voice is edgy and demanding. Her eyes dart at Juliette.

'Ah, Nina, yes. I'll be with you right away.' Charles stands at once, reaches his hand out to Harry, turns to wave goodbye to Julie and Dwight, then back to Harry. 'Great pleasure to meet you. Hope you'll come over to Oak Court next time you visit Dwight. Sorry I've got to run. I'll leave word at the bar for them to look after you.'

'Be seeing you.' Harry bares teeth in understanding, then turns to Dwight. 'Lost his job and gained a woman, all at the same time. Sounds expensive.'

'Guess not. We should be getting along as well,' Dwight says, gulping the bitter lemon.

'After all that build up, we're driving back without even the mother?'

'What can I tell you, bud? She turned me down flat.'

'That so? What's she after?'

'Alan Penn-Winton, young guy keeps saying he's engaged to Emily. Valerie spotted him as a patient in the psychiatric wing of the hospital. Jumped to the conclusion he's the sicko maiming animals and setting forest fires.'

'That a fact? Has it all figured out, I guess. Guy hanging round the girl's the fall guy.'

Dwight grasps that Harry knows as well as he does that it's

unlikely to be Alan who's responsible for the woodland atrocities. Much too slick, too pat a solution. Besides, he already has an outlet. His illness is recognised and catered for. He doesn't need to take it out on anything else.

'So what's the plan, Harry? I can take you to the depot, or you can stay over till the morning and I'll give you a lift back. I want to stick around till Jock comes by for Sheba. I don't like leaving her on her own after that fire.'

Harry rolls his eyes in mock annoyance. 'OK, Dwight. First the girl, now the bitch. You sound broody. Why don't you settle down?'

'No chance of that. She has dozens of guys coming round.'

'I wasn't being particular. You have a stableful of beauties.'

'Where do all these young men come from, Dwight?' Julie, apparently, would not have sniffed at them.

'I guess they're neighbours,' he says, eyeing the competition. Depressing there are so many candidates.

'Neighbours?' Juliette laughs. 'The place is miles from anywhere.'

'They've found where she lives. And they stick to their own kind. I guess she wouldn't go for a Yankee.' Dwight parks the Bentley in front of the house. He's pretty sure Harry will want to get back to London that night.

Once inside he removes the guard keeping the coals from rolling on to the parquet or the new rug. A fine mild steel fire bed is heaped with smouldering coals. He takes a poker and stirs it into life, then leaves to fetch the drinks.

A sudden scream from Juliette makes both men turn as a glowing coal, showering sparks, splutters on to the elegant Chinese carpet Dwight has recently acquired. He rushes for the fire irons, takes the tongs off their ledge and skilfully replaces the coal on the fire bed. A dark singed stain stares out at him from glinting blue. Ashen and sinister, a one-eyed monster.

'It just jumped out of the fire,' Juliette squeaks, backing away towards the windows. 'Leapt up in the air and jumped.'

'Too many gins.' Harry mumbles amiably, putting an arm around Julie. He puts the fireguard back in place, grinding the burnt piece on the carpet with his heel.

'I didn't realise the coals can fall that far,' Juliette's open mouth

118

comes back to life. 'It's really scary. That piece seemed to jump up like a firework and then land on the carpet.'

'Sometimes there's a pocket of gas inside coal,' Dwight soothes her. 'Something like a small explosion. Fires are beautiful but dangerous.'

Strong emotions are dangerous. The woodland fire was started by someone who feels trapped, someone who wants out.

Will whoever it is start a fire at The Woolhouse? And then another, even more frightening, thought grabs Dwight's mind. Did he know someone would set a match to the woodlands, just like he knew about the forest fire in his childhood? Is that how he escaped both times?

'You forgot to douse the fire, Pop.'
'Sure, son. You go ahead.'

'I've had an idea,' he says, poking the coals apart to cool them. 'We can take Sheba to the Fox and Hounds. That's my local bar. I can leave her with the barmaid, she's a fan of Sheba's. Jock always eats there, he'll take her back with him after his evening meal.'

'Great,' Harry says. 'Let's go for that. Maybe we'd better put that fire out first.'

They don't intend to stay at the pub, but their entrance causes a certain amount of excitement. Dwight walks ahead towards the bar, smiling his greeting at the landlord.

'Good evening, sir.'

'I wonder ...'

''Be you t'chap from T'Wool'ouse?'

A bent old man, wearing a torn tweed jacket, faded trousers bicycle-clipped over stout work boots, stands up from his stool.

'Sure thing.'

'Arrh. Mrs Brooke were on 'tus 'bout yer.'

'She was?'

'A does 'er diggin' for 'er, an' t'grass.'

'Of course.'

'Said, did 'un?' The old man's raspy voice is high-pitched.

'I think we met your grandson. Fishing in the millpond.'

119

'Young Pete, that be 'im.'

'I promised him a replacement for the net he lost.'

''E did say summat ...'

'I'm not here during the week, you see.'

''E c'n wait ...'

'Perhaps you'd get it for him, or ask his father to do it.'

'Me daughter be on 'er hown.'

Dwight fishes out a ten pound note and hands it across, embarrassed but not clear what else to do. He promised the kid, and then forgot.

'Queer goin's on,' the old man says, pocketing the note. 'Young Pete ain't harf as keen on fishin' has 'e were.'

Both he and Valerie realised the kid had seen something, frightened enough to drop his net and hare off as soon as he heard them running towards him. Frightened of what, and when? Just a man with a dog? Must have been more to it than that. And it can't have been that day, or he wouldn't have stayed on his own. The kid must have come across something suspicious some other time – the day before, maybe.

Dwight nods at the grandfather. 'We got the feeling Peter is frightened.'

''E says 'e leggo 'is net 'cause yer chased 'un.'

'We ran round the edge of the pond to see what was going on, yes. We'd only just come from the new plantation.'

'Hall 'em trees topped.' The old man sits down and Dwight signals another of what he's drinking. 'T'were t' trap that did get 'un.'

'Trap?'

''E stumbled into t' snare. Set for rabbits, like years hago. Hillegal now. Catched 'is foot and goes sprawlin', no 'arm done. Does giv'un a turn, though.'

He's strung between two branches, wings dangling limp, head hanging loose.

The pond scene comes back to him. The oval shape, reminiscent of a wire snare, floating on the water. Dwight turned the net into a snare in his mind, now has an inkling of impending – catastrophe. He's sure someone is trying to catch an animal – a live one, this time. To kill it. And he's recognised the omen: a noose.

He's nervous, same way he'd been nervous as a kid. Not just animals. Someone, somehow, somewhere is plotting a crime against a human being. He can sense it, feel it, almost smell the evil of it, the festering of a twisted mind.

''E thinks t'bloke as'd set 'er are hafter 'im for wreckin' 'er.'

'He could have been caught in the trap himself.' Dwight frowns. 'Surely he shouldn't be out in the woods on his own.'

'If t'were good henuff for me when I be a nipper, it be good henuff for 'im.'

None of his business. Dwight turns his attention to the barmaid, Lily. He's got to know her reasonably well, reckons she can be trusted.

Another tenner and he's arranged that Sheba stay with Lily until Jock comes in. Dwight turns and waves Harry and Julie out.

'I'll drive you back. We can eat on the way.'

'Living in the city ain't a patch on the country,' Harry announces, leaning back against the luxurious leather, rolling an unlit cigar in his mouth. 'I might even get into it.

CHAPTER 16

'Rye? Bourbon?' Dwight's snowy eyebrows lift as he looks towards his friend. 'I guess they have some.'

'Make it a double. Scotch will do.'

Harry Solferino uses his thickset shoulders to force a passage through the crowds. The Boat Show visitors have tired of boats and everyone, it seems, wants a drink. Dwight catches the bartender's eye.

'I got to hand it to you, Dwight.' Harry shakes his head, squinting, then grins. 'I don't know how you swung it. I sure didn't credit anything could come of that shed set-up! The blonde's a real hummer!'

'Real cutie, too.'

'Sure thing. You signing her up?'

'Not a prayer. Valerie insists she finish school. Don't see how I can pry her loose.'

The solid shoulders shake with laughter. 'Don't know how? For chrissake, Dwight, you make her'n offer she can't refuse!' Suddenly the laughter stops and Harry's blackcurrant eyes gleam understanding. 'She's under age.'

'She'll be eighteen in the fall. No problem there, Harry. They don't run on money.'

'C'mon, pal, gimme a break.'

'Honest to goodness, Harry. The mother's in charge, and pretty sharp.'

The little black eyes all but disappear as Harry's lids close almost shut. The cigar clamped between jagged teeth is bared by fleshy lips drawn back into a leer. 'You bet! Trussed you like a turkey for Thanksgiving.' Harry's lips surround the cigar again, then part. 'Tell her your intentions are honourable.' He sees Dwight isn't laughing with him and composes his face into more seemly lines. 'Just kidding, old buddy,' he says, taking a large gulp from his Scotch.

'Sure, sure.' Dwight sips his bitter lemon. 'I'm driving the girls home as soon as they've changed and packed. I'll stay on at The Woolhouse after that. Be in touch Monday, Harry.'

'There we go, Sophie. Right to your front door. You be OK or shall I see you in?'

'This is fine, thank you very much, Mr Delaney.'

'Dwight, Sophie.'

'Dwight. It's been lovely. I had a smashing time!'

'Great. Be seeing you.'

''Night, Em. Bright and early tomorrow morning, remember. Landrover's longing for us to exercise him. Mummy's not feeling that brill.'

'I know, Sop. I'll be there.'

The Bentley slithers smoothly into the dark. The white leather-cover seats are soft and springy. Dwight likes to think of them cushioning Emily's tired back. She hasn't complained, but Dwight has watched her sitting on the side of motionless boats hour upon hour for several days and sensed the strain she's under. He's noticed that though Emily's mouth was curved into a constant smile, her right hand occasionally, surreptitiously, strayed for a few seconds against the small of her back. The Show has clearly been more tiring than all the exercise she's so used to. The Ipswich air, loaded with salt spray, winds eddying around thin clothes, has taken its toll. Emily, shivering, has roused Dwight to insist on wrapping his coat over hers, pulling it snug around her shoulders.

Even so, he notices with alarm she's begun to cough again. The beautiful eyes are already less lustrous, the sheen on her skin less silken, the tilt of her head a hint less high. Released from duty she rushed to change into her frayed jeans and T-shirt, and slung her old anorak comfortingly around herself. Maybe a workout with Landrover is exactly what she needs.

'I hope you're going to wear your gloves,' Dwight mentions, voice as throw-away as he can make it. A good ploy to edge into what he wants to say.

'But it's all over now, Dwight. I'm back to my usual chores.'

'I thought you might consider more work.' He drives as slowly as he can, creeping silently along the lanes.

He can feel Emily tense beside him. 'More modelling, you mean?'

'Right. I'd be happy to sign you up for any type of modelling you care to do.' Dwight waits. Will she be pleased, surprised? Throw her arms around his neck and hug him?

But Emily doesn't respond at all. The Bentley lurches as he turns it into the bumpy, pot-holed drive leading to Bramblings. Dwight slows to crawling pace and creeps up to the grass. 'Here we are, then, Emily.' He turns the Bentley deftly in the small space at the top of the Brookes' lawn. It's a ploy to ready himself to drive away, but in fact he's giving himself as much time as possible. He feels he's getting quite good at tactics. He backs on to the lawn as far as he dares. 'I can't get any closer with the car,' he finally says. 'I'll walk you to the door.'

His eyes linger on the girl, waiting to catch a glimpse of her when the courtesy light comes on. He can't help the softness he can hear in his voice, has to make a special effort to restrain his arm from fingering the graceful shoulders. Dwight aches as he remembers touching them, steering Emily through the Boat Show crowds. He hasn't been able to restrain the impulse to bring a red rose to pin on her outfit. The only way he's been able to hide what he's doing was to bring one for Sophie, too. Not red. He made it a yellow one for Emily's friend.

He sends a dozen roses, crimson red.
'Don't waste your money, son.'

'Of course not, Dwight. That would be ridiculous. It's only a short sprint across the grass!'

He gets the message: she doesn't want him to hang around, wants to be rid of him as soon as possible. 'Think about what I said, Emily. You could have a great career ahead of you.'

Dwight senses the hesitation. The passenger door is already open but Emily seems to be waiting. Does she want more encouragement? Promises of success?

'You think I'd make a good model?'

'The best.' How can he get it across to the girl that she's sensational, but that he really doesn't care about that. All he wants is to help her on her way.

'Pink eyes, pink eyes!'

The Pink Rabbit, Dwight thinks, bitter about his defect. That's how the locals thinks of him. Can't ask a girl like Emily to settle for that. 'I've seen some talent in my time, Emily. You've got whatever it takes, and then some.'

'So that's what you think I should do? Become a model?'

The words are gentle, shy. What does she mean? Is she asking him if modelling is a better bet than carrying on with her schooling which, according to Valerie, she not too good at? Or taking some uninspiring job whilst waiting to choose the best from among her many suitors? 'I think one has to grab at any special opportunities life offers.'

'And that's what I'm being offered? Modelling?'

'I know you have many other choices,' he sighs. His soul is in that sigh, his world is at her feet. 'I guess I think this is the one you can make the most of. It'll make you independent, Emily. In charge of your own life.'

She slips out of the car. 'Mummy will be waiting,' she says, quiet resignation trembling through the huskiness.

Too late it filtered through Dwight's mind that perhaps Emily wanted something more intimate, just maybe she does want him to ...

'Thanks for everything. It was lovely.' Gently she clicks the car door shut, a tiny muted sound.

He's prevaricated too long, left it too late. Eyes pricking, Dwight presses delicately on the accelerator and noses the Bentley down the drive. The big car steals immediately, noiselessly, away. Small salt drops trickle down his cheeks. Emily is walking away from him. He sees her walk sideways towards the beech hedge, then pries his eyes from the rear mirror.

Gliding away, with that assurance that comes from driving a familiar route home, his headlights pick out the myriad pink eyes of rabbits lining the lanes. Nocturnal creatures, out in full force. Their reputation for sweetness and innocence is belied by their depredations of the farmers' crops.

'We're having a shoot,' Jock informed him a couple of weeks before. 'Cut down on those damned pests. If you want, you can follow and see Sheba working.'

A clear offer of friendship. Dwight's maintained all along that he wants a working dog. What he hasn't fully thought through is the kind of work the dog will do. Maybe he should have settled for a sheepdog rather than a retriever. But whatever type of dog she is, Sheba is a wonderful companion – loving, generous. He's very happy with her, adores her.

Sheba isn't in the kennel when Dwight arrives at The Woolhouse. It isn't merely that he needs her company – he feels uncomfortable without her there. Not that she's in any sense a guard dog, but he's sure her presence staves off intruders. She is, after all, a big dog. No one who doesn't know her would guess how mild she is.

Not that it should matter. Just as Valerie prophesied there have been no further incidents in the woods while Alan was in hospital. And, Dwight admits to himself, they started again as soon as the guy got out. Nothing much, perhaps not even connected. Large swastikas carved into the big oaks, the gate leading to woodland from the Pontings' garden left open so deer fed on some choice shrubs, flowers slashed in the Brookes' garden. Enough to make everyone nervous but not enough to cause real alarm.

Dwight had brought Juliette down to Sussex again two weeks before the Boat Show. The two of them and the Brookes were sitting on the lawn, enjoying lemonade, when Alan turned up at Bramblings, unannounced as usual. He was his usual well-turned-out self: pristine white shirt, trousers with knife pleat creases, blazer immaculate.

126

He was furious about Emily's modelling engagement. 'I don't think that's at all suitable,' he snarled. 'I hardly think it's the sort of work someone with your upbringing would want to consider, Em.'

The implication was, Dwight took it, that modelling is something 'not quite nice' or, as Alan might have put it, aping his father, 'infra dig'.

Emily smiled and made no reply at all. Valerie, sharp, quick to point out that at least they can now live in their own house during the summer, broke up further complaints from Alan with requests for tea.

It occurred to Dwight, not for the first time, that Valerie has an uncanny knack of treating Emily as though she were some sort of family retainer. If Emily resented that she didn't show it. She went on smiling with her lips, showing small even pearly teeth. Her eyes stayed distant, her manner aloof. Precisely the look of hauteur a successful model needs.

Dwight drives on through the night, wistful, dreaming.

CHAPTER 17

Dwight garages the Bentley and looks round for signs of Jock and Sheba. It isn't really late, around nine-thirty. But Jock has normally dropped the retriever off by this time. He'll come by soon, Dwight comforts himself. Within the hour for sure.

All on his lonesome.
Owlet is dead.

He turns the front door key. The house seems silent, waiting. Mrs Dean has laid a place for supper, the furniture gleams polish and the smell of beeswax scented with lavender brings on a migraine. He badly needs a short walk with Sheba. Where in hell is Jock? Should he drive down to the Fox and Hounds, dig him out?

The grandfather clock in the hall begins to chime: seven, eight, nine, ten. By the time he gets down there it will be near closing time, and Jock is likely on his way already. He'll wait.

A feeling of oppression envelopes Dwight. How can he escape the curse of his albino body? Emily will not have him as a suitor, fair enough. But she won't even consider, let alone take on, the outstanding job he's offering her.

He doesn't understand that. The girl isn't academic, Valerie has told him often enough that she doubts whether she'll pass the three Higher Certificates she's studying for. Nothing too academic, at that: Art, Horticulture and Domestic Science.

'Appearances are so deceiving, honey.'
'I guess, Mom.'

Julie calls Emily a natural. The stint in hospital has helped smooth the skin on the young girl's hands, and Emily's eye for make-up is almost uncanny. Her posture, her walk, the way she wears clothes, all fit her for a career in modelling. What's holding her back?

Idly Dwight turns towards the hi-fi. Mozart, perhaps, something nice and jolly. The stack of CDs almost winks at him, then, as he brushes by, strews all over the floor. He's emotionally disturbed again, clumsy, ham-fisted. What now? Just because the girl doesn't want to become a model? It's ridiculous, the way he obsesses about her. It's as though she's spun a charm around him, is keeping him bundled up to suck his blood at will. A real spellbinder.

He picks the discs up, puts on the Mozart, then goes through to the kitchen. There is a shattering sound as he knocks a mug off the dresser. The earthenware crashes on the quarry tiles. Fortunate he isn't using the bone china he bought recently.

He bangs his head on the low-slung lamp. Will the Mozart be soothing enough, or does he need a pill?

Milk and honey, the healer he'd consulted insisted. 'Honey calms the nerves,' she droned on; sugar sweet sounds but not much help. The swinging kitchen light plays shadows on the wall as he warms some milk in a saucepan.

Two shapes entwine. Two profiles in silhouette.
They pull apart, one holds up a long narrow shape and menaces the other.

As the shadows flow into each other on the blank wall the kitchen lamp begins to steady, then stops. Dwight suddenly visualises Emily. He senses danger for her, is sure she needs his protection. Dejected, he sits down at the wooden table and begins to sip the milk and honey drink. It brings him back to his senses. There is no way that he can know what's happening to Emily at this moment. He's in

The Woolhouse, and she's safely with Valerie. He'll absolutely insist Valerie cancel the rest of the summer bookings, press the necessary money into her hands. Why is he worrying? Mother and daughter are safe and snug at Bramblings. He's just dropped Emily there himself not more than an hour before.

Mom pushes Pop away from her, pushes hard. He staggers backwards.

In spite of his reasoning Dwight cannot get the feeling of danger out of his mind. A rattle at the side door, a rapping at the kitchen window, makes him jump. There he goes, imagining things again. He turns his back to the kitchen window and begins to walk towards the living room when the rapping, more persistent, starts again. It's so lifelike that he turns, resigned, expecting to see nothing but the blank black void of kitchen window-glass.

But there is something there. Dwight thinks he can make out a face looking at him through the pane. It seems to leer at him. Where in hell is Jock with Sheba?

With a start he recognises Sheba's gentle eyes beside the face, and understands that this is Jock. But an excited, grimacing Jock, trying to get his attention. What's he playing at? Why is he so late? Is this illusion, too?

'It be me, Mr Delaney, sir. Jock.' The face at the window looms nearer, the voice is loud. 'Open up, will you?'

Dwight forces himself across the quarry tiles and into the small scullery beyond. He draws back the bolt, opens the door. Sheba greets him rapturously.

'Sorry we're late. There's been trouble at Bramblings.'

'Trouble?' He knew it – he just knew it! Why didn't he stay, see her inside?

''Fraid so.' Jock hesitates, then splutters: 'Emily's been stabbed.'

'Stabbed?' Dwight grasps at the door frame to stop himself from falling. 'But I only left her about an hour ago ...'

'*You* were with Emily? Tonight?'

'Did you say stabbed? Is she ...?' His voice begins to break, he can't bring himself to finish the sentence.

'Not as bad as that. They took her off in an ambulance.' Jock

130

stops, looks at Dwight. 'When were you with her?'

'I brought her back from the Boat Show – Ipswich. You know, dropped Sophie off at Oak Court and Emily at the top of their lawn.'

'That's when it must have happened.'

'What must have happened?'

'Someone must have been lying in wait for her. Sheba and I were walking back from the Fox and Hounds when I heard Raffy making one hell of a racket. I ran down to the cottage to check, just to make sure everything be all right, but the place were all locked up. I could see the light inside, and the fire, but Mrs Brooke wouldn't let me in. She'd drawn the bolts. I knew right off something had to be very wrong. Never locks anything.'

'My God, Jock.' Dwight has gone into the kitchen and slumped down on a stool. 'She OK?'

'Mrs Brooke?'

'Emily.'

'All I can tell you is that I got help up there as quick as ever I could.'

'You? What in hell were you doing there?' He's heard Raffy, OK. But what was he doing near Bramblings in the first place? It flashes through Dwight's mind that Jock had the opportunity to carry out all these odd happenings that have plagued the district for the past few weeks. Jock, too, is sweet on Emily. Just like Alan, and half a dozen others he probably hasn't come across as yet. But would Jock be here if he were the attacker?

'Just bringing Sheba to you. Thought I'd take the short-cut through the woods.'

He sees the guy look at Sheba, then at him. Notices that Sheba's with them and not locked into her kennel. Is even Jock afraid?

'After my supper. Thought I'd just walk through the area, check to see if there's anything unusual.'

Jock – everybody – knew Emily was coming back that night. Can't blame him for trying to catch a glimpse. And using Sheba. Well, that's what they're training her for. To catch the woodland ghoul. Jock is only carrying out Dwight's suggestions.

'I offered to see her to the door. She turned it down. Said her mother would be waiting.' Dwight's hands shake as he brings the mug of warm milk and honey to his lips. 'Help yourself to something, if you want.' He takes a sip, pulling out a chair and beckoning to Jock to sit. 'Where is she now?'

'I grabbed their bike and rode hell for leather to Oak Court. Got them to ring for the ambulance from there. By the time I'd cycled back I could see Mrs Brooke had Emily settled. She was on the floor, lying by the fire.'

'Valerie let you in?'

'I looked through the window. Told me I'd have to stay outside. Can't blame her, really. Sheba and I kept watch until the ambulance turned up. I saw them take her off. And Mrs Brooke. That's all I know.'

Jock poured some water, drank it almost greedily, then turned to Dwight. 'Who'd know you were bringing her back tonight?'

'Who wouldn't? They all knew Sophie and Emily were modelling at the Show, they all knew when it was due to end, they all knew the girls would be coming back latish tonight.'

'Dare say.'

'It has to stop, Jock. It's gone too far. Now the police will have to be involved.'

'They'll be round asking questions, don't you worry!' Jock scuffs the tiled floor.

'Valerie – Mrs Brooke – actually saw the attacker?'

'Dunno 'bout that. She shouted at me that Emily'd been stabbed and was bleeding. That's all she said, enough to send me running.'

It struck Dwight that Jock might, after all, have been the assailant. He could have attacked the girl, realised the mother was there, watching, let the girl go and come back again, the valiant rescuer. 'So how did you catch on something was wrong? Why were you actually near the place?'

Jock looks at him sideways but answers all the same. 'I did say. Walked Sheba over to you after the pub, like usual. Thought I'd check everything was all right on me way. That's when I heard Raffy barking his head off.' The shoulders straighten as the fiery hair is tossed back. 'I know when a dog's barking at danger,' he says. 'I was listening out for anything different. Just luck we were near the bridle path to the cottage.'

'The overgrown one.'

'The track. I sent Sheba on and followed right behind. We gets there just as Mrs Brooke is pushing home the bolts inside.'

'And she talked to you?'

'No, I tapped on the window but she took no notice. She was on the floor, by Emily. I has a bit of trouble getting her to understand I wanted to help. It's Sheba's barking as does it in the end, must have recognised that. Anyways, she wouldn't let me in. Just shouted to fetch help quick as I could.'

Long, tall shadows flickering on white-painted walls.
Mom's hair flows back, hands cover her face. He sees the stick raised in Pop's hand.

What possessed him to let Emily walk those last few yards alone? What the hell is wrong with him that he's allowed this to happen? Hasn't he had enough premonitions, hasn't Valerie said, time and again, that Alan is dangerous?

'D'you know which hospital they've taken her to?' Dwight asks Jock, trying not to tremble and stirring more honey into the milk.

'Chichester, I dare say. There's nowhere else that's properly equipped.'

'I'll go and pick up Mrs Brooke.'

Jock glances at Dwight, then down at the floor. 'Best let her stay the night there. They'll send her back in a taxi in the morning.'

'I guess.'

'I'll be off, then.'

'Thanks for bringing Sheba over.' Dwight returns to his sitting room in a daze. Emily is wounded. He can't wait, he has to know how she is. He gets the hospital number from enquiries, dials it.

CHAPTER 18

'But she *is* all right?' Dwight asks. He tries not to sound too agitated.

'She's not going to die, if that's what you mean.' Valerie, her bulbous, sycamore-wing nose sharpened to ash, looks dour. Her usual optimism, though not entirely gone, is clearly dented.

Dwight rushes over to Bramblings as soon as he feels he decently can. His strong sense of guilt tells him it's his fault that this outrage happened. Emily wouldn't have been in the garden at all if he hadn't brought her back late. He was afraid to keep the girls in Ipswich for another night after the Show finished, afraid Valerie would suspect his motives. If he'd thought about Emily instead of himself, if he'd brought the girls back today ... He feels disgusted with himself, furious – and impotent to do anything about it. Just like the bad old days.

'One has to count one's blessings,' Valerie says. 'She's wounded, and terribly shocked – but the doctor assures me she'll recover completely.'

He sees the stick raised in Pop's hand.
'No, Earl!'

She'll never be the same again, Dwight worries, bleak at the thought. There'll always be that lurking fear within her, the trauma will be lodged – for ever. He hasn't done enough, he nags at himself, he's prevaricated, made excuses. This time he won't be stopped.

134

He'll find that damned attacker before he can strike again.

'Where, exactly, was she stabbed?' He needs to know because it will help him work out what actually happened. But at some level he's afraid to find out, it seems too intimate a question, too indelicate.

'You mean which part of her anatomy? In her left side, just under her breast.'

That last word jolts Dwight almost into panic. 'That could have pierced her heart!' He fights down nausea.

'The doctor says it's a narrow miss. Not just her heart, her lung might have been punctured. She's incredibly lucky. The knife wasn't really driven in with much force at all, it sort of glanced off one of her ribs. A nasty-looking flesh wound. The surgeon says the scar will hardly show.'

Not the physical one, no. 'But they have to keep her in?'

'For the time being, just to check there's no infection.' Valerie's eyes stare, unseeing, over Dwight's shoulder. 'Em's in a state of shock.'

'Of course. And you must feel quite ghastly, too.'

Eyes refocused, Valerie seems assured, unusually composed. 'I know she's safe now,' she says, strong vibrant tones. 'That's the main thing. My greatest feeling is of relief.' Her mouth automatically turns into a shallow moon as she looks at Dwight and motions him to sit. A reflex, or does she genuinely think she has something to smile about?

'Am I intruding? Do you want to be on your own?'

'I'd rather have the company, talk it through.'

'In that case I'd like to know exactly what happened.' He sounds calm, confident – in charge. A charade. 'If you can manage it.'

'It'll help to talk it out.' Valerie stands erect, lined up by her mantelpiece, a small dumpy woman in her early fifties, Dwight guesses. Her normally alert eyes are half closed with tiredness.

'I didn't hear your car last night.'

An accusation? He should have sounded the hooter to tell her they were back? 'I turned round on the grass.'

'Your Pop slips into harbour, like a ship in the night, and steals out again before I've woken up.'

'It's so luxurious, I didn't even hear the door slam.'

He remembers how Emily shut it slowly, carefully – noiselessly.

135

A tiny click.

'If I had, I might have been able to prevent the whole thing.' Valerie is now crouching in front of her magnificent Tudor fireplace, rattling her enormous poker through the ashes. The great hearth, charred by a succession of logs burned there for over four hundred years, has a small mound of grey topped by a desultory flame licking a long, and evidently green, log. It's been wet and cold since early morning, and Valerie likes to light the fire on such days, even in summer. She stares at the glowing ashes as though mesmerised, tosses in a newly-smoked butt, another Player already lit from that. 'There isn't enough ash yet.'

'You heard Emily scream? That's what alerted you?'

'Mom!'
He hears her say his name, calling him, yet knows that is the past.

'She didn't scream, not that I heard.' Valerie stands up, puts back the poker, returns to a decaying wing chair squatting at the right of the fire and taking a long drag at her cigarette, inhaling slowly. Dwight is struck once again by her owlish look. She stares, unblinking, her eyes completely rounded now, into the fire, then exhales and breathes in again before returning to her story. 'I just sensed it must be time for her to be back, felt her presence out there, and opened the front door. Raffy, of course, was with me.' She puts her hand down on the terrier's head and fondles it lovingly. 'It was one of those nights with clouds scudding across a fairly full moon – well, you remember. At first it all seemed very dark, and then I saw a figure walking slowly by the beech hedge – I couldn't really make anything out, but I never doubted that it was Emily. Who else would be around here at that time of night? I was just about to shout 'Hello' when my eye caught some sort of movement by the wall. A deer, I thought to myself, gleeful that Em had caught it in the act. They're terrors in the garden, you know.'

'And?'

'I was about to send Raffy to help chase it off when the clouds cleared and I realised it wasn't an animal at all – it was a human being. A man, I was pretty sure, from the height and size, though

136

obviously I couldn't see too well.'

Short-sighted, Dwight had worked out early on. He recognised the signs only too well. And, naturally, Valerie doesn't bother with glasses.

She draws on her cigarette again, slowly, intensely. 'Emily saw it – him – too, I think, but probably didn't grasp it wasn't me. He'd have been almost swallowed up in the shadows from her angle of sight. At any rate I heard her call 'Hello', then stop short. She must have realised it wasn't me at that point.

'The figure was, by now, rushing towards her. I heard that. Presumably to cut her off from making a dash for the cottage door. Somehow, I can't explain why, I was rooted to the spot – I just couldn't seem to move.'

She left the cigarette in her mouth as her right hand goes once more towards the poker. Dwight sees that it's trembling.

'Then everything happened at once. I shrieked as loudly as I could, hoping to frighten off whoever it was, and Raffy ran towards the two figures now sort of locked together.'

Two shapes entwine. Two heads in silhouette.

Dwight remembers his instincts that something was happening to Emily when the shadows cast by his kitchen lamp flickered across his wall. What use was that? Always too late. Why hadn't he escorted her to her door?

'Raffy started to snarl, maybe he even bit the man's leg. I rushed towards Emily, she was heaving to push the man away. I yelled blue murder all the time. Raffy was in a frenzy, barking like mad. I think the noise finally unnerved the man.' She looks into the flames once more, rummaging through the ashes. 'Emily sort of fell backwards, almost into my arms, and practically landed on top of me. It's then I knew she'd been hurt, punched, or strangled, I suppose I thought. I dragged her arm around my neck and hauled her, as fast as I could, towards the door. Somehow we managed to get in, I drew her over towards the fire on to the rug in front of it as quickly as I could.'

'What a terrible experience.'

Valerie looks at Dwight carefully. 'How did you hear about it so quickly? Have the police been to question you?'

The police; he hasn't thought about that. 'Jock brought Sheba back last night, afterwards. He was so late, I was worrying and waiting for him. He told me how he'd heard Raffy barking, and ...'

'That's how you heard?'

'He came straight over, after he watched the ambulance take you both off.' Does he detect a note of caution about Jock? Or – the thought only just surfaces – about him? 'What exactly did the man use to stab Emily with?'

'A knife, just an ordinary pruning knife anyone might have carried. I had no idea about that, then. I thought Emily'd been throttled, that she was petrified with fear, not physically damaged.'

A pruning knife.

Her throat is cut, wide open, slit.

The rabbits, Dwight remembers, were deliberately slit from spine to belly. Full, gaping slashes which could easily have been made with a pruning knife. Something else is triggering in his mind. He can't place it for the moment, he'll have to work that out later, when he's on his own.

'Then I saw something sticking out of Emily. He'd plunged something into her, I grasped, something with a hilt. Into her left side – it was still there. I was absolutely terrified. I didn't know whether to leave it there, or pull it out, or what to do to save her life. I suppose I just prayed for help.' Valerie inhaled deeply, staring into the distance.

Dwight waited patiently. Is he a prime suspect? She's not acting that way. How can he prove it wasn't his doing?

'It was all settled by Emily drawing the knife out herself. She just pulled it out and let it drop, and the blood started oozing through.'

Bright scarlet streaming down, a rush of red he tries in vain to stem.

'Even at the time,' Valerie goes on, 'I realised dimly that it was oozing, not spurting, and that struck me as a good thing. I took the nearest cushion and pushed it against her to halt the flow, while I rushed to get a wet towel and something to bind it to her.'

'She was only wearing a thin T-shirt under her anorak, which was unfortunately open. Otherwise it might have stopped the blade. Anyway, all I knew was that I must staunch the wound, that I must make sure some sort of makeshift bandage would hold something tight against the flesh, and that I had to keep her warm. And get help as quickly as I could.'

Her eyes sweep past Dwight as she sighs, a tear sliding down her cheek. It takes several moments before she can speak again.

'I steeled myself to feel under the shirt. I felt a sort of deep gash under her left breast. Of course I had no idea how to deal with such an injury, or what damage it might have done, or how I was going to get help, so I simply pushed a wet towel against it, then took my scarf and tied it over that as tightly as I could. Then I took that rug' – Valerie turns and points at the sofa draped with the tartan Dwight noticed on that first day he'd strayed into the little garden – 'and put it over the poor darling to keep her warm. I shoved a cushion under her head. It's at that point that I heard Raffy, still outside, barking on and on.'

Valerie looks at Dwight and grins, rueful, almost wry. 'It's only then that it struck me that the fiend, whoever he is, must have left. After all, the door was wide open, anyone could have come after us. I finally grasped Raffy was just barking, nothing more.'

She'd gone out to call the terrier in and bolted the door behind him, she tells Dwight. That's when Jock appeared at the window and asked to be let in.

'Of course we all know Jock McClough, he's a good sort and simply not the type to go round stabbing people. But I was overcome with fear and worry, just the sight of a young man made me shudder.'

'A phone would have ...'

She waves her hand, impatient. 'And Jock could be carrying a pruning knife, or something much more lethal.'

'He carries a survival knife, quite a vicious-looking thing.'

'I wouldn't know. Anyway, I refused to unbolt the door, I just shouted through the window to get to the Pontings' phone as quickly as he could and call an ambulance.'

So she didn't tell Jock that Emily'd been stabbed?

Valerie looks at Dwight solemnly, her round eyes fixed on him.

'He tried arguing at first, but he could hear the urgency. I shouted that Emily'd been stabbed and was bleeding, and he sprinted off. I watched him through the window. He'd gone for the bike and was pedalling up the lawn, with Sheba after him.

'After he'd gone I reasoned I'd better not rely on him. It might have been him, after all. How could I possibly be sure? Coming back to try to help us could have been a clever ruse.'

'Sure thing.' He'd been just as suspicious himself. 'Except for Sheba.'

He sees her mull this over.

'You mean Sheba would have barked as well? I didn't cotton on to that. At the time I simply didn't understand what he was doing here.'

'He was walking Sheba over to me after his meal at the Fox and Hounds.'

'Past Bramblings? Bit out of his way, wasn't it? Hoping for a chance to come across Emily, I dare say,' she says drily.

Dwight laughs. 'Knew she'd be back around that time, like everybody else. Probably hoped to catch a glimpse of her.'

Valerie turns to the fire and pokes at it again. 'Raffy fetches the newspaper every morning from the village shop, you know, so I got a label and wrote:

'HELP! EMILY STABBED. BLEEDING. GET HELP, GET AMBULANCE!!

'He was sitting in front of the fireplace, panting after his exertions.
'Fetch the paper, boy,' I said. 'Go fetch.'

'He looked up at me and cocked his head, but didn't make a move. Maybe he knew it was the wrong time of day!'

'If you'd trained him properly ...'

Valerie frowns. 'Let me finish, Dwight. I said 'Fetch, boy, fetch.' And he finally got up. I drew the bolt back very slowly, very quietly, and let him slip out. Just then the moon came out and I saw him start off up the lawn.'

'Good dog.'

'There didn't seem to be anybody around. I shot the bolts back as quietly as I could. Of course I realised if it wasn't Jock, that madman – that ghoul –

might still be out there and I might have alerted him to Raffy.'

'You have to have a phone, Valerie. This is going too far in the simple life. I'll order a line for you tomorrow.'

'No, Dwight. I'll order a telephone if *I* think fit.'

Stubborn as ever. He can't force her, of course. Maybe he can get the doctor on his side. Or that solicitor she's always talking about?

'I don't mean to interfere. It's just that I feel responsible. I should have walked her to the door.'

'That's really nonsense, Dwight. Young girls must be allowed to walk about their own grounds, even at night. Whoever it was was lying in wait for her. Even if you'd been back two hours earlier the same thing might have happened.' Valerie gets up from her kneeling position by the fire and sits back in the chair.

'I take it the police are investigating.'

'They took some statements from me, yes.' She doesn't seem to think that that will help track down the man who stabbed Emily. Is she just tired out, exhausted, not up to it? That seems unlikely. Perhaps she doesn't think they'll bother.

'You don't think they're going to follow it up?'

'I have my doubts,' Valerie says bitterly. 'They don't seem all that interested.'

'What happened to the knife?'

'The police have it.'

'Jock's been training Sheba to track. Is there something else the attacker might have touched? Something Emily was wearing?'

Valerie looks blank. 'Wearing? You can't get fingerprints ...'

'For Sheba to get the scent.' Something caught on the bushes, fallen out of a pocket. Raffy might have torn a piece out of the man's trousers. 'Something Raffy might have brought in? A scrap of cloth, maybe.'

'I'll look for that.'

'And I was thinking, if you can let me have a list of everyone – absolutely everyone – Emily knows, we can get to the bottom of this.'

'That will be quite a list.'

'I guess we can eliminate most of them before we even start. But if there's any chance at all that one of them might be responsible we will eventually track them down.'

'Bloody waste of time, Dwight. Very good of you, but a complete waste of time. I think you know as well as I do who it was.'

He stares at her. Is she accusing him?

She sees the look on his face. 'It's perfectly obvious,' Valerie says succinctly. 'Alan Penn-Winton.'

So that's why he's off the hook. She presumed him innocent because she's targeted Alan. He should have guessed: suspect number one and only one. 'Just to humour me,' Dwight persists. 'It can't do any harm.'

'I'll think about it, Dwight. Don't think I'm quite up to it at the moment.'

'You bet, in a day or two. And what about your visits to the hospital? May I order you a cab?'

'That's very good of you,' she smiles at him. 'But actually it's all arranged. Anne is going to give me a lift.'

'Anne? You mean Anne Pontings? Really?'

'Not entirely charitable. She's looking for a boutique in Chichester.'

'What d'you mean? She's intending to buy a store?'

'She's always wanted to run one, and I've always encouraged her. But up to now she felt she ought to spend her time running the house.'

'So what's changed?'

'Chas has changed. He's really involved with Nina. Not like the others. This time he might leave Anne.'

'Meaning he's all for her branching out?'

'Doesn't know about that. She's got some capital her parents left her. Going to find a place and use that money to fund it.'

'Exactly what Juliette always wanted to do. Fact is we scouted round the marina the day Emily was taken to hospital with pneumonia.'

'Did you see anything good?'

'Sure. Harry – my friend Harry Solferino – snapped it up. Says it's a bargain.'

Valerie just looks at him.

'He's buying it for Julie; they had something going at the time.'

'And?'

'Point is that Julie's looking for a partner. She's still with me, she doesn't want to – can't afford to – leave until she's sure the business will work out. That might suit both Anne and her. Julie knows her way around the rag trade, especially the fashion end of it. She and Anne could be absolutely right for each other.' Pitching in there.

'It sounds a good idea, Dwight.' Valerie busies herself with the fire again.

Has she smelled the stinking rat? 'They can hold a little fashion show for their opening. With Emily and Sophie.'

'Emily's in hospital, Dwight.'

'Right now, Valerie. But you said yourself it's only a flesh wound. She's very fit, she'll get over it in no time.' He takes a deep breath, walking towards the window and looking out. 'Do her the world of good to have something to look forward to, away from ...'

'Away from her roots, you mean?'

'It's a good half-way house, Valerie. She'll forget more easily if she's busy. And she won't be far away.'

CHAPTER 19

Valerie, unusually animated, rushes out at the sound of an approaching car, leaving Dwight in mid-greeting by her door. Dwight watches her short legs scissor their way – snip snap – across the lawn. The grass, though trimmed short by old Jem only a day or two ago, hugs rain, squelching mud water into every step.

Dwight can hear Valerie's welcoming voice. 'It's very good of you to come, Matthew.'

She chatters on, rumbling low, so he's not able to decipher what else she says as she and her new visitor walk towards the cottage. He backs into the living room and watches Valerie open her front door wide and motion 'Matthew' through. He ducks under the lintel and walks in, cautiously keeping his head lowered. He beams genially around as he flattens himself against the wall to let Valerie through, his light-blue eyes and soft fair curls giving him an angelic look.

'This is Matthew Sunnington,' Valerie introduces him briskly. 'My solicitor's son, come to stand in for him. Matthew, this is Dwight Delaney.'

Dwight watches again as the young man's stoop gives way to his full height, his hair in danger of brushing cobwebs from the ceiling.

'Dwight's our new neighbour at The Woolhouse. He's here at my request.'

'Delighted.' Matthew holds out his hand.

'Hi, there.' Dwight stands as tall as he can, puts out a shy hand.

The young man's grasp is firm and sure. Dwight strengthens his own.

He cowers in corners, alone at playtime.

Dwight turns to Emily, sitting demurely silent by the fire. 'Hello, Emily.'

The girl lifts her head, a languid look and no response at all. Dwight manoeuvres proprietarily towards the sofa and eases himself into the seat nearest her. He leans towards her, handing her a small elaborately wrapped package of Belgian chocolates. 'I hope you go for candy.'

Emily forces a brief smile. Sheba has padded over and settled by the fire. Emily begins to pat her head, ignoring Dwight.

He sends her candy.
'You know I'm on a diet, son.'

'I brought these for you,' Dwight says, handing the chocolates over.

Emily takes her time to even acknowledge the packet, eventually accepting it without any sign of interest and placing it, unopened, on the hot mantelpiece.

The big black hearth is alive with scorching flames, breathing fire. They curl eagerly round stout logs crisscrossed above the now larger mound of ash. Emily turns towards a tray just behind her holding four pewter goblets and begins to pour a thin green-yellow liquid from a quart beer bottle.

'Miss Hopkins said urgent and private,' Matthew is saying, an eager spaniel wagging his tail. 'My parents have just gone off to Crete for a fortnight's break. Thought I'd better come out and see what the problem is before handing you over to partner Tim.' His smile continues, eyes fastening on Emily. The muscular body appears to fill much of the small space. The country tweeds, a mixture of fawns and browns, give his sturdy frame a decidedly bulky look, staid, solid, virtually middle-aged.

Emily crouches on her little stool, not bothering to look up. Dwight's satisfaction that even such a healthy specimen of manhood should be disdained uncoils tight belly muscles.

Matthew Sunnington leans towards Emily as his smiling eyes begin to shine. 'Long time no see, Emily. Glad you're looking so well.'

Emily busies herself with the poker, unsettling a happily burning log. 'Hello, Matthew.' Almost a monotone.

'Do sit down.' Valerie waves the young man to the sofa next to Dwight. 'What about some elderflower wine. Last season's, so it's quite heady now.'

'Lovely.' Matthew bends himself in half to give Raffy a friendly pat, then cranes his face sideways to feast on Emily. She shies away.

'Tim's very good, of course. But my father mentioned you'd popped in to see him about a couple of weeks ago and you said private, so I felt ...'

There's a rapping at the door and it opens gingerly, showing Anne Pontings restraining Tatman from rushing in.

'May we come in?'

'Anne! This is a surprise.'

A puffy white-faced Anne blunders over the gum boots knocked into her path by Tatman in his rush to join the other dogs.

'Oh, dear. This is quite a little gathering, isn't it? Not much room for any more!'

'Actually, it's a meeting, Anne.'

'And I'm de trop.'

'Really, my dear. That isn't what I meant at all. We're just about to discuss Emily's contract with Dwight,' Valerie assures her, smoothly and glibly. 'Do join us in a glass of elderflower champagne.'

So Emily has mentioned ... And then Dwight remembers that he's discussed possibilities of signing Emily up with his agency with Valerie herself.

Though Anne's eyes betray a certain reluctance for the proffered drink she chooses to overcome this in favour of joining the gathering.

Emily lifts the tray holding the goblets and is about to offer them round when Dwight takes the tray from her.

'Let me,' he says, anxious to do something concrete for the girl. 'I expect you're still very tired.'

146

He's rewarded with a peevish 'Don't fuss, Dwight,' as she allows him to take over and promptly disappears into the tiny kitchen off the living room.

'I'll pour, shall I?' Dwight hands round the brimming goblets, decanting more liquid into the glass which Emily just fetched and now holds out. There's no more pewter.

Everyone dutifully lifts their drinks and waits, politely, for Valerie to start.

'Your healths,' she says, then corrects herself. 'And particularly Emkin's. We all know what happened, and we can probably guess who the culprit is. So here's to justice!'

'I'm glad you think you know who's responsible,' Anne says sourly. 'I wouldn't like to say, myself.'

Which is why Valerie is tolerating her, Dwight feels pretty sure. She wants to pump her before the meeting proper is begun.

'I'm sure you have your suspicions, Anne.'

'Don't like the look of Earl's kid.'

'I know who it jolly well isn't,' she says aggressively. 'It's not one of the locals, that much I can vouch for.' She looks at Dwight venomously. 'But we've has such an influx of all kinds of people, there's no knowing what they're capable of.' The look has turned to open hostility.

'You're thinking of someone in particular,' Valerie prompts quietly, almost softly.

'I simply mean,' Anne is now flushed bright red, 'that we've had something of a flood of newcomers. First there was Nina, then Dwight, and now that beautiful Old Cottage in Lickfold has been sold to Buddhist monks.'

'You think a Buddhist attacked Emily? Honestly, Anne. They may be odd but they have a philosophy of peace.'

'You know I don't mean them, though they do have the most peculiar ideas.'

Red herring. Is she going to accuse him openly? Dwight feels the familiar prickling in his armpits. The room seems overpoweringly hot.

'I don't want to be rude,' Anne persists 'but we only have Dwight's

147

word for it that he dropped Emily off.'

It's out in the open at last. Dwight feels he'd just as soon shoot that one down immediately. 'I ...'

'No, we don't, Anne,' Valerie interrupts. She seems prepared for such an accusation, sounds strangely soft and gentle. 'As a matter of fact we know it can't have been Dwight.'

'What is to stop him getting out of the car and following Em?'

'Nothing to stop him doing it. Plenty to prove he didn't.' Valerie takes a sip from her goblet and seems to savour it. 'It's a good vintage year,' she says.

'So prove it,' Anne prods obstinately on.

'Lay off, Hank. Just ain't got no pigment in his skin, is all.'

'The man who did it was in front of, and to the side, of Emily. By the beech hedge, above the garden wall. Dwight was, originally, in the car and let Emily out. He'd have to have turned off the lights, sprinted out of his side of the car, shut his door to turn off the automatic inside light so I wouldn't spot the car...'

'He could have turned that off before.'

' ...shut the door without making any noise ...'

'He could have left it open.'

' ...taken even more time to go round the car, and then bolted towards the side and got there before Emily. All this without making any noise, or otherwise attracting my, or Emily's, attention.'

Dwight is amazed to hear it set out so precisely. She sure knows how to speculate logically when she wants to. And she's given quite a bit of thought to his possible implication. Must have, right from the start.

'And I saw a rather tall man, I told you that. Quite apart, of course, from the fact that Emily would have recognised Dwight.'

It sure annoys the hell out of him that Valerie uses his lack of height as circumstantial evidence. Why not draw attention to his white hair and pale face standing out against the dark while she's at it? A fleeting memory of something he can't quite catch flitters through his mind.

'So you're saying it was some stranger she's never seen before.

Some vague – but tall – person who just happened to be there and happened to want to stab Emily. What an extraordinary solution!'

'I certainly don't think he was a stranger. I think he's someone we all know quite well...'

'Then Em would say!'

' ...and Em didn't recognise him because he was, at that moment, unrecognisable. Not his normal self. That can't have been Dwight. Not just his height, Em had just said good-night to someone in a perfectly ordinary state of mind. I don't see how anything could suddenly have made him feel outraged enough in that short space of time to decide to knife her. If he'd wanted to attack her he could have done it properly, away from here.'

Dwight hadn't felt murderous, no. Depressed, dispirited. What Valerie has inferred is wrong, but she can't know that, since Emily obviously hadn't even bothered to mention his latest offer, let alone considered it – well, presumably there hadn't been the opportunity. OK, then, neither of them had any idea how much Emily's reactions might affect him.

'That wouldn't have been very bright. Dwight would have been suspected right away. He was, after all, bringing her home. That's the whole point. It's a perfect cover,' Anne says.

'So how did he get away with it?' Matthew looks at her, intrigued.

'For goodness sake! It wasn't Dwight, I'd hardly not recognise him!' Emily explodes from her corner.

'Pink eyes, pink eyes!'

Exactly, Dwight thinks ruefully. She'd recognise him anywhere – the Pink Rabbit. A *short* pink rabbit.

'It wasn't Alan either. I'd have recognised him, too,' Emily almost mumbles. Her hands are up by her temples now and she is rocking back and forth.

Dwight has the feeling that no one apart from himself has even heard her.

The girl suddenly drops her hands, grasps hold of the poker with both of them, and begins to rattle the logs in the fire, sparks flying in all directions. Her strength is as startling as it is unexpected.

149

Valerie goes over and gently takes the implement away from her.

'What about Jock McClough, then? His is rather a thin story, don't you think?' Anne tries a new tack.

'It can't have been McClough,' Valerie says composedly, almost smug. 'He had Sheba with him, and Raffy would have spotted – well, scented – her, at once. She's still on heat. Only something very unusual – like an attack by someone not accompanied by a bitch on heat – would have kept him from her. And, anyway, I'd have heard her bark.'

All figured out and, so far, rational.

'Have it your own way,' Anne says brusquely. 'Tatman and I have to be going. I've got someone coming round to see the house.'

That's what she came about, Dwight now realises. A heart to heart with Valerie.

'As bad as that?'

'Not too good at the moment.' Anne looks defiantly around the room. 'Oak Court's already on the market, and the boat has to go as well. Chas has gone off to Ireland with Nina – no doubt spending that derisory tin handshake from Stoare Vantile.'

'But he's sending you enough to keep you going?' Valerie asks, sounding quite anxious.

'He's looking after number one. He has promised half what's left from the sales.' Anne's nostrils enlarged unpleasantly. 'Not that he doesn't have to, even if he hadn't spent my capital.'

'He spent your capital?'

'I let him handle it.'

'He's got to send you something to live on, isn't that so, Matt?' Valerie's concern is clear.

'You can apply for a maintenance order, yes.'

'Only if the husband has a job,' Dwight slips in snidely. 'I gather Charles doesn't.' No way Harry is going to look at Charles Pontings unless Dwight gives him the nod. Anyway, Harry's already sucked Charles dry.

'Not my field, of course,' Matt inserts cautiously. 'My father would be the one to consult. But I'm pretty sure you can stay in your home if you have underage children. You can't be forced to sell it, the name on the title deeds is neither here nor there.'

150

'And live on social security. I know.'

Sussed it all out already. Fast worker.

'They're hardly going to pay the mortgage for Oak Court. And even if they did, it wouldn't cover the rates ...'

'You mean the benefits cover the mortgage now?'

Anne stops, aware that Valerie, in her time of need, wasn't helped. 'Things have changed for the better in some cases. Not really mine, I won't have the money for next year's school fees unless I can arrange a decent sale. Then I'll have to use some of the capital.'

'The house must be worth quite a bit.'

'Not once the mortgage has been paid off.' Anne sounds brittle. 'So good at money, you know.'

The crash – Valerie must have got it right about Chas losing his shirt.

'You mean Sop might not be able to carry on at school? Then I'll leave, too!' Emily almost shouts.

This time all eyes turn to Emily. Never one to join in, positively uncommunicative, they're shocked into hearing her at last.

She wants out, Dwight realises. Just out. Any excuse.

'How sweet of you, Em. We'll have to hope it doesn't come to that, but Sophie might have to change to Midhurst Grammar.'

Anne grabs at her goblet and looks into it fixedly. Dwight sees that she's almost choking, bringing it to her lips, pretending to drink. 'A terrible blow in her A-level year, but she really mustn't allow her parents' marriage problems to get in the way of her education.'

'I'll talk to the Governors,' Valerie assures Anne quickly, eagerly. 'Admiral Brooke would never have tolerated a girl leaving in the last year for financial reasons. I'm sure I can persuade the present board of governors to let her stay.'

What *is* she talking about, Dwight wonders? How can she approach the governors with Reginald Brooke on the board?

'You can?' Anne looks at her carefully. 'What about Reginald?'

'Exactly. He won't argue with me. He'll back me up.'

Does she have something on her ex? Something she hasn't mentioned?

A genuine smile lights up Anne's face and Dwight can see her eyes are moist. 'That really would be marvellous, Val. Walkies,

151

Tatman,' she rasps, stumbling towards the little vestibule. 'Sorry I've got to go. Be seeing you.'

'I'll walk the dogs,' Emily announces and follows Anne, calling to Raffy and Sheba. She doesn't bother to ask Dwight whether he has other plans.

'Good luck with the house.' Valerie clicks the door shut behind them, brisk and ready for action.

'And now, to the point. You both know what happened to Emily. You also know that there have been some unsavoury – frightful – happenings in the neighbourhood. Up to now we've had no idea at all of who the culprit might be. But now I'm sure I know.'

A deep, long draught of elderflower as she appraises the two men sitting together on the little sofa, opposite the fire. Matthew's gentle face is grave and attentive. Dwight can feel himself far too red. The fire is hot and the little room is overwhelmingly stuffy. Why has she shut the door? Valerie douses the flames down by poking the logs apart. She opens the small leaded window.

'It really is good of you to come, Matthew.'

Dwight recalls his helping out for weeks and she's never even mentioned it. Is she taking him for granted?

'Your father will have to do the honours eventually. But I can fill you in meanwhile, and you can give me the benefit of your advice.'

Just a whipper-snapper, Dwight finds himself thinking. He could mop the floor with him.

'Unqualified, as yet.'

'Never mind. Good enough, I'm sure. Just like your father.'

Valerie has, Dwight thinks wryly, an uncanny way of getting the best out of people. She's simply determined that, if she knows them, they're the very best. It's almost as though her projection of superb qualities gives her nominees the very gifts they need. It's a remarkable attribute, and Dwight only wishes he had a small part of it.

'When I was waiting for them to settle Emily at the hospital – you remember, when she had pneumonia – I came across Alan Penn-Winton, as I've already told Dwight.'

Neither man makes any comment. Matthew has, perhaps, been alerted by his father. Or maybe worked it out for himself.

'I know you both think I'm imagining things, and I know Gilbert thinks I'm overreacting. So I did some investigating on my own. I've gets friends in high places, you know.' She titters slightly, almost nervously. 'Perhaps I should say low places. That's often much more useful.'

So why insist on Grove House Chapel, Dwight thinks.

'I happen to know one of the nurses at the hospital, Jenny Arbitage. Her aunt's a very good friend of mine.'

'Your friend Loretta?'

It takes Valerie a couple of seconds to place how Dwight knows that. 'Exactly; my friend in Scotland. I promised to keep an eye on the girl while she's finishing her training. The next time I visited Emily I got in touch with Jenny and took her to tea. It wasn't at all difficult to discover that I'd been quite right. Alan is a regular patient in the Psychiatric Department.' Valerie pauses, looking round, waiting for a response. There isn't one.

'He's schizophrenic. And before you tell me that that's all controlled with drugs now, I already know that theory. But you have to keep taking the drugs, and the reason Alan constantly has to go back to hospital is because he doesn't bother.'

'That doesn't make him Mr Hyde, Valerie.'

'Where are you off to, Dwight?'
'To play in the woods, Mom.'

'He often gives a pretty good imitation of Dr Jeckyll,' Valerie goes on, unabashed. 'I'm quite clear Alan's the man we've been looking for all along. He's Emily's attacker, and he's responsible for torturing slowworms, slashing dead animals and setting fire to the woods – among other things.'

'That's quite some accusation,' Dwight says, frowning slightly. 'I thought you said he's often away in Paris.'

'For Paris read Chichester Hospital.'

'But still away – often as far as Oxford.'

'It's not that far. He's got a car, after all.'

Matthew is staring into his goblet, concentrating on the pale fluid, petillant and clear. 'It's rather jumping to conclusions,' he says, measuring his tone. 'All you have to go on is hearsay and that you think Alan is a patient.'

'I know he's a patient. Apart from anything else, I personally saw a nurse escort him to the ward.'

'He might have been in an accident and been concussed.'

'And we've heard nothing about it. That's carrying legal caution too far, Matt.'

'It does sound pretty damned convincing to me as a friend,' Matt agrees. 'But legally speaking, that's another matter.'

Dwight, his colour even higher, the translucent skin unable to mask it, looks challengingly at Matthew. 'Emily hasn't been able to identify him, she keeps saying it isn't Alan. We do have to pay some attention.'

Matthew faces him, eyes clear and imperturbable. 'And in my profession you have to be sure,' he agrees amiably. 'She's a sweet girl, she probably can't imagine someone she knows actually knifing her.' He smiles his profession's patronising smile. 'But we can look into the matter further. There's certainly a case for asking serious questions.'

'Can you get things moving, Matt? So that we'll have something concrete to show Gilbert when he gets back?'

'I don't see why not.' He smiles engagingly again, smooth cheeks crinkling into runnels. 'It's nothing anyone can take exception to. Just preliminary enquiries, which I'll enjoy making.'

'And what about the police?' Dwight asks. 'Surely they're looking into the case?'

'You do have to remember Penn-Winton's profession and his standing in the local community.'

'That's a very salient point,' Matthew agrees with Valerie.

'They still have to do their job, don't they?' Dwight demands, but there's no reply.

His lone voice crying in the wilderness, he guesses. Two voices, Dwight corrects himself. Emily is on his side.

154

CHAPTER 20

'Emily's still recuperating, we don't want her to overdo it. Honest, I'll be glad to drive you.' Dwight tries not to sound too eager. 'Jock hasn't brought Sheba over yet. I have nothing pressing to do.' Dwight has left London early that Friday, looking forward to a long weekend in the country.

Valerie hesitates for just a moment, glancing briefly at her daughter. 'In that case you must come into Gilbert's office with us. Help me persuade him to bring a charge against Alan.'

'I guess that won't work too well. He doesn't know me.'

'At least you're a man,' she blows the assertion away with a smoke ring, 'and therefore, in his eyes, level-headed.'

'Won't Matthew have filled him in? I thought he was rooting for you.' Is the guy opting out?

'He's done some sterling sleuthing, but he's gone back to that boring job in London.'

'Job? I thought he wasn't qualified yet.'

'Conveyancing. Some sort of apprenticeship these solicitors do in a law firm. He's going in for that.'

Dwight begins to wonder which profession Valerie does approve of. 'So he's not here to back us up?'

'We're on our own,' Valerie says, almost as though she relishes it. 'You and Emily and me. An unlikely trio, but we'll win through.'

Emily turns away wanly. Since the stabbing her reserve has often

155

shown as sullen looks, the silence converted into impatient twists of her body, leaning away from whoever speaks to her. The blooming apricot tint of her skin has changed to palest rose. She's drawn her hair back tightly from her forehead, catching it in a drooping pony tail. Her hands, though not as coarse as before the Show, haven't been manicured again. It's as though she's simply functioning on automatic pilot.

Both Dwight and Valerie have tried to lure her out of her private world. Dwight has bought tickets for Chichester Theatre, attended polo matches in Midhurst with the girl, included Sophie in sailing trips on First Lady. Emily has simply suffered these attempts at friendship, doesn't respond in any way.

Valerie, on the other hand, tried a different tack. She's convinced that finding the culprit and bringing him to justice will bring Emily round. Her theory is that the young girl is afraid as long as her attacker is on the loose.

'Sure, Mom. I know you mean well.'

Dwight doesn't buy that. Something is bugging the girl. He can't put his finger on it, but somehow he senses Valerie is pressing her too much. Crowding her, crowded her all her life, Dwight reckons. And more than ever now. But how? Valerie doesn't stop her daughter going out, doesn't even put an end to the hours the girl spends tramping alone in the woods.

Dwight has done his best to talk to Emily. She simply doesn't converse at all, just answers in monosyllables when absolutely forced to. That's no way to gain new insights into what's upsetting her so much. And she isn't worried about roaming the countryside on her own, she does it more than ever before.

'Just going to fetch some kindling,' she's announced more than once as soon as Dwight appears, and then rushes off before either he or Valerie can stop her. Even more curious, she doesn't bother to take Raffy. That certainly seems to rule out Valerie's theory. If Emily were afraid of her assailant surely she wouldn't venture out on her own.

It's extraordinary. Emily wanders off without the excuse of

exercising animals. She even refuses to replace the jobs she used to be so keen on. The summer visitors are no longer there, of course, and the Pontings have no horses to exercise. Myra Stanhope no longer needs Emily as she's become too arthritic to ride. But the girl has made no attempt to find new work.

Dwight is aware that Emily herself might be responsible for some of the odd happenings in the woods. She has real opportunity – more time than ever – to etch symbols into tree trunks, to build altars, to gather floral offerings. But can he really imagine Emily hacking a hedgehog to pieces? Can such a keen nature lover enmesh live slowworms in plastic netting, slice the tops off a whole plantation of saplings? Preposterous! Even if she were responsible for marking up trees it needn't follow she's done the rest.

It has crossed Dwight's mind that Emily might be mentally disturbed. Perhaps she's attracted to Alan in the first place because she's schizophrenic, too. There's no question that she's in deep depression now. Perhaps her illness, undiagnosed, has progressed to a catatonic phase.

'This is Dwight Delaney, Gilbert.' Valerie introduces the reluctant Dwight. 'He's as keen to get to the bottom of all this as I am, so he's come along.' Valerie smiles sweetly at Gilbert. 'He ran – owns! – Models International. I expect you've heard of it.'

'I'm the president.' Dwight tries disarming Gilbert Sunnington. 'My shareholders own the business.'

The solicitor bows briefly at Dwight. Strait-laced, early sixties, his old Oundelian tie blending in with his shirt. 'How d'ye do.' An unwilling handshake.

'He's been kindness itself,' Valerie twitters, roguish and slightly out of breath. 'I don't know where we'd be without him.'

'I believe he simply dropped Emily off at the top of the lawn that night,' Gilbert says quietly, 'and you had to manage by yourself after that. I still don't know how you did it.'

'There wasn't all that much I could do. It just all solved itself.' Her eyes unveil slowly, deliberately, as she opens them to their full extent and devours Gilbert with them.

'Emily was saved because she was attacked with a Saynor pruning knife,' Dwight puts in, determined to be noticed. 'Fortunately that blade is reasonably short and stubby – and it's a folding knife. It must have gone in at an angle and then begun to close up again. I guess it hadn't been clicked in place to hold it open.'

'The point is it cut right into Emily.' Valerie, dismissing Dwight's careful analysis as irrelevant, sounds crisp. She pauses to reassemble. 'What I did grasp was that my poor darling would almost certainly survive as long as I could stop the loss of too much blood.'

Valerie begins to describe the incident again. Dwight observed before that she doesn't seem able to stop herself. "Best if we don't move you,' I told her. 'She was quite snug in front of the fire and on the floor.' Valerie gives a deep, expressive sigh. 'I piled more wood on and brought down the eiderdowns, cocooned her as best I could.'

'You're all I have, Dwight, honey.'

Cocooned, exactly that. Dwight understands the situation only too well. Emily is a butterfly ready to spread its wings, unable to escape.

Valerie shrugs. 'Fortunately Emily didn't take the warm drink I offered her. They told me at the hospital afterwards that that was just as well, otherwise they'd have had trouble about the anaesthetic.'

'I think you were absolutely wonderful, Valerie,' Gilbert interrupts suavely, glances up, then pauses. 'But don't you think Bramblings is a little on the isolated side for two women on their own?'

The bristle is instantaneous, round eyes consume him. 'I would have thought it's much safer than anywhere else. There are muggings even in Midhurst, Gilbert! This was a personal attack, that's why we're here. So we can bring the fiend who did it to justice, and to stop him doing it again. Living in Midhurst would hardly be protection against someone like that.' The great orbs are intense, settled on Gilbert who shifts uneasily under their steadfast gaze. 'Ordinarily we have the nicest people round us. There's just this one ...'

'Now, hold on, Valerie ...'

'This raving psychopath ...'

'Schizophrenic, yes.' Gilbert returns her gaze steadily. 'We've established that Alan is being treated for schizophrenia, and that

158

he often neglects to take the prescribed medication. But the doctors are adamant that his being off medication would by no means result in the sort of behaviour you describe.'

'They don't say he can't have done it, they say it's unlikely he would do it as a result of his illness. It's not all that likely that anyone would do it, schizophrenic or not. Knifing people is fairly infrequent, even nowadays.' Valerie sits there, composed and certain.

Dwight decides it would be a good deal safer if it were he and Jock, helped by Sheba, who tracked down whoever was responsible. Valerie might easily make matters worse. True, Alan makes a ready target. He's obviously crazily in love with Emily, he's probably green-eyed about all the rivals he knows of, and of the dozens more he cannot foresee. But Emily has always, and will always, attract many admirers – why would he wait until now to stab her?

So what does he think happened? Emily has, after all, been stabbed. And a man was involved, both Emily and her mother have testified to that. Dwight wishes for the umpteenth time that he'd waited to see her safely in, but the truth is he was upset that she hadn't even bothered to answer his suggestion about the job. He allowed her to go unescorted. He had, as usual, been thinking about himself, concentrating on his own problems.

'Where did you get that knife, honey?'
'Pop asked me to look after it for him.'

And then suddenly Dwight sees the knife, disembodied, lying – where? The answer to the riddle lies in that. Where has he seen that knife before?

'We can, of course, issue a summons in the magistrate's court. No one can stop us, though the police have told me that they're making their own enquiries and would prefer not to have members of the public interfering. They'll prosecute if they find there's a case to be answered.'

'Of course they'd prefer it! And we all know why.' Valerie looks round aggressively, her head slumped into her neck, thickening it. 'They all stick together. Penn-Winton is, after all, a governor of Midhurst Grammar School, a brilliant barrister, a respected citizen, a former mayor of the town.'

'That makes absolutely no difference, Valerie.'

'Don't be such an old fogey, Gilbert. Of course it makes a difference. We all know the old boy network is working overtime on this one. Only they're not going to get away with it, not this time.'

'This time?'

'Like that time with Reginald. They all stick together when it comes to the crunch.'

A movement across the windowpanes changes the light. Emily is fiddling with the old-fashioned catch which keeps the casement window in its place. She unhooks it, then clicks the dent into a different hole to open the window wider.

Gilbert frowns deeply. 'Are you referring to that alleged business about Reginald being involved in badger baiting? There was no evidence at all.' He looks down at his papers, uncomfortably shifting them about, levering one file over another.

'My point exactly. Evidence melted away. In any case, we have to bring the case, whatever comes of it. You can see for yourself, Emily's nature is completely changed. She doesn't ride, she only occasionally walks Raffy, she disappears for hours on end or just sits at home and mopes. The only way she's going to recover is if her attacker is brought to justice.'

The girl stirs again, once more unhooking the window. It swings in a wide arc. 'I wish you'd stop going on like that, Mummy. I've told you, over and over again. It wasn't Alan. I'd have recognised him.'

There is a sort of dull persistence, the repeating of a refrain. Her voice remains low, hardly distinguishable in fact, the outside roar of traffic almost drowning it. But she did bring herself sufficiently out of her lethargy to speak. It constitutes a Brownie point for Valerie.

'How could you possibly have recognised him, Em?' The voice is softened but still dismissive, insistently dismissive. 'It was dark!'

'I saw the face, he was right on top of me. I didn't recognise him.'

'It won't have been the way you're used to seeing him. He wouldn't have been recognisable.'

'You're always saying that.' Emily shrugs, resigned, then makes what looks like an enormous effort. 'I know Alan very well. I'd

160

have known him whatever his state of mind.' She's shut the window, wrenching the handle tight.

'All twisted up, with bared teeth...'

'Did he speak at all?' Gilbert interrupts. His quiet, modulated tones gain from the contrast with Valerie.

'I don't think so. I can't remember anything.'

'Then you can't possibly have recognised him, Emkins. He was beside himself, and he didn't speak because he was too busy going for you in a fit of jealous fury. You weren't expecting an attack, you'd never seen Alan in that state, you couldn't possibly have identified him!' Valerie finished up in a crescendo of righteous anger.

Emily twists back to the window and gazes across to the new houses sprawling Chichester into the surrounding countryside.

'You're trying to put words into her mouth, Valerie. That isn't any good. Just leave it for a bit and see if you don't feel all this is best left behind you.'

'I seem to remember your advising me to sell Bramblings, too,' she snaps acidly. 'No, I won't leave it and see how I feel. I'm taking Alan Penn-Winton to court, and I'm taking on his father, and if you don't want to act for me I'll find someone who will!'

Gilbert's original shocked reaction changes to his smooth look. 'Of course I'll act for you, you know that. But, even if I waive my fees, do you know what you're letting yourself in for if the verdict goes against you?'

'Legal aid,' Valerie says smugly. 'I haven't got a bean.'

'That's where you're making a mistake, Valerie. You've got Bramblings.'

For a moment her determination seems dented, but she recovers in a very short space of time. Reaching for the pack of cigarettes in her bag she lights one and draws in the nicotine, exhaling with relief. 'Then it's a proper use for Bramblings,' she announces, inhaling deeply, encompassing the world in the motion of her arm.

'If you lose, you may have to pay Alan's legal costs.'

She puffs more rapidly.

'Penn-Winton will go for 'malicious' prosecution. The damages can be enormous.'

She shrugs, not even listening.

161

'Even if you win, and that really is extraordinarily unlikely, you won't necessarily get back your costs.'

'Anything else? We might as well have the full extent of the possible damage.'

'They're bound to make counter accusations.'

'She encouraged him to stab her, you mean?' Valerie positively cackles.

'If there's any doubt, if the magistrates get confused, they'll simply bind both parties over.'

'Bind over?'

'To keep the peace.' Gilbert draws himself up, face grave and long. All he needs, Dwight thinks somewhat frivolously, is the black cap.

'In my professional opinion the best you will achieve is that. And it can cost you the home you've fought so hard to keep.'

Dwight tries to catch the solicitor's eye. He will be more than happy to pay the expenses. It makes absolutely no difference to him and he'll be glad to do it, if it helps. The sight of the glorious girl sitting there so unresponsively, virtually in a state of catatonia, makes the spending of money nothing more than a passing hiccup. Anyway, he has more than enough. What else is he to do with it?

But Gilbert Sunnington shows no intention of even acknowledging Dwight's presence, let alone conspiring with him for the Brookes's benefit.

'As I said, I'll be glad to waive my fees.'

'There's no need for that,' Valerie brushes him off haughtily.

'If you insist on going ahead – and perhaps I can at least persuade you to think it over for a day or two – we might try for the Crown Court. I think that gives us a much better chance.'

So the solicitor knew all along that Valerie would go for a private prosecution. 'I'm sure the money can be worked out,' Dwight puts in loudly, moving his chair nearer Gilbert's desk, 'that really isn't the problem. The problem is getting evidence. Emily says the person who attacked her wasn't Alan...'

Gilbert swivels his back on Dwight, levers up and walks over to Emily.

'Was it definitely a man, Emily?'

The young girl is still by the window, looking out, her forehead pressed against a pane of glass. She turns, her eyes blank. 'I wish you'd all leave it alone. I don't care who it was, or why he did it. I just want to forget it.'

'It was a he, then, Emily. You said he.'

The girl says nothing.

'What about the future, Em? None of us will feel safe. If it wasn't Alan the whole situation is even worse. We can't just sit back and do nothing. A serious crime has been committed!'

His Mom strokes his white hair out of his eyes.

'Even if they leave you alone, they'll bully somebody else. Do you want that on your conscience?'

'I don't want to fight them, Mom. Maybe I can dye my hair?'

Perhaps Emily's beauty is a form of disability. People are drawn to her much as they're repelled by him, Dwight thinks. Either way, singled out. He can hardly stop himself from smiling at this idea.

Emily finally turns right round. The light haloes her hair, drawn tight against her head, just a few wisps curled softly round her ear and so pointing to the hollows in her cheeks. 'I think we might assume that whoever did it, did it to me. No one else is going to be in danger.'

She knows, Dwight understands. She knows who attacked her, that it was a personal attack. And she's protecting him. That's unlikely to be Alan – why should she bother about him? He doesn't mean anything special to her. It has to be someone closer than that. But who? An unacknowledged boyfriend? Her father? A psychotic Valerie?

'That's not true, Emkins. He didn't just attack you, he's also done these odd things in the woods.'

Has Valerie noted the significance of what Emily said, Dwight wonders? He doesn't think so. Valerie assumes Emily is protecting Alan, that she's too kind-hearted to let him take the rap. Has Sunnington understood? If he has, he certainly isn't going to mention it. Perhaps he thinks it's just something Emily has dreamed up to get her mother off her back.

'You don't know that either,' Emily insists coldly and emphatically.

163

'You're just making one assumption after another, and I wish you'd stop.'

Sure she knows, Dwight reasserts to himself, listening to them. But whether she knows she knows is quite another matter. Could be an hysterical suppression.

It's hard to distinguish Emily's expression, carefully hidden by sitting in the window against the light. Dwight watches her movements closely, carefully, trying to remember something, somewhere, which stirs within him.

'I hope you're not expecting to raise the matter of slashed animals and forest fires at the same time,' Gilbert says coldly. 'It will be hard enough to establish any connection with Alan and the stabbing, let alone rushing all over the place with red herrings.'

Red – blood red. He sees the oozing blood from the rabbit spreading into the *Financial Times*. Perhaps his mother was right – one thing does lead to another. Perhaps if he'd been more enthusiastic to find whoever slashed the dead rabbits Emily might never have been stabbed. The girl was nearly killed! As it is, she'll always have a scar – two scars. One physical, one mental.

So is he simply worried about her not becoming a model? At least, he grins to himself, it will stop her modelling topless.

Why is Emily so keen to protect Alan? There can be only one answer. She knows it wasn't Alan. That's precisely what she keeps saying, though Valerie, for one, doesn't seem to hear her. It's obvious she isn't in love with him, why would she be protecting him?

'You know I don't like you to carry a knife, Dwight, honey.'

The pruning knife! The answer is to do with that. If Alan were the stabber it certainly would be unlikely he'd use a pruning knife. So where did it come from?

And then Dwight finally sees it. You bet! The pruning knife was in Emily's anorak. Her pruning knife. Exactly, her pruning knife – and Valerie's. Emily, however much she protested, had almost certainly become anxious about the woodland maimings. Anxious enough the carry the pruning knife around with her, almost equally anxious not to let anyone else know of her misgivings. So whom

164

does she suspect? Someone close to her, evidently. Someone – like Jock? He shrugs that off, she's not involved enough with Jock to care.

Does Emily suspect her mother of the woodland atrocities? That has to be the answer. She's keeping the knife away from her mother. That explains why she'd eyed the newspaper parcel in that peculiar way. She was expecting it, and Dwight, to bring the matter to a head.

That is also the reason Valerie eyed it so nervously. She had the opportunities, she isn't squeamish, she could be the culprit. Question is – does Emily suspect her mother?

Melodramatic nonsense. There has to be another answer. The woodland atrocities could turn out to be a quite separate problem. The one that concerns him now he's almost sure he's solved.

The pruning knife is Emily's own – that much is obvious. She might have wandered dreamily across the lawn along the beech hedge, still day-dreaming about her time away from home, might have seen a figure there, would have assumed it to be her mother.

She would have called to her, confirmed in her idea that Valerie prowled the woods at night, committed odd acts ... Then she'd quite likely have seen the figure swoop towards her, grasped it wasn't her mother after all, and taken fright.

She could have been terrified enough to have clasped the pruning knife in her right pocket, to have pried it open and grasped it in her hand, to have taken it out of her pocket and thrust it forward.

The figure, he can work out from what Valerie maintained, kept coming. By the time he reached Emily the momentum might well have been great enough for the knife to deflect from the attacker's coat – perhaps a button or a belt – into Emily herself. And the blade could have begun to fold again. That's why it entered at that odd angle – that's why there'd been no serious damage. The knife hadn't been thrust into her – it had simply caused an accidental deep flesh wound...

' ...don't you agree, Dwight?'

'Emily doesn't want you to persecute Alan, Valerie. She's said so many times.'

'Persecute? Of course not. Prosecute!' She waves her arms about. 'Emily isn't herself,' she continues relentlessly, 'and she's under age and my responsibility. I'm pressing charges against Alan.'

Even if it had, against all likelihood, been Alan, Dwight can see why Emily wouldn't wish to acknowledge this. He might have rushed at her, might have hit her, possibly even intended to strangle her, but he hadn't intended to knife her. She can't even be sure that he'd meant any physical violence at all, though undoubtedly he intended to attack her verbally. Because he was jealous...

Whoever it was, and he was almost certainly a man, had unquestionably been jealous. Emily's many admirers, her absence from home, her chance of a glamorous career, the fact that she will soon leave West Sussex – all this could easily overwhelm a jealous lover, or would-be lover.

That description would pinpoint anyone who was keen to keep her there. Jock, Alan, Matthew, Charles Pontings – even, in a flight of fancy, Reginald Brooke. Or, indeed, Valerie!

That isn't really fair. Valerie allows her daughter the freedom of the woods, has never actively discouraged her from modelling.

'So, if you don't object Gilbert, I'd like to bring a private prosecution against Alan Penn-Winton.' Valerie looks coolly at her solicitor. 'And I'd like you to act for me.'

CHAPTER 21

'The police are keeping the knife as evidence, Jock. We have to find something else which might have belonged to him. So that Sheba can get the scent.'

'Back to square one.'

Not quite. Dwight remembers very clearly how he showed Jock the matchbox he'd picked up near the topped saplings, and how the young man pocketed it without any comment. Why had he let Jock do that? At the time Dwight told himself it was so that Jock could train Sheba, but that was clearly absurd. The truth was that he simply hadn't liked to ask Jock back for the matchbox because both of them knew it was, somehow, connected with the Brookes. At that time neither of them wanted to go into it further.

But now Dwight badly wants that matchbox back, has asked Jock for it, indirectly but quite clearly, for the very reason he'd let him keep it in the first place. Is he hearing Jock right? Dwight decides to play it cool, but firm.

'Well, no Jock. I guess not. What about that matchbox? I know we can't be certain whoever's responsible for the woodland atrocities is the guy who attacked Emily, but it's better than nothing. Let's find him first, and then we'll take it from there.'

'Matchbox?' Jock shifts from one foot to another, evasively disappearing behind the door.

'I gave you the matchbox I found when I was walking Sheba,'

Dwight persists. 'You remember, the day before the fire. About six weeks ago.'

'Oh, that.' Jock wipes his boots uncomfortably, stepping off the door mat into the scullery, looking for firmer ground.

'Yes, that!' Dwight warms to irritation but holds himself to an even reply. Maybe Jock just used it, forgetting what it was. 'Did you lose it?'

'Not exactly,' Jock says, reddening his embarrassment.

'Not exactly.' Dwight's voice softens into camouflage. 'What happened to it?' He looks beyond Jock.

Jock follows his look and returns it, goaded into a literal rendering of what happened. 'I showed it to Mrs Brooke. She says it's probably hers, but of course it can be anyone's. It's just an ordinary matchbox.'

Valerie? Jock went to Bramblings and showed it to Valerie? Where Dwight thought he has a partner, he only has someone he pays to train his dog.

'You promised to give me a hand, Earl.'
Pop vaults down the stairs and out.

Dwight is dumbfounded. Why would Jock go and ask Valerie about a piece of evidence which he, Dwight, found. As it turns out, an important piece of evidence. Is Jock implicated in this curious story, after all? Is there more to the connection with Emily than he's realised? Have they, at one time perhaps, been lovers, and Valerie found out and put a stop to it? Is this Jock's way of ingratiating himself with the mother?

'You gave it back to her?' It's hard to keep from shouting his astonishment.

'Not that. I still got 'un.' With that Jock fishes the matchbox out of his trouser pocket. The plastic Dwight so carefully wrapped it in has gone.

'But that's made it useless as far as Sheba is concerned!' Dwight explodes, outraged. 'It has your scent all over it.'

'And Mrs Brooke's, and even Emily's.'

'Emily's?' Finally getting to the bottom of it. 'She doesn't smoke, does she?'

'She lights the paraffin lamps, cleans them and lights them of an

168

evening.'

Cinderella Emily uses matches, and kerosene for that matter. 'So you're saying, in effect, that whoever set the woodland fire knows the Brookes.'

'Looks like it.' Jock sidles towards the back door.

Why is Jock being so uncooperative? What's happened to make him so unwilling?

'I really don't think I'll have the time to spend on this, Mr Delaney,' he mumbles. He takes small uncharacteristic shifts away from Dwight, edging towards his exit.

'All of a sudden?'

'The governor's keen I get the pheasants going ...'

'You said you'd done all the work on that.' Inspiration bursts light into Dwight's mind. 'It's probably one of the people who rented the Brookes' cottage,' he explains to Jock. 'That's obvious. It could easily have been one of their early summer guests. Who was that first couple? The Mastertons?'

'Can't be them,' Jock says laconically, 'they'd been and gone by the time of the fire.' But he stops edging off, a flicker of interest in his eyes.

And then Dwight remembers that the sliced rabbit was what led him to the Brookes originally. In fact he sees Anne Pontings' point, as far as he can tell the weirdest happenings only started after he joined the neighbourhood.

'More'n likely, if you asks me, to've been some silly tourist walking through and throwing away his match – '

'You know the firemen found evidence of arson, Jock. You know as well as I do that the fire was deliberately set, that the vegetation round it was doused in ker... in paraffin.' What was it Jock said? Emily always sees to the paraffin lamps, that's what she uses the matches for.

So is it Jock, after all? Stealing a date with Emily, depressed at the state of affairs, taking the matches and a bit of paraffin and going off, infuriated, to set fire to the woods?

Jock slashing dead rabbits? The whole idea is absurdly out of character. He shoots rabbits, you bet, considers them vermin, just like rats and crows. Jock skins and eats rabbits on occasion, but he doesn't slice them up and leave them lying round the woods. And he certainly doesn't build altars to display the slashed corpses. It

169

can't be Jock, and it's time he thought more productively to try and find the real culprit. Otherwise Emily will continue to be in danger. And surely so will everybody else.

'I forgets.'

He forgot? Well, he might not have been responsible, but it sure sounds as though he's covering up for someone he thinks was, or at any rate might have been, responsible. But who? One of his cronies at the pub? There isn't that much love lost between Jock and the other locals. He's the gamekeeper, they're the potential poachers. No way that he's collaborating with one of them. So, who?

The trilling of the phone breaks across his thoughts.

'Hello.'

'Dwight, old buddy.'

'Harry!'

'Surprise, surprise.'

'How in the world?'

'Julie.'

'I gave strict orders no one is to have my country num...'

'Among friends, old buddy.'

'I've got to go, Mr Delaney.'

'Hold the line a minute, Harry.'

Jock is already out the back door when Dwight starts after him, quick as he can make it. His left leg is giving trouble again, and he hobbles, gasping in pain and irritation, slipping and just catching himself on the huge kitchen dresser, making a note to tell Mrs Dean not to polish the quarry tiles so much. He lumbers out into the garden.

'I'll see you at the Fox and Hounds,' he shouts to the disappearing figure. 'Around eight. OK?'

No answer.

'Jock?' he shouts. Nothing. He shrugs and hobbles back to the house, rubbing his shin. He doesn't remember Harry till he sees the receiver off the hook.

The phone still swinging, off the hook.

He picks up expecting to find the line dead. It isn't.

170

'Sorry, Harry.'

'Just one moment sir, I'll reconnect you with Mr Solferino.'

'Problems?' Harry's voice comes cackling on the line almost immediately. 'I thought that's what you're doing down in that godforsaken funk hole, Dwight. Escaping problems!'

'Sure, Harry. Just seeing to the training of my dog.'

'A major venture. OK, OK, dogs need training.'

What is this? What is Harry after? They don't do much business together. What in the world can he be ringing for? And hanging on?

'You kinda got me going on that Chichester marina,' Harry is chuckling down the phone. 'Thought maybe I'd come down and drum up a little business.'

Dwight laughs. 'And you wanna boast how well you've done right away and meet for a drink,' he chortles.

'Sure, we'll have a drink. But, listen, buster, you're living in that huge pile with no one in it. How about letting me shack up for a coupla days?'

Harry wants to stay at The Woolhouse? In the middle of the country, away from the roar of traffic?

'Why, sure,' he says, 'anytime.'

'I was thinking tonight.'

'In the middle of the week?'

'I told you, I'm aiming to do some business in Chichester.'

'Well, OK Harry. Help yourself. Get here by seven. I'm meeting someone in Lodsworth at eight.'

'A local flame! You been holding out on me?'

'My dog trainer, at the Fox and Hounds. You been there.'

'Sure thing, the old retainer! I should've known it wasn't no chick. OK, catch you at seven.'

CHAPTER 22

'So what's the low down, Harry? Let me in on what's doing.'

'I told you. Chichester.'

'C'mon, this is Dwight Delaney you're talking to. You hate the boonies, why aint you staying in the best hotel in town?'

'I'd be lonesome all by myself.'

'What's with Julie? I thought she filled that gap right now.'

'You're so cynical, Dwight. Julie and I are all washed up.'

'Does she know that? From the private info you left I guess she doesn't.'

'Maybe I'll take over one of these old piles, myself.'

'You? Live in the country?'

'Maybe not quite so far off the beaten track as you. But nearby, say Petersfield.'

'What is this, Harry?'

'A good investment, pal.'

'You're going into the real estate business?'

'Just somewhere near Chichester.'

'Since when do you live near the marinas? Your beat is London, or New York, or maybe Tokyo. But Petersfield? C'mon, Harry. What's on your mind?'

But Harry has no intentions of explaining what, precisely, he's doing here.

'C'mon down to the local. You know it absolutely grabs you.'

The smile broadens as Harry's little eyes twinkle in anticipation. 'That's real friendly of you.'

'We may come across Jock – '

'The famous Jock!'

'We're trying to sort out what the hell is going on around here. You're pretty shrewd, Harry. You can sing for your drinks.'

Sing isn't quite the word to use to Harry, but he let it go. 'Let's take the Lambourghini.'

The bright red Lambourghini is sitting in the middle of the turning circle in front of The Woolhouse. It looks incongruous there, the streamlined body contrasting uneasily with the leaded windows of the house.

'I was going to walk.'

'I'll drive you,' Harry says magnanimously. 'You can steer me round these tracks.'

Why is he getting the feeling that what Harry has really come about is to orient himself to the area? What possible reason can Harry have for living here? He hardly needs investments.

Vague memories of *The Godfather* flitter through Dwight's mind. Is Harry about to found a 'family' home, here in West Sussex? Is he intending to bring his mother and his sisters here? It has never been anything but an open secret that he's escaping from too close a family involvement. So what in hell is he doing here?

A sudden idea that somehow Harry can be involved in the weird happenings in the woods. His friend wouldn't find it hard to slice up dead rabbits – or even live ones of the human kind. Didn't he always say ...

'If you need help, Dwight, you know where to come,' Harry is saying as the car screams blind corners at a furious pace.

'For chrissake Harry, use your hooter!'

They swerve noisily around the next bend, about to crash into a girl astride a horse, head on. The roaring red of the Lambourghini, throttled back to second gear, terrifies the animal which promptly rears, the girl's eyes and mouth dropping wide in horror.

'Stop!' Dwight shrieks as Harry is about to engage the clutch in first and accelerate away.

The car brakes hard enough to tighten their seat belts. 'Why?'

'We have to make sure that girl's OK –
'One of your friends?'
'Never seen her before, Harry. It's the custom to slow down for horses.'
'They pay road tax?'
'You'll have me in trouble with the neighbours. I want to live here, Harry. I like it here. I want to be friends with the locals, not get their horses rearing up and unseating their riders.'
'You're in my car.'
'And easily recognised.'

To his surprise Harry drives off sedately, creeping round the blind corners like an old pro. It has to be the family, what other reason can Harry have for staying with him and then attempting to follow the rules?

The pub is almost empty. One very old man, sitting in the corner by the empty grate, is drinking something long and dark – stout, by the look of it. The landlord is nowhere to be seen. The middle-aged barmaid, buxomly true to type, is polishing glasses as though her job depends on it.

'Rye?' Harry asks.

'I doesn't quite catch that, sir. What does you want?'

'A double Scotch and Malvern,' Harry says, resigned. 'What's for you, Dwight?'

'The same.'

They sit and wait at the bar. Lily – her name, Dwight remembers now, is Lily – turns and fumbles for what seems hours while she finds the right glasses. She stares at the bank of bottles. 'Teachers?' she says.

'D'you have a malt?'

Lily looks baffled.

'Glenfiddich?' Dwight puts in helpfully.

'Up on the left,' Harry directs her.

She finally makes it. Slowly, infuriatingly slowly, she manages two measures into each glass, then is about to add the water.

'That's OK,' Harry says quickly. 'Just leave it as it is. We'll take the Malvern with us.' Reaching over the bar he takes the glasses and goes off to the table by the window at the side. 'Just bring the water, Dwight.'

'Add some crisps and peanuts,' Dwight says to Lily, smiling uncertainly.

'Yes, sir,' she says, and hands him two packets so quickly he isn't ready.

Harry comes up to pay.

'I don't think we got change for £50, sir,' she says, looking at the note he holds towards her as though it might bite. 'Not this early in the evening. The lads be still out beating, been quiet so far today.'

So that's why the place is virtually empty and there's no sign of Jock. Dwight produces the right change and the two men sit beside the window, looking at the daylight greying into the woods. It will be dark soon.

'So what's on your mind, Harry?'

'Had this idea I might open a little office in the marina.'

'Give me a break, bud. You don't come down in person to scout for office space. What you after?'

'Gee, Dwight, if you can fall in love with the place, can't I?'

'I guess it's not something I'd immediately associate with you.'

Harry looks at him, widening his mouth and showing teeth more lengthened than he normally cares to show. Dwight isn't fooled. 'OK, I have a reason I'm keeping close.' He laughs, patting Dwight's shoulder. 'But you'll be the first to know if it comes off.' He smiles again. 'So where's this powerful dog-handler of yours?'

'I guess he's still out at the shoot.'

'The shoot?'

'They rear pheasants, then invite their friends – or clients – down. The beaters come and beat the birds out from under cover, the guests shoot and the retrievers get the booty back to them.'

'Sport.'

'Real sport.'

'And that's his job? He's a beater?'

'He's a gamekeeper. Clanesbury owns the Smithbrook estate just round the corner from me, Jock's his head keeper. Rears the pheasants, looks after the woods, culls deer, organises the beaters, keeps down the number of foxes, makes sure there aren't any poachers taking his boss's game ...'

'Game? They play games?'

'Their word for deer and shooting stock.'

'Shooting stock? What the hell is that?'

'Pheasant, partridge, grouse ... that sort of bird.'

'Sounds my kinda game.'

'I guess it is, Harry, now that you mention it. I guess it really is.' Dwight laughs. 'Is that what brings you down here? You're going to buy a country estate and invite your pals to a shoot?'

'Not sure they need inviting,' Harry grins, 'but it's a new one on me.'

Dwight hears the sound of a truck turning on the road outside. The door swings open and seven or eight men troop in, approach the bar and order drinks. Landlord and Lily seems to draw pints with ease, no fumbling and no search for rarely used bottles or glasses. Dwight puts his horn-rims on to see if he can recognise any of them. Not likely, since he's never heard of Charles Pontings coming to the pub, nor any of the other men he's met at Valerie's.

'Wondered if you'd still be here.' Jock's voice behind him.

'So there you are.'

'I've got to talk to you.'

'Join us,' Dwight says. 'Harry, this is Jock McClough.'

'The famous Jock,' Harry laughs easily.

'Jock, this is my friend Harry Solferino. He's staying with me...'

'I don't want to be rude, sir. But I have to talk to you privately.'

Dwight looks at Jock, his face tense, his hands tight fists.

'Something's happened?'

The strong young man hunched weak and, somehow, vulnerable.

'Take this,' Dwight says, handing him the drink he's hardly touched. Jock empties the glass in one gulp.

'Don't worry about Harry, Jock,' he says. 'He'll lend a hand if we need it. Right Harry?'

'Right, buddy boy.' Harry's eyes are twinkling. 'Said I belong.'

'God awful thing's happened.'

Emily attacked again ... 'Emily? Is she OK?'

'It's that Penn-Winton bloke.'

Can Valerie have been right all along? 'Alan? Is Emily...'

'Nothing like that.' Jock grabs Harry's glass and knocks the contents back. 'There's been a hanging in the woods.'

'Hanging?'

'By the new plantation, from one of the old oaks there.'

Owlet, strung by his neck.
The beige wings beat a rhythmic dirge against dark branches fingering
the broken body.

Dwight sees Emily's face, the glorious hair around her like a halo, the tongue protruding, the eyes almost out of their sockets. He should have made sure the Brookes stayed in Chichester. Damn Valerie and her insistence on the bloody cottage. That beautiful innocent wonderful delicate girl – Valerie has no right to keep her there, doing those ghastly chores, everlastingly exploited by mean-minded guests who lap up the atmosphere but don't do the dirty work.

'Alan Penn-Winton. When we was coming off the shoot, we thinks we'll walk and take the short-cut Lodsworth way.' He puts the glass down.

He sees the movement. Dense firs obscure, but the metronome sway is
clear.
He ran, heart beating, aware of tragedy.

'I'll get another.' Dwight raises his hand and signals to the barmaid.

'We was just going along and suddenly Sheba veers off the path. I calls her back but she just wouldn't come. I be getting really mad at 'er, thinking I'd have to give up 'er training if yer jest let 'er do what she likes when I'm not there, but I still follows 'er. Tracking, she were. I'd given 'er 'is glove to get the scent.' Jock's cheeks seem to have sunk in, and his eyes.

'Glove? Whose glove?'

'I finds a glove lying around at the top o' the Brookes' lawn.'

And never mentioned it. 'You did? Just when was that?'

Jock looks at him dully. 'And then I sees 'im. The bank above the lane, 'e's dangling there, from an oak branch over'anging it.' He shudders.

'I think we need the bottle,' Dwight says.

'Sure.' Harry catches Lily's eye. 'Can you find us a bottle? We'll have it here.'

'I can do you Teachers, sir.'

'OK, OK.' Dwight nods impatiently and turns towards Jock, then shouts after the departing Lily. 'And another glass!' And almost immediately regrets it. She'll take several more hours finding what she considers appropriate.

'That's the guy I was telling you about,' Dwight says to Harry. 'Young guy with mental health problems –'

'I didn't think ...'

'Valerie thinks he's the one who stabbed Emily. She can't prove it and the police did drag their heels. His father is quite a force around the place. We're trying to untangle the mess.' He looks at Jock steadily. 'Jock and I are working on tracking him down with Sheba.'

'Sheba?'

He screams.
'Owlet! Who did this to you, Owlet?
The wind sighs back, then gusts into his eyes.

'My dog, for chrissake. The one I keep telling you I'm – Jock – is training.'

'Didn't know she's a bloodhound.'

'She's a Labrador trained to retrieve. She can learn to track. Jock's teaching her.'

Harry looks at Jock reflectively. 'You can teach her that?'

'Not that difficult.'

'What possessed him to go that far?' Dwight turns to Jock.

Jock shrugs. 'Wouldn't know about that. 'e were up there again. That be 'is glove, I sees the other on 'is left hand.' Jock looks tired, worn out. 'There's all that talk of an 'earing in the Magistrates'. Maybe 'im can't face it.'

Hounded to death.

'You promised, Earl!' his Mom cries out, a bucket at her feet. 'I haven't enough buckets to catch the drips!'
Pop vaults the stairs and out. The big front door slams shut.

'I suppose that's it,' Dwight sighs. 'We should have gone into it sooner.'

'Wouldn't 'ave done no good.'

So it's over, Dwight muses, dazed and dispirited. Penn-Winton is their man, just as Valerie maintained all along. It's finally all over, done with, finished. Nothing more to do.

CHAPTER 23

'I certainly didn't think he was so depressed that he'd commit suicide.' Anne Pontings' high-pitched squeak sounds like a reprimand.

'Depressed? Afraid of the whole thing coming out, you mean.' Valerie has no inhibitions about speaking her mind even about the dead.

'Guys don't kill themselves because they have to go to a hearing.' Dwight's voice sounds quite harsh. He feels sick, ashamed. Should he have done more to protect Alan?

'They might – if they're guilty, and their whole family can be involved.'

'Such a polite young man.' Anne seems genuinely surprised he's impolite enough to put them out with his suicide.

'Don't think we've anything to blame ourselves for. No one could have predicted anything as drastic as suicide, Dwight.' The excitement in Valerie's voice, though clearly under some physical control, is hardly seemly. 'I kept telling everybody he's seriously disturbed.'

The smile on the face of the tiger.

'I still can't believe it. He comes – came – from such a good family!'

The British, apparently, are snobbish even unto death. Anne's touching belief that the 'right sort of people' inevitably bred the 'right sort of children', though patently disproved by Charles' abrupt departure for Ireland with Nina, seems not to have led to any change in household gods. To Dwight's mind, formed in New England rather than in Ye Olde Realm, a family who makes 'good' is often an assertive bunch of hoodlums. He sees Harry in the part. No Rubens, of course, more of a Picasso or a Braque. A short hunky practically bald guy on the wrong side of forty-five. But he has drive. Those gleaming black eyes are laser sharp, what he holographs them on endlessly reproduces itself to his advantage. A contemporary robber baron is hunting his way through rural West Sussex. He'll scoop them all up on his way to Chichester.

Anne Pontings, trimmer than Dwight remembers her, has Tatman with her. She always walks him herself now her income has ceased to exist. As she comes closer Dwight notices her face is blotchy, as though she's been crying. The dog is on the leash, a curious development since Anne, like Valerie, believes in the freedom of dogs to roam the neighbourhood.

Valerie has also registered Tatman's leash. 'Have you been walking Tatman past Tom's new flock of Jacobs?'

'Because he's on the lead, you mean? No, we've been all over the place. I just don't want him rushing off somewhere, like Ruskin.' Anne's hands describe a wide arc, embracing both the woods and the fields beyond Bramblings. 'I've tried absolutely everything I can think of. No sign of that cat anywhere. It's been four days now.' She looks around her eagerly. 'You haven't seen him, by any chance, have you Valerie?'

'Ruskin? I'm afraid not. You know toms stray, Anne. If you insist on keeping a tom...'

'He's never been away more than a day or two before. Of course he hunts and goes courting, but he always calls in – to stoke up, if nothing else.' An attempt at a smile.

'Ruskin's a missing cat?' Dwight asks. Is the woodland fiend at work again?

'My tomcat,' Anne says. 'I'm particularly fond of him.'

'I didn't even know you own a cat.'

'He's shy with strangers, always rushes off as soon as he hears anyone on the drive.'

'What kind of cat? Pedigree?'

'No special breed, just a long-haired ginger moggy. Marvellous hunter.'

She knows he's been killed, Dwight takes in at once. Keeping Tatman on the leash because she's afraid for him as well.

Anne takes a deep breath and reverts back to Alan. 'What I find peculiar is that Alan should choose to do it here. Almost as though these woods somehow cast a spell on him, brought him here against his will.'

'There's a very simple explanation, Anne. He was scouring the woods for Emily.'

'Just playing in the woods, Mom.'

'He's dead, Valerie. Haven't you hounded him enough?' Dwight can't stop himself. And it's all starting again. Alan might have been involved in Emily's stabbing, though Dwight doesn't believe that. But he sure isn't in a position to commit any new atrocities. And Ruskin's disappearance is too much of a coincidence not to point to further trouble.

'What on earth are you talking about?' Valerie rounds on Dwight. 'I'm hardly responsible that he couldn't face the court for what he'd done.'

'He might have had the decency to find somewhere else,' Anne puts in as though Alan failed in his duty.

'He lives in Midhurst, Anne. Difficult for him to get away from other people there. It helps to be alone when you want to finish yourself off.'

'But to come to our woods to do it.'

Dwight looks at Valerie but she's studiously looking away. She's no keener on Anne's company than she used to be, she confided to Dwight. But Sophie is Emily's best friend, and the Pontings always went out of their way to include Emily socially when she badly needed it, so Valerie isn't about to turn her back on Anne now. In fact she intends to do all she can for her. 'She's always wanted a boutique,' she reminded Dwight a few days ago. 'You mentioned something about a friend of yours looking for a partner.'

'And you think Anne can handle a business?' he asked her,

protecting Julie.

'I think she's got a pretty shrewd grasp of practicalities,' Valerie surprised him with. 'I always tried to encourage her to do something before now, but she wouldn't hear of it.'

Valerie smiles at Anne now, encouragingly. 'There's a glut of May Duke this year,' she says, forgetting Anne's huge garden full of all kinds of fruit. 'We can all go out and pick you some. It's the perfect day for it, fine, with a slight breeze, so the gooseberries will be completely dry.' She turns to Dwight. 'Otherwise they'll go off almost immediately.'

Hot summer sun is flooding the little holding, harsh and relentless. Valerie's garden, highly productive and geared to paying guests as well as herself and Emily, is in full bearing. Peas, beans, lettuces, courgettes are all ready to crop as Valerie has finally succumbed to Dwight's nagging and cancelled the rest of the summer visitors. She has more than enough to spare.

'Old Jem's surpassed himself this year.' She waves over her riches. 'His swan song. His nephew's taking over. Do take some vegetables with you, Anne. I can't possibly get through them all.'

'That's very kind of you.'

'If you hold back that netting, Dwight, Anne and I will pick.'

They pick a full bowl of gooseberries in about ten minutes. As far as Dwight can see it makes no appreciable difference to the look of the bush.

'Where's Em?' Anne asks, looking sideways at Valerie.

'She's gone off with Matt somewhere. She's seeing quite a bit of him. Such a nice young man. He really is doing his utmost to be fair to Alan but he certainly dug up enough evidence to make a case to answer for.'

'Matt?'

Valerie turns to look at Anne. 'Matthew Sunnington, Anne. Gilbert's son.'

'You think she's out with Matt?'

'I know she is. They went off in his car this morning.'

'Does he drive a red Lambourghini? I thought he was just a student.'

'He's articled to Dumforn and Dumforn, in the City. Doing very

183

well, I understand.'

'Not well enough to run a Lambourghini, I wouldn't have thought,' Anne persists.

Red Lambourghini. How many red Lambourghinis can there be in the area? Harry, Dwight knows immediately. So that's it, he's after Emily. Dwight wonders just how he missed such an obvious development. Hadn't he heard what Harry had said? Hadn't he seen the look in his eye? Does he need a diagram?

Familiar pricklings in his neck, sweat moistening his scalp, Dwight tries to subdue his fury. What the hell is Harry doing, holding out on him? Does he think he'd try to stop him?

Maybe he would have, at that. Emily and Harry? No, he sure doesn't like the sound of that. Besides, it's clear that Emily has, somehow, substituted seeing Matthew Sunnington in Valerie's mind for seeing Harry. Does Valerie even know Harry?

He recalls she has, briefly, met him. The day when Emily was diagnosed with pneumonia and he walked Harry and Juliette over to the cabin to meet them, not knowing what was going on.

But why is Harry keeping the romance a secret? He knows damn well that Emily isn't going for Dwight, no one knows better, he told Harry so himself. He was already seeing the girl, sure thing. Or was he? How did he swing it? Is that why Emily's so evasive? Is that, in fact, why she spends so much time, ostensibly alone, off in the woods?

'What car does Matthew drive?' Dwight asks Valerie, looking for magic.

Blasts of backfire pop his ears.

Perhaps his father loaned him ...there's no way Gilbert Sunnington would drive a red Lambourghini. It's unlikely that Matthew would, even if he had the cash to do so.

Valerie doesn't answer immediately, she concentrates on the vegetable patch, cutting a dwarf cos lettuce near the soil to keep it fresh, yet high enough to avoid the sandy loam getting into its leaves. Finally she looks up at him. 'Will you have one, Dwight?'

'One what?'

'Lettuce,' Valerie says composedly. 'I'm offering you one of my Sugar Loaf lettuces. They're absolutely superb.'

'Yes – no, thanks all the same. I don't know when I'll be driving back to town.' Almost unconsciously Dwight has picked up their way of talking. 'What car does Matthew drive?' Surely she should be concerned that Emily might have misled her?

'I really didn't pay much attention. Some sort of smallish car. Not red, though. An ordinary colour, grey, I think. Or perhaps blue.' She smiles and shrugs. 'I really can't remember. Cars don't mean a thing to me.'

She's mentioned that Alan drives a noisy red car, so she does at least remember colour. Dwight reflects again how irritating Valerie can be. Always this sloughing off of things she can so easily do without, but which other people find necessary for their lives.

'I'm happy on my old two-wheeler,' she's grooves on happily time and again. 'I can see the countryside so much better. You can't see a thing, whizzing past in one of those glossy modern cars.'

Whizzing isn't a word he'd apply to any car negotiating the West Sussex lanes. He grins as he thinks of Harry's driving, then frowns as he remembers the near misses.

'Well, I saw Emily in Midhurst, in the car park by the Post Office, only last week,' Anne goes on, 'and she was standing by a red Lambourghini which a fat little man with no hair was getting into. It certainly wasn't Matt.'

Valerie smiles, smugly wiping earth off her hands. 'Just someone she knows, I expect,' she says sweetly to Anne. 'She knows such a lot of people. They're all so attracted to her – like moths to a flame.' She laughs gaily. 'I never thought, living out here, that there'd be such hordes of admirers,' she tinkles, hell bent on Matthew. 'But they almost scent her out, we just can't keep them away.'

Another thought appears to strike her. 'Alan drives – drove – a red ... You might have seen his car last week,' she finishes rather awkwardly, probably already knowing the answer.

'He wasn't bald, and he didn't drive a Lambourghini. I know the difference between a Lambourghini and an MG, you know.'

'I'm sure you do.'

Sophie, Valerie's often mentioned to Dwight a little spitefully, has great trouble finding any boyfriends. One of the reasons she's so keen on Emily, Valerie is convinced, is that she has the pull which fascinates the men. Sophie feasts on Emily's leftovers.

'Money isn't everything,' she'd finish up triumphantly. Does anyone, Dwight wonders, even Harry, think it is?

'I dare say she was waiting for Matt to meet her there and give her a lift back. I'd probably asked her to do some shopping for me.'

'Waiting by someone else's car?'

'Obviously she wasn't getting into it,' Valerie points out swiftly, and logically enough. 'Just spotted one of her friends. I told you, she knows simply hordes of people.'

The list Valerie had given Dwight, though fairly long, cannot be described as exceptionally lengthy. Is she holding out on him, has she screened them according to her own preconceptions, or does she simply not know all of them?

Valerie walks slowly to a row of peas and brushes her hand across it caressingly. 'Just look at these fat pods,' she gloats. 'Even the mange touts are filling up. I'll have to pick them over carefully.' And she begins to pick.

'She looked to me as though she was going to get into the car as well,' Anne persists stubbornly.

'Really, Anne. You just said a fat old man was getting into it. You see embroilments where there aren't any. I expect she was just saying goodbye.'

'That's exactly what I must do,' Anne snaps, suddenly tetchy. 'I just hoped you'd seen Ruskin. Be seeing you. Walk, Tatman.'

She strides off, holding her head up high, rounding the beech hedge and out of sight.

'She'll be all right.' Valerie looks after her. 'She has all the makings of a first rate businesswoman.'

'So Chas is doing her a favour.'

Valerie sees what Dwight is getting at and grins agreement. 'Well, there we are then, Dwight, end of an era. It's so kind of you to help us as much as you have. And Matt, of course.'

All settled, finished, no more to say. Maybe so. Dwight thinks he can still smell a pretty nasty smell.

CHAPTER 24

Emily was meeting Harry all along. That's why she spends long hours away from home. How in the world did Harry set that up? How did he see off Matthew Sunnington? It sure isn't the kind of riddle Dwight can solve with Jock and Sheba.

'Will you and Sheba like to join Raffy and me?' Valerie asks. 'We're just about to go down to the water garden. It's lovely there, and we haven't really been out today.'

Dwight accepts gracefully. He wants the opportunity to warn Valerie that, though Emily might not have been a passenger in the Lambourghini last week, there's no way Harry will even pass the time of day with a girl if his intentions aren't dishonourable. No way he'd even be in Midhurst.

'It's really wonderful to feel we can walk the woods again and be quite safe,' Valerie burbles, swishing brambles aside, her little legs shearing through overgrown paths. 'This is my very favourite walk. Lord Sandings always said he doesn't at all mind my using it.'

'I doesn't realise this is private property.'

'The Smithbrook estate. Lord Sandings was very decent to me. Always got one of his men to cut down my fallen trees, or leave manure, or suggested we glean corn for the chickens, that sort of thing. Didn't you say you know Jock McClough quite well? Clanesbury took over the estate a couple of years ago, when Lord Sandings died. Jock's his head gamekeeper.'

'Sure I know that. What I didn't know was that the estate actually adjoined your land.'

'Bramblings is the original gamekeeper's cottage on the estate. I bought it from Lord Sandings.'

So Jock is entitled to come very close to the cottage – and has plenty of opportunity to see Emily on the quiet.

'It's terrible, of course, that Alan should have taken his life,' Valerie muses aloud. 'But I understand that being schizophrenic at his age is quite a dreadful fate. I hear the drugs work for a time, then they have side effects.'

'By the time he got to that stage they might have found something better.' Dwight doesn't bother to hide the brusqueness in his voice. He's getting antsy. Does Valerie believe in the final solution for incurable disease, by any chance? After all, on that basis he himself is a candidate. 'It's not a reason to commit suicide.'

'He was disturbed, Dwight.' No retreat, no hesitation. 'That's the whole point. Even that useless Coroner's Court said the balance of his mind was disturbed, and that's why he hanged himself.'

'The standard garbage, Valerie. Be fair. He couldn't cope with the accusations. That's why his parents tried to stop it all.'

'It's easy to be on his side now,' Valerie slightly raises her voice, losing her usual cool. 'But at the time you entirely agreed with me...'

'I did no such thing!'

She glances at him, shrugs. 'All the evidence pointed to Alan. He was known to be roaming the woods that night, and the Crown Court would have convicted him.'

'That's pure surmise...'

'His father offered to settle out of court! Pretty convincing proof.' She stops to throw pieces of wood for Raffy to collect. Sheba, entranced, is joining in the game.

'I'm not saying it wasn't a tragedy. But the boy must have been a trial to his family. In some ways they must find it a relief.'

Dwight, shocked more than he cares to admit, feels the chill weight of his albinism. Just as disposable? Thinking of his inheritance makes him think of his mother. She's been his bulwark against the world – and now she's gone. Grief grips him.

All he has left is money, the colour gold. It makes him yearn for Emily to share his affluence, his beautiful house, even walking Sheba with him. Valerie, for all her poverty, has Emily to share her life. But for how long?

'Do you remember meeting Harry?'

Valerie is walking along a trickle of a stream, astilbes feathering the banks. The plump leaves of variegated hostas are shaded by copious plantings of mock orange showering fragrance. Sparkling nature at its best, green fingered behind the scenes.

'Harry? Is he someone I should remember?'

'It was his stand at the Boat Show where Emily did her modelling. And Sop.'

'Sophie, yes.'

'He's the guy from New York. A friend.'

'No, I don't think I remember meeting him.'

'He visited the weekend Emily developed pneumonia.'

'No doubt I was taken up with other things.'

'We planned to have dinner with him and Juliette. They came down, you may remember, to meet Emily.'

'Ah, yes.'

'I think he's taken quite a shine to her.'

She walks quickly ahead, turns round. 'To Juliette?'

'To Emily.'

'That's nothing new.'

Valerie's indulgence fires Dwight to further onslaughts. 'He's quite a hit with the ladies.'

'A little old for Emily, wouldn't you say?'

Not only remembers him; taken that on board.

'And isn't he married?'

'He's always married,' Dwight spells out, 'but it doesn't make a whole lot of difference. He gets unmarried as easily as he gets married.'

'How quaint. And expensive, I suppose.' Valerie flips a burr from her clothing, watches it disappear among the brambles.

'He can afford any number of wives.'

'I don't think Emily will ever go for someone like that.' Valerie picks seed pods of wild balsam pops them under her boot, grinning at Dwight. 'I can't resist them,' she says, popping another.

'He drives a red Lambourghini.'

'So that's who Anne saw her with.' Valerie takes a deep breath, then pops another round, white seed ball.

Dwight resigns himself to weather the avalanche of justifications.

'I've brought Emily up to be very discerning. She has a lovely home, in spite of everything. We live in one of the most glorious parts of England. It's peaceful, beautiful, and except for the unfortunate interlude with Alan, free from crime. It's all on tap for her, she has no need to settle for anything not up to that standard.'

'This is my home, Dwight, honey, and a fine one, at that.'

'She's a lucky girl,' Dwight says. And means it.

'Why don't we sit here while I have a smoke?'

They've left the river garden and walked into a nearby field. One long lonely tree trunk lies in the centre, an isolated meadow tree felled by a recent gale. Valerie pats it invitingly, sits back and lights a cigarette. Slowly, luxuriantly she pulls at it. The smoke hangs, still and unmoving, above her, like a wispy, transparent cloud she doesn't know exists. Dwight sees it there, hovering, not dispersing, watches it grow, envelop the whole of her. Raffy is lying at her feet. He sees it enlarge and engulf him, too.

At first the light is dimmer, the sun behind a veil. The smell, acrid, pervading, doesn't leave his nostrils.

He splutters, coughs, runs towards the house.

Danger is lurking over Valerie, Dwight senses. Some cloud is hanging over her, and Alan's death has done nothing to disperse it. She and the dog, somehow they're caught up in it. The air, so luminous and clear, looks less so where she sits.

'The most important thing was to make sure Alan couldn't harm Emily again. That's why I insisted on serving a summons. No special antipathy to the poor chap. And now he's dead. I can hardly believe we're free of that.'

Only free of Alan, Dwight thinks. 'You have no doubts that Alan was responsible for everything?'

'You're just not willing to admit you were wrong.'

'I'd be delighted, Valerie. It's just I have this hunch. Alan was often up at Oxford when those atrocities were committed. I don't quite see ...'

'You're affected by Alan's suicide, you don't like to think ill of the dead.'

'You know real well I never subscribed to your theory. There surely is more to it than Alan.'

'He has a car, Dwight, he could easily have driven down at any time.'

'It takes organising to catch all those glass snakes, for instance. And even the rabbits. How could he have been sure there'd be a shoot?'

'He sliced up the rabbits because they were there, he found some sort of cache of slowworms and then worked out the pit...'

'And found the netting?'

'Took it from Myra's soft fruit, actually. Anyone would know about that.'

'Something's bothering me. I haven't worked it out, but something's still not right.'

'I wish you'd relax Dwight. Everything is back to normal now.'

They start back. As they near the drive Dwight senses another happening, right then. 'Did you hear that?'

'Dwight, honey, stay with me. I think it's a bad one.'
It's worse than bad, it's life-threatening. The fire is moving towards them, moving fast.

'Honestly, Dwight ...'

Both Raffy and Sheba set up a chorus of barks. Dwight already has the leash out and clips it to his bitch.

'Stay, Sheba, stay.'

'If we worried every time a dog barks... That's enough, now, boy. We're almost home.'

They walk the last yards along the rutted driveway. The cottage, familiar and glinting up ahead, is bathed in the mellow light of late afternoon. The coarse green of summer is overpowering now, long days without rain have browned the grass and the weeds stand rank and high.

Dwight has his glasses on. He glances from left to right and back again. Nothing, nothing wrong at all. Is it really that he's thrown by Alan's suicide? Does it bring back his mother's death? Is he getting neurotic? More than that, sick? Should he see a shrink?

'Why not stay and have supper with us. I'll just go and find us some eggs.'

'Are you expecting Emily?'

'She knows when supper is. Do let Sheba off the lead, Dwight.'

He let her go and follows Valerie to the chicken run. As they near it he can feel the evil, almost like a presence, oozing out of it. Someone, something, was here in their absence.

'That's odd, I thought I'd left this door latched.' Valerie pulls the rickety door, a haphazard construction of chicken wire and posts now slightly ajar, open wide, shuts it behind her and walks towards her hen house. She lifts the egg flap and puts her hand in, then draws it back, fingers dripping yolk and white mixed into slime. She stares, opening the flap wide. 'A fox must have got in. All the eggs are smashed!'

A wolf more like – all dressed in sheep's clothing. 'Eggs?' Dwight is surprised. 'I thought foxes go for the hens.'

'Probably a vixen, they take the eggs for their cubs.'

'Why aren't the hens here then? Where have they gone?'

'Hiding inside, I expect.'

'Or dead.'

'Just Reynard come to call, as they say around here. Wily as ever.'

'Sure thing. We'll see.'

'Something else – crows – could have been after the eggs. You really are letting your imagination run away with you, Dwight.'

'So who opened the door?'

'I'm sometimes absent-minded,' Valerie insists. 'Maybe I forgot to hook the latch. A fox can push it open. I expect the hens just panicked and ran off. They'll be around.'

No sign of feathers? No traces of any kind of struggle? What sort of fox is that?

At first there isn't anything to tie in with the hens. The birds have vanished. A search all over the garden and into the nearby woods brings nothing further to light. Raffy begins to snuff at a small dark hole overhung by a tree. He barks with excitement, rushes inside and chases out the beige-feathered bodies of several Buff Orpingtons. They flutter away, dithering from thicket to tree, squawking their terror.

'Raffy. That's enough, boy.' Valerie calms him down. 'Heel.'

Dwight and Valerie herd five of the hens back into their enclosure. The cock and another hen are missing.

CHAPTER 25

Can Harry be implicated in Alan's suicide, Dwight wonders? He's utterly ruthless, has disposed of wives, wolfed down a couple of children, and several business partners he's even swallowed whole. But he'd have known Alan was no kind of threat, so he'd hardly have gone after him. Unless he held him responsible for the stabbing. Way out.

Is he himself, somehow, responsible for Harry? Has he opened a Pandora's box for Emily, did he put absconding with Harry into her mind?

'This is our home, and this is where we stay,' he remembers Valerie told Gilbert Sunnington.

'I make good money now, Mom. You could be much more comfortable.'
'I'm happy here, Dwight. This is my home, was ours. All my happy memories are here.'

Does Emily agree with Valerie? Dwight guesses not. That's why the girl's so clammed up, avoids contact with him when she can. Maybe she even keeps away from the cottage and his regular woodland routes just in case he calls by. In case he, somehow, got wind of the fact that she's gone for Harry.

Dwight goes out to the kennel, calling Sheba. He'll walk her while he puzzles it out. Harry turned up in Midhurst to see Emily, maybe

194

he's even met her in the woods. That could mean just another affair for Harry, but Dwight is sure this time it's more than that. Harry exhibits all the signs of a lothario who's finally been caught.

'Sit, Sheba.' The big black bitch sits, her soulful eyes on him. He opens the gate and 'Heel' brings her out sedately, stationed by his side. Jock has her trained for tracking now.

Lured by some unseen force Dwight and Sheba walk in the direction of Bramblings. Not to call on Valerie. He wants to avoid that for the moment.

There's something to look into, something to investigate. It pulls at Dwight, tugs at him with unseen hands.

Investigate? Surely all that's behind them now? Alan is dead, the maimings have ceased. Only a fox, or vixen, marauding in the natural course of nature – a hazard of country life. No malice or premeditation.

Dwight and his bitch walk along the well-worn track leading to Lodsworth and Oak Court. The little footpath to Bramblings is quite near, but Dwight is determined to keep Sheba from going off on it simply by repeating a command. No leash. She's trained to obey his words.

'Heel,' he insists sharply as Sheba trots away from him. She slows, teeters back and follows. Summer, hot and coarse, sees the vegetation opulent and swollen. It hides some of the views he's come to love.

'I never like late summer much,' he remembers Valerie said earlier. 'The spring's over and autumn isn't here yet. It's much too rank for me.'

He sees her point. Everything is overgrown and dense, no delicate shades of green, only a single boring verdant mass of uninspired vegetation not even enlivened by the rhododendron mauves of spring or the bluebell haze of May. He can see a few light dots of cuckoo spit.

A gleam of something large and pale, fluttering in an unusually clear space a few yards off the wide track, catches Dwight's eye. He's deliberately not wearing his tinted glasses. One of the advantages of all that stolid growth is that it shields his eyes from the sun – when it's there. But even Dwight doesn't need glasses to recognise the flapping of light against dark, or to be aware that a space has been hacked clear.

The old feeling of dread grips him as he pokes his stick through to the light, then stops. 'Sit,' he commands Sheba as he puts his glasses on.

He sees the movement.
Dense firs obscure, but the metronome sway is clear. He runs, heart beating, aware of tragedy.
Beige wings brush against dark branches fingering the broken body.
He screams, the wind sighs back, then gusts into his eyes.

Cold blood thickens in his veins. He realises he's heard as well as seen. Two largish birds, hung by their necks, their light-beige wings spread-eagled out and pegged to a rope strung between two branches. They flap slowly, their wings like sails catching the wind and soughing a doleful dirge of death. Strung up in much the same way that farmers hang up crows as warnings to other crows who threaten their crops, but the wings are somehow different. They're spread out, pegged out full width. And these birds aren't crows, or magpies.

Dwight feels oppressed. It definitely isn't over – the woodland ghoul has struck again. Worse than that, this sure isn't Alan's doing. The sickening realisation, already known but carefully suppressed, comes out with fierce intensity.

'Just playing in the woods, Mom.'

It wasn't Alan Penn-Winton. It's someone Dwight knows, and knows quite well at that, someone who's laughing at him. No way they've been released from the horrors. Alan was just another victim of the monster.

Dwight shudders in the warm evening. He knows the person, whoever it is. That's as clear to him as reading a detective story in which he's been given all the clues but hasn't quite marshalled them in the right sequence. He knows who the culprit is, but he can't – yet – name him. Brooding, looking around for leads that might give Sheba a scent which can identify this ogre, he mentally scans the list

Valerie gave him for likely suspects.

Is it Jock, after all? He has the opportunity, he has the skills, he also ... and then Dwight sees Jock, lips compressed, freeing rabbits caught in snares, exploding into curses. He sees Jock gently caring for his pheasant chicks, his hands cupped so as not to frighten them more than is necessary. Above all he sees him with Sheba: stern but fair, insistent but gentle, demanding but loving. A constant, dependable Jock, always the same. He knows very well it isn't Jock.

So what about old Jem? Valerie's gardener, now over seventy, West Sussex country bred and never out of his native village. Besides, he lives in Lodsworth, a couple of miles away. Too far for him to cycle out at night just to slash saplings, or dead rabbits, or hack hedgehogs to pieces. Old Jem is failing and sick, it isn't him. Even if he were fit enough there's no reason for an old man to change habits bred through many generations of countrymen who tilled the soil.

Dark red, Dwight takes in now, a splash of something dark nearer the track, to the side of the birds. Surely they can't have bled that much? He'll figure it out later.

Charles Pontings? A non-starter. He left the area weeks ago. And, though Dwight doesn't rate him, he knows Chas will never commit ungentlemanly acts against animals. Only women.

But Emily has many other admirers. Matt, for example. Matt might have found out about Harry and not liked the thought of Alan and – that's absurd as well. He's pretty clear that if he looks into it Matt will be found to have been in London when a number of these events occurred. It's not the young solicitor.

Perhaps they're the local cockfighters Valerie mentioned darkly several times. Perhaps even Reginald Brooke among them. Maybe they went to steal Valerie's cock, and let the hens out for good measure. Then, after the fight, they'd strung the dead birds up.

And suddenly, quite without warning, the image of his mother comes to Dwight's mind again. What is she doing there? Why now?

He sees her, gentle, middle-aged but looking elderly, grey hair grown long, cascading down her back. Her soft curves are, as always, enveloped in voluminous unfashionable skirts and tops, flat shoes, welcoming smile. But those warm eyes turns cold whenever his father is mentioned, turn to steel when she's negotiating terms for her cookies and when demanding payment for goods delivered.

And then he understands. The psychopath who's done all these dreadful things isn't necessarily a man. Women are just as capable of them. He sees his mother wring the neck of a chicken they're to have for dinner. It never crossed her mind to even think about it.

'Chicken for dinner, honey! Hurry on down.'

Chickens, a cock and a hen. Valerie's beloved Buff Orpingtons. He forces himself to look at the birds again. Undoubtedly two domestic birds, one with a cockscomb. Are these Valerie's missing fowl? Was reynard – vixen – a woman?

Anne Pontings? Is that why she's so vicious, so keen to point the finger at him?

The saplings, for example. It could quite easily have been Anne. He's seen her with those classy secateurs of hers, that's all it would have taken for young trees. She's a keen gardener, after all, always pruning – pruning knife!

And now he thinks about it, it's curious she had no idea that Charles and Nina... because she'd only just come in herself! That display Anne put on for him and Valerie, when they found her snipping shrubs in her border, could simply have been a convenient cover.

The woman is strong, too. A good horsewoman, a member of the local hunt, quite capable of lugging boulders for her rockery like a navvy – boulders. The slowworms.

He needs a tangible clue. Red rag. To the right of the birds, by a bush, he sees it. Some sort of blanket, a mixture of red and black, apparently thrown in a heap.

He goes over and inserts the point of his shooting stick to lift it up. Caught by some thorns, or by a stone, it won't budge. He moves closer, pokes about. Something heavy wrapped up in the material. Dwight already knows what he will find. Some ghastly corpse, some unfortunate rabbit, perhaps a squirrel. The package looks about that size. Maybe a hare this time. He doesn't want to touch it but he makes himself kick the thing over, finds the loose end and pulls it, chary, with the metal point of his shooting stick.

Slowly, bit by bit, he unravels the material. A furry leg, not grey, more brown. A definite paw but not a rabbit's. Long, ginger hair streaked with white, the pointed ears of a cat. Quite dead, the eyes almost popped out of their sockets, the neck virtually severed by the wire it was garrotted with.

Her eyes, still blue, gaze their unseeing stare at him.

Ruskin, presumably.

'He doesn't like strangers,' Anne said about him only yesterday.

How was he caught? Anne Pontings clearly loved that cat almost as much as she loves Tatman. Is she so sick that she would kill her own pet in a fit of – frustration? Nonsense again, it wasn't Anne. If Charles were around he'd be a better candidate. And Nina even more so.

Dwight stares, deflected from his purpose, only one thought now in his mind. Hell is let loose again. Accusing Alan, the poor guy's suicide, has put the search for the real culprit back for a couple of weeks. Alan had no hand in the macabre happenings in the woods. Dwight always sensed that. Now he has proof.

The sound of approaching horses makes Dwight jump. No way he can afford to be associated with finding Anne Pontings' dead cat. She'll pursue him as relentlessly as Valerie pursued Alan. He'll have to snatch what evidence he can and disappear.

He grabs the coloured cloth, trying to tear a piece off it. He can hear the riders chatting to each other, coming nearer, and begins to panic. Another lunge and the corpse falls right off the rug and thuds down a small slope away from him towards the sandy track. Still the material won't give. He gulps and grabs the whole thing, bloodied and filthy, with his hands, but it's caught on brambles and won't budge. Desperate, he grabs at a piece of fringe and dislodges a few strands. Then he scrambles, blundering down the steep slope towards the millpond. It isn't where he wants to be, but it's better than running into the riders.

He can't stop stumbling all the down the little sloping path, the momentum is so great. But he has the evidence he's looking for. Triumphantly he looks at it wedged in his hand.

The horses stop right above him.

'Stay, Sheba,' Dwight sibilates at his dog. Just a few yards away, they'd hear his heavy breathing if they listened. He crouches beside his bitch, the darkening green of the rhododendrons affording good cover. There seem to be two horsemen and a man with a bicycle. He hears them dismount. Have they seen him? Are they looking at the dead cat? Will they find the birds and sniff him out? He crawls into the bushes, pulling Sheba towards him, his arm tight around her neck.

'Right, Fangs. Stay.' A curt clipped baritone which carries well. A low male voice, assured, in charge. Dwight recognises the tones of an 'old boy'. Something faintly familiar about it.

'That's a quick find. Looks like a big one.'

'Not quite as easy as that,' the baritone laughs. 'Had my eye on this sett for some time. Walked straight into a whole family last night.'

A cigar butt lands near Dwight. He watches its glow retreat to grey, the smoke curl out, the odour floating to him. Where did he come across that smell before?

'That's the ticket, Williams. Get cracking.'

'Right you are, guv.'

Dwight hears the steady scrunch of spade in earth.

'There's a bloody dead cat 'ere, guv.'

'What if someone comes along? We're pretty near the path, old man.'

'What?' A low growling laugh. 'Just plugging for tomorrow's hunt, don't y'know. What's wrong with that, eh?'

'Trust you to figure it out, Reg, old boy.' The loud nasal guffaw reminds Dwight of Charles Pontings. Can he be back?

'I can feel 'im now, guv.'

Badger baiting, Valerie said. Her ex goes in for badger baiting.

The loathsome sounds of a dog attacking a badger seem close enough to Dwight to feel they'd dug the sett right down to him.

They're evidently unearthing live badgers for a session later on. Lurchers set against badgers. His heart pounding, Dwight can only pray the lurcher will not sniff him and Sheba out and come after them.

Sounds like they're experts. Dwight guesses they're stuffing several badgers into sacks. The pounding of blood in his ears makes him feel faint.

'Fill her up tight, Williams.'

'Will I shove the old cat in?'

Another guffaw. 'Splendid stuff, and keep that dead fox beside you. You know what to say if anyone comes.'

And they're gone, riding off at a stiff trot. Dwight reasons that Williams, the man they've left, is unlikely to trouble him. He creeps out from his hiding place as quietly as he can and carefully places the few pieces of fringe into the plastic coverings he now carries round in case he spots evidence.

The millpond is ahead of him, calm and darkening in the evening light. That's where he and Valerie came to see the kingcups, so many weeks ago. Peaceful, usually solitary. He strolls across, remembering the topped saplings, Pete's fishing net. No question it was a trap, that's what the kid came across. Traps set by men like the ones he's just overheard. Out for sports like badger baiting and cock fighting. The kid might even have seen the men. No wonder he was terrified until he recognised Valerie.

Is that what is behind the disappearance of Valerie's Buff Orpingtons? Were they after the cock? Cockfighting, and someone – worse than the cock fighters, maybe one of the guys he's just heard – strung the birds up later. The woodland fiend.

Legs outstretched, leaning back on his elbows, Dwight gazes across the pond. So still, so peaceful. Does man have to savage everything? He watches languidly as wide grey wings circle over the glinting water, a sudden dip and the heron snatches its prey. He shivers at the cold kill, watching the great wingspan flapping the bird's body up and away. Nature red in ...

Not nature. The cock and hen were deliberately killed and strung up, the cat garrotted. Man's – or woman's – doing.

He can't let it ride, not this time. Emily is in danger again. He calls to his bitch and makes for Bramblings. The sooner he sorts out this latest development the better.

He takes the long way round, hoping to feel calmer by the time he arrives. At first he even walks past, leaving the drive and walking towards his own house. They have a phone now, he can give the Brookes a ring.

No, he'll face up to Valerie. He zigzags back and takes the little path leading straight to the garden. 'Anyone at home?' he calls, walking across the lawn and towards the little cottage.

Something shiny and bright reflects light into the corner of his eyes. He turns his head, something glinting red. Red? Alan is dead, so ...?

He's about to look more closely when the front door opens wide. At first he can't make out the figure standing there, in the dark of the cottage doorway. A man, a short thickset man. A new admirer, perhaps?

'Dwight, old buddy,' the figure says, coming out and putting an arm around his shoulder. 'Come on in. We were just wondering where you'd got to.'

CHAPTER 26

Raffy, scenting Sheba, rushes out to squeeze between Harry's legs. Small and podgy, they're planted astride, immobile, adamant. Dwight sees Harry cross his arms and stand, keeping hold against Raffy's blunt push between his left leg and the door. Intrigued, he watches the dog, defeated the first time, change his sideways tackle and wiggle through the larger centre. Harry's expletive is muffled. Dwight grins at just how subdued it is.

'Harry!' is all Dwight can manage in response to his friend's greeting, glad the dark glasses are shielding his eyes. There's no way he was looking to find Harry at Bramblings.

'Is that you, Dwight?' he hears Valerie call out by the open window, raising her voice above the barking of the dogs. 'I thought you might have left for town already. Mr Solferino was only just saying he wanted to call on you. I warned him you might have gone.'

She comes out, following Harry and Raffy, wearing the same plaid dress she'd worn when they first met. A cigarette is trembling in her right hand, ash wind-whipped. She walks towards him and stands close enough to make him feel uneasy.

'Mr Solferino was just driving up the lanes to your house when he spotted Emily,' she says, voluble and laughing, 'so he gave her a lift home. Wasn't that kind.'

Emily, beautiful in an Anna Sui number in dove grey, her glorious hair wound in a soft chignon, stands framed by the lead lights of the cottage's south window. A sudden burst of firelight blazed a golden halo around her head, and then, as suddenly, dimmed. She walks out, exquisite Italian leather on her feet, her legs clad in the sheerest denier haze. Dwight has trouble taking his eyes off her.

'Hello, Dwight,' she says, husky and gentle, her whole face turned to him. Her lips, full, pouting, are delicately lipsticked a dusky pink, her eyes highlighted into happiness.

She's hardly managed a greeting for weeks now, but today all that has changed. He recalls once again how, physically, she's recovered from the stabbing astonishingly quickly. The hospital doctors were astounded. Today she blooms as enchantingly as in the past. A metamorphosis – it strikes him as positively miraculous.

'She's quite exceptionally fit and strong,' Mr Rulings, the surgeon who'd looked after her that traumatic night, marvelled more than once to Valerie. 'I know she's young, but you hardly ever come across anyone as healthy as Emily these days.'

'It's all the exercise she gets, riding and walking the dogs,' Valerie'd boasted to Dwight, rather more often than he enjoyed. 'It keeps her hale and wonderfully well. That's why she has such a glorious complexion, and why she's so beautifully built.'

And she certainly doesn't get a chance to overeat, Dwight thinks to himself. Mentally, he guesses, Emily began to live in another world for some time now. Which world? Harry's world? Has he been seeing her for long?

Or is she just living away from her mother in her imagination? Does she conjure up the world of London, exciting, adventurous, remunerative? Has she developed a taste for the glitz of fashion modelling and is trying to find a way to ease Valerie into the idea of that becoming her career?

As far as Dwight knows all the money he paid for the work Emily and Sophie did has gone to the respective mothers. There's no way Valerie spent Emily's share on designer clothes.

'Emily's just been to Chichester to get herself a new dress,' Valerie chirps, a tiny quiver in her voice. 'With some of the money she earned from you,' she adds, smiling coyly at Dwight. 'Doesn't she look lovely?'

'Emily would look lovely whatever she wore,' Dwight answers

diplomatically, his eyes masked behind their tinted glasses. He doesn't look at Emily or Harry.

'Mr Solferino ...'

'Harry will be just fine, Valerie.'

Dwight sees her flinch at the familiarity, then resolutely snatch back her authority.

'Of course.' She turns to Dwight again. 'Harry has very sweetly asked us out to dinner. He was just about to ring you and ask you to join us. That is, if you're free?'

'Sure thing,' Dwight says, looking at his friend. 'Haven't had time to talk to Harry in a long while now.'

'We can have drinks here,' Valerie announces. 'Last year's elderberry is particularly good. Just like a port.'

Dwight waits, amused, for Harry's response.

'Not quite my style,' Harry says, beaming a mouthful of gold. 'I use rye or malt whisky. Sure know that's hard to find around here, so I carry a few bottles.' He's already on his way towards the Lambourghini, missing Valerie's polite 'of course'.

She looks after him for a moment, then turns and beckons to Dwight to follow her into the cottage.

The little porch is filled with gumboots, walking sticks and a trug to carry the fir cones Valerie always collects on her walks. 'They have such a lovely scent when I throw them on the fire,' she's explained to Dwight. He wonders just what Harry is making of all this. Probably hasn't noticed.

He enters the little living room, the white-washed walls grey-streaked with smoke, the big black beams only nine inches above his head. The glorious fireplace is mounded deep with ash, a charred log flickering intermittently in the centre. He walks towards the mantelpiece. Two matchboxes.

'I wonder if you can help me out,' he says, smiling ingenuously at Valerie. 'I've run out of matches. May I help myself to some of yours?'

'Have you taken up smoking, Dwight?' she laughs at him. 'Of course you may, my dear. Just help yourself.'

'I'd love to sample some of that elderberry.'

'Absolutely. Emkins ...' Her eyes, puzzled at first, spark into understanding that Emily has gone with Harry. 'I'll just fetch us some glasses.'

He slips his hand into his pocket to whip out his small isolating cover, then remembers the threads, the other piece of evidence already wrapped in it. He looks round for a tissue, cursing himself for not bringing more covers. There isn't a thing he can use as far as he can see. Then he notices some letter paper on the little table Valerie keeps near the window. He helps himself to some of that.

Seed packets, all torn open and some thumbed back to hold the seeds Valerie hasn't used, lie covering a muddle of envelopes. One has a stamp which seems familiar yet oddly different: from Scotland, he notices. Perhaps her friend Loretta. He pulls a sheet of airmail paper he thinks will work for him and uncovers a cheque – ten pounds, signed Reginald Brooke. Ten pounds.

He can hear Valerie in the little kitchen and hurries over to the mantelpiece, picks the matchbox up and folds the paper round it methodically. He puts it safely into his pocket just as she walks in.

'Aren't they back yet?'

'Just coming, I guess.'

Does Valerie suspect there's something between Harry and Emily? Dwight can't tell, though Valerie is no sort of fool. Should he report what he's found in the woods and what brought him here? He decides not to. What's with him now?

Tartan. He found Ruskin wrapped in tartan, in colours just like Valerie's dress. He thinks of the plaid rug, and its usual place on the back of the sofa opposite the fireplace. He turns to look. Missing from where it's always been before. Valerie used it to cover the worn upholstery.

Loretta lives in Scotland. Had she sent down a tartan rug? And was that used to wrap poor Ruskin in?

'It's gone, Dwight! The twenty from the cookie jar. You seen it someplace?'

'What happened to your rug?'

'You noticed that,' Valerie says, animated. 'It's really very odd. I often wear it as a shawl and make it do double duty as a picnic rug.

206

I know I had it the day before yesterday, it was quite chilly early on. But I simply can't remember where I put it.'

'Maybe you took it on a walk, left it somewhere?'

'I don't think I'd be likely to do that.' She smiles. 'I do sometimes drop it outside the hen house, by the low wall.'

'Isn't it the same pattern as your dress?'

'No, no, Dwight. This is from Marks and Sparks, not the same thing at all. Your eyes aren't sharp enough to tell the difference. Loretta sent me the rug, it's a real Cunningham. That's her clan, you see. She sent me the genuine cloth. Matter of fact she weaves it herself, clever girl.'

'She knows how to weave a tartan?' Emily and Harry have walked quietly in.

Jeez, Harry taking an interest in tartans?

'You know about tartans, Harry?' Valerie looks at him as though, possibly, he belonged in the cottage after all.

'I'm having one designed for me.'

'Tartans aren't designed for people.' Valerie laughs indulgently.

Dwight can't help a grin. Her habit of assuming ignorance in others isn't likely to go down well with Harry.

'You either belong to a clan, or perhaps a district, or you don't,' she lectures.

Dwight sees Emily give a little smile, a knowing little smile.

'Mine's a ...'

'You mean your friend actually knows how to weave a real tartan?' Harry's eyes peck Valerie over.

'It's a relatively simple sett. She spins the yarn used for the rugs, dyes it and then weaves it. I wish I could show it to you. It really is magnificent; virtually indestructible.'

'Yeah. Maybe another time. Better get going.'

Dwight can tell right off Harry's already seen the rug. But where? Did Emily pinch it for them to lie on?

'Does your friend Loretta belong to a clan?' Dwight decides to distract Valerie.

'It's really a district tartan rather than a clan tartan.'

He's completely lost. 'I guess I don't know what that means.'

'Well, anyone who lives in a particular district – in Loretta's case Cunningham, a district in Ayrshire – has the right to wear the colours. Even if they don't live there now, but simply come from there originally.'

'I thought anyone could wear tartans.'

'There's no law against it, no.'

'One wouldn't be able to enforce that, anyway,' Dwight muses.

'I go for having one of my own,' Harry says gravely. 'I reckon that's a great idea. Is why mine's being designed for me right now.'

Valerie remains silent this time, looking into the fire and rattling the poker.

'So, what'll it be? Where's a good place, buddy?'

Emily puts a hand to her forehead. 'If you don't mind,' she says, a dutiful smile widening her mouth, 'I'll just stay here. I do have rather a head.'

'You two boys go off on your own,' Valerie takes up her daughter's excuse with alacrity. 'I'll make sure Em's all right.'

CHAPTER 27

The low-slung Lambourghini has trouble with the rutted drive leading from Bramblings to the lanes.

'I'll get you there,' Harry insists, crashing gears and rocking the car. 'Don't guess your fucking Bentley's that great in these twisted dirt tracks.'

'Depends on what you mean,' Dwight says coldly. 'It's pretty good at delivering passengers, but not so good at making off with them. Not quite my speed, pal.'

'How d'ya guess?'

'I know you, buddy. And I can tell an Anna Sui when I see one. Besides, you were spotted in Midhurst last week, talking to Emily.'

'Jeez. Bloody fuckin' spies.'

'It's country, Harry. The real McCoy, you gotta take the rough with the smooth. And it's mostly rough-edged.'

'You bet.'

'You been seeing her long?'

'A while now.'

'Since she got out of hospital?'

'Sorta.'

'Drop it, Harry. While there's time.'

'We got something special going, buddy-boy.'

'You always got something going, Harry.'

'Honest, it's for real. She's what I been looking for all my life.'

'Maybe, Harry. But what's in it for her?'

'You'll think it's money.'

'Not me, bud. Not Emily's style to go just for the cash. Already wise to earning that herself. I've spelt it out for her often enough. She don't run on that.'

'In that case, old buddy, it's beauty and the beast.'

This is a different Harry. No dirty jokes, no innuendoes, no sly references to parts of Emily's anatomy.

'She's such a sweet kid, Dwight. So shy and unassuming.'

Dwight sees it then. The golden yashmak covering the blank innocent face – hiding it. And he recalls Emily looking through it at him. The jade green eyes scrutinised him, assessing carefully, calculating his worth.

Since then, now many weeks ago, Emily's life has changed a whole lot.

'You'd think she's been to one of those modelling schools,' Julie marvelled, right from the start.

'Maybe she's practised in front of a mirror.' Dwight laughed. 'It's just that she's been so protected. That grace comes from leading the healthy outdoor life. Let the girls in on it. Horse riding, walking the dogs, that's what'll give them her style.'

And Juliette giggled. 'Go riding in the Mall? Is that what you want me to tell them, Dwight?'

'Rotten Row,' he giggled back.

'All I really needed to do was show her how to put the make-up on, give her a few tips on what to use, and get her to learn how to dress her hair the right way to go with the clothes she's wearing.'

Emily wants out, and she has no idea how to tell Valerie. Who already knows – of course she does. All that masquerade about Harry picking Emily up. Dwight saw the set of the mouth, the hard lines forming, the steel in the normally serene eyes, the forced gaiety. Since when did Valerie accept invitations out to dinner? He can hear her saying it:

"I don't need expensive restaurants, Dwight. I have everything I need on my doorstep. What can be better than a dish of chanterelles from the woods, with parsley new potatoes grown in my own garden? Drunk with the latest elderberry champagne? You can't get that in your expense-account restaurants."

He guesses Emily's had her fill of elder, port or champagne, and that Valerie knows it. So is the girl taking her frustrations and disappointments out on the woods and the inoffensive wildlife? She certainly has, still does have, the opportunity – and the grit. He fingers the little matchbox wrapped in airmail paper. He'll stay over at The Woolhouse, take Sheba tracking tomorrow.

'It's still going on, Jock.'

'What is?'

'The happenings in the woods.'

Jock shows no surprise. Does he know? Has he come across anything himself? 'What be going on this time, then?'

'Two chickens, strung up by their necks, their wings pinned out and hanging from old rope slung between two branches. The undergrowth's been hacked away. They're swaying there, like a couple of ghouls.'

'Chickens? You mean hens?'

'A cock and a hen; two of Valerie's Orpingtons.'

'Mrs Brooke's birds? That's rum.'

'We found the gate unlatched when we arrived back from a walk the day before yesterday. All of them were gone. We rounded up five hens, but the cock and a hen were missing. I guess I found them.'

'That a fact.' Jock's eyes search his face, turn away. 'When d'yer come across 'em, then?'

'Yesterday, latish afternoon. Walking Sheba down in back of Bramblings, that wide sandy track.'

'Know where yer mean a'right.'

'Just before you get to that dandy old house.'

'Ditches Hall.'

'Is that the name? Yea, I guess Valerie did mention it. Where the old lady lives on her own. Anyways, just before you get to that, up on the ridge, there's a couple of venerable oaks about fifteen yards in.'

'Know that a'right,' Jock agrees, pensive and even quieter than usual.

'Wasn't wearing my glasses, but my eye was caught by flapping. Maybe it was the sound. Odd, kinda swishing.' Dwight looks from

Jock to Sheba. 'You have an hour to spare? Thought we might test out Sheba's tracking skills.'

'So yer've decided who dunnit.'

'I'm keeping an open mind. But I do have something belonging to my suspect.' He pulls the matchbox, still wrapped in paper, out of the plastic bag he's placed it in. 'We'll let her sniff it when we're about five hundred yards away. That makes it fair.'

'What's that yer've got?' Jock sounds intrigued.

'You'll see. Coming?'

''Spose I can walk on to the Fox and 'Ounds from there.'

The grudging tone doesn't fool Dwight'. Jock is as puzzled, and as curious, as he is. Dwight would prefer him not to have the same suspicions as himself. Somehow, he feels, that would make his case much stronger.

Sheba walks to the left of Jock. When the gamekeeper's there Dwight tends to be overlooked, though Sheba's affection never wavers. But it's Jock's voice she obeys.

'Let's 'ave it, then.'

Dwight pulls the little package out of his pocket, pulls the box wrapped in paper out of the plastic with a pair of tweezers, unravels it without touching the matchbox and lays it, on the paper, on the ground.

'Another matchbox?' Jock raises eyebrows. 'From Bramblings?'

'There aren't that many people it can be, Jock.'

'Could be me an' all.'

'I've given that some thought. I guess I don't think that fits.'

'Fetch, Sheba,' Jock says. 'Fetch, girl, fetch.'

The dog has already scented the matchbox, and she's off. Straight as an arrow, without any hesitation whatsoever, she goes down the track and then veers right. The two men follow slowly. The dog will bring her booty back to them, or stay. Dwight doesn't wish to influence her in any way.

Sheba doesn't return. They hear her barking, jumping, unable to reach the target. Deliberately, unhurriedly, they walk on to where she is. Just as Dwight said, the undergrowth has been hacked away, the little clearing stands revealed, and Sheba is in the spot where the Orpingtons were hanging.

Except there isn't any sign of them, or anything else. Not even the rope they'd been strung up on – or the tartan rug. What they do see, what Sheba has fastened on, is a scrap of the plaid material. The bitch is jumping at some limp strands hanging from a couple of tall brambles. She jumps high and gives one last tug, gleeful, bringing bits of frayed dark-coloured yarn to them.

'Valerie's,' Dwight says triumphantly. 'I just know it.'

'I does recognise a bit of that old blanket Mrs Brooke's so keen on,' Jock says. ''Ardly needs Sheba to identify it.'

'It's just bits off the fringe, Jock. Could be from anything. The point is it has the Bramblings scent on it.'

Jock searches the area around. 'No sign o' dead birds.' He clears his throat and Dwight waits. 'Daresay Mrs Brooke were walking Raffy and slipped that blanket on for warmth. Often seen 'er at it. Likely one o' them fringe things got entangled on a bramble. She do slip down to the millpond from this spot, and she be quite short-sighted. Probably jest didn't notice she'd lost a piece.' He smiles. 'That blanket be falling to shreds.'

'It's pretty tough. I tried to tear a piece off it and couldn't.' Dwight has his glasses on and is peering round the little clearing, intent on proving his case. He isn't going to be made a fool of by the critical Jock.

He spots the feathers, a little clutch of them stuck in a clump of grass grown tall with summer. It hasn't been chopped back like the other vegetation. 'Here's the evidence.'

'There's blood, too,' Jock agrees, now scanning the earth. 'I can see as yer didn't imagine it none. But there's nothing as we can do 'bout that,' he adds. 'Can't go round accusing people of dire deeds when all us has is a bundle of old cock feathers and a few threads o' material.'

Does he sound relieved? 'It'll happen again,' Dwight says composedly. He takes the plaid remnants down with his tweezers, folds one of his covers round them and places that in his pocket. 'This is a better source, in any case. And I promised to bring the matchbox back.' He slips that into his other pocket, carefully putting the paper it was covered in into another plastic bag. 'I think I'll meander along to Bramblings now. I'll walk as far as the turning

213

with you and Sheba.'

'You thinking of walking back through they woods without Sheba?'

'Have to get back to town.' Is Jock nervous for him? 'D'you think it might be Valerie?'

'Mrs Brooke? Never!'

'I rather think you're right. Any ideas?'

'Can't rightly say.'

They part at the little fork where Dwight had his first sight of Bramblings. It's there: small, cosy, serene – almost smiling at them through the brambles.

Dwight thinks he knows for sure now. It has to be Emily. Poor shattered mind which can't stop itself from taking its frustrations out on the woods, and the animals that live there.

Once Jock is out of the way Dwight pulls out the other scrap of material, puts his glasses on, and concentrates. They look the same. He can't be sure, his colour blindness makes that difficult. He'll have it checked out professionally.

He can see it all now. Emily comes home, sees her mother isn't there, and vents her rage on the eggs. The hens panic and Emily, infuriated, shoos them out. One less chore for her to do. Perhaps the cock goes for her and she, frenzied, wrings its neck. Then adds a hen for good measure.

Possibly the rug is lying near the chicken run and she simply used it to wrap the birds in. And walked off to the woods to string them up, grisly and menacing.

So his theory of cockfighting was all wrong? Then where did the blood come from? Just oozed down slowly from the dead birds, presumably.

And Ruskin? Why would Emily become so vicious as to kill Ruskin? Can she really have done that?

No, he doesn't believe she can. The cat was probably caught in the illegal traps set by poachers for hares. Then he remembers that the cat was garrotted. It's more serious than he's bargained for. Except Emily doesn't need to garrotte the cat, he works out with relief. That was the trap's doing. She'd simply come across the corpse, seen the wire snare round the cat's neck, and pulled the body out. Used it, just as she'd used the already-dead rabbits and the hedgehog. This time she used the tartan rug to wrap the corpse in. Is that a sort of replica of what she thinks her mother is doing to her, cocooning her? Is she trying to point the finger at her mother? Perhaps that's all a little far-fetched.

What Dwight is sure of is that the girl is seriously disturbed. Should he tell Harry? Will Harry listen, let alone understand? Or will he simply assume that Dwight is jealous, trying to give him a bum steer. Is that what he's doing? Is he trying to puts a spoke in it for Harry so he can pick up the pieces for himself?

The girl actually smiles when Harry is there, seems to be revived by him. That was the first time he'd seen her make herself look gorgeous since the stabbing.

'Beauty and the beast', Harry said. But which one, exactly, is the beast? In this case certainly not Harry.

Beauty. There's been a different pattern to the atrocity this time. No altar, no flowers. Is this a different ogre, after all? Was Alan responsible before his death, and now someone else is taking over? Or is it that there wasn't time. Someone, something, came along and disturbed this particular sacrifice. The cat was wrapped in the tartan. Maybe that was decoration enough.

CHAPTER 28

'You really didn't have to return the matches right away,' Valerie is saying. 'What a treasure you are, Dwight. So reliable.'

'Emily doing anything exciting?'

Valerie's eyes blank out. 'She's off on one of these long rambles she goes on in the woods.'

'Without Raffy?'

Valerie looks a little frosty. 'All on her own. She won't take Raffy because she says she's gone too long, it will exhaust him.'

Of all the lame excuses Dwight has heard this takes some beating.

'I don't really like it. I know Alan's dead and she's quite safe, but somehow I don't feel about the woods the way I used to.' She meets Dwight's eyes. 'I'm worried about her,' she admits. 'I know there's something wrong. Has been, ever since that awful stabbing. But the doctors just think I'm an old fusspot, and Emkins – well, Em hardly says anything at all except hello goodbye.'

'But she always comes back at night?'

'Sometimes it's very late but, yes, she always sleeps here.'

'And spends the days in the woods ...'

'Not always. Quite often now she's off to Chichester, first thing in the morning.' She sees Dwight look knowing. 'To help out Anne and Sophie!' she says defensively. She tosses her head. 'I know that's true, I've checked with Anne.'

Dwight feels she's still holding out on him. What is he fastening

216

on? He looks around the little room: nothing different. The big hearth, not lit today, the great mound of ash littered with cigarette butts. The little table by the window, some wildflowers in a jam jar. The threadbare furniture ... The rug!

The rug is there, slung over the back of the worn-out sofa. He's leaning against it. He bends forward in alarm and horror.

'I'm afraid it's still a bit wet,' Valerie says, seeing his reaction.

'Wet?' More blood? He almost chokes.

'The rug,' Valerie explains calmly. 'I had to wash it, it was revoltingly dirty.' She doesn't look furtive, seems merely to be relating fact. 'I found it caught up in some brambles in the woods. Absolutely filthy.'

She has to know about the Buff Orpingtons, right? Yet she's still letting Emily roam the woods. And she must be suspicious about Ruskin, too. Sure thing, but ...

Well, he's pretty convinced who the woodland ogre is now, and, he guesses, so is she. The answer to the missing birds flashes itself into his mind. Sure thing her rug is back, because Valerie walked the woods with Raffy last night, maybe looking out for her tartan. She'd have come across the birds strung up and put two and two together – especially once she'd spied her rug. Can't he see what is staring him in the face? Valerie spotted her dead birds, and she took them down herself! How come he had trouble figuring that one out? Clear as the nose on his face.

'You're all I have, Dwight, honey.'

So he's been right all along. Valerie, like Dwight, knows enough psychology to recognise that these outrages are a cry for help. She's covering for someone, and who would Valerie cover for? Beaconing out like the white of his hair, who else but Emily? The little girl who loves the woods, the plants, the woodland animals. The child of nature who grew up on wild berries and sweet eglantine. The *Sleeping Beauty* of Bramblings, buried behind stinging nettles, choked by brambles, rotting in compost. Valerie is protecting Emily, smothering her.

She can afford to let her roam. She knows the girl is safe enough,

217

physically, because she knows it's the girl herself who is committing these dreadful atrocities.

The burgeoning young woman has turned in on herself, and Valerie doesn't know how to help her daughter. She's tried interesting the medical profession. She's tried talking to Emily, and found her unresponsive. Now, probably as a last resort, she's come to him for help.

What can he say? Does Valerie admit what's going on with Harry? As he stares out of the window his eye is caught by a large expanse of newly-turned earth. It's set out in careful ridges. Trench digging.

'I see old Jem's been up to dig the garden,' he says, playing for time.

'Old Jem?' Valerie looks puzzled. 'He's been down with bronchitis, actually. Well, I know it's more than that.' Valerie looks Dwight straight in the eyes again. 'I've seen death walking beside him. He's had enough.'

'I've seen death in Gramma's eyes,' his Mom tells him. 'Don't stay away too long.'

'Had enough?'

'He can't garden the way he used to, so that's it. He wants to call it quits.'

'You think he's decided to die, so he's going to?'

'Exactly.'

'So who does do the digging for you? You can't have done it yourself.' He smiles. 'There's too much of it, and it's too deep!'

'Oh, that. Em did it last night. A couple of minutes after you left, she said she felt so strange in her new clothes, she was going to change into her old jeans and wash her hair. And later she said she needed some fresh air to get rid of her headache. Put on her Wellies and started in – by moonlight!'

The old laugh that he's come to know so well. This is the daughter Valerie knows and understands. The girl who likes muck on her hands.

Dwight sees it differently. He sees a girl who sits through drinks pretending she doesn't know Harry, pretending her Anna Sui is something she picked up at Next, pretending she doesn't know one end of a Lambourghini from another. All that pent up pressure has to be released. He just wishes Emily had always used such a safe way of doing it.

Alan! What happened about Alan?

That isn't Emily, she surely wouldn't – couldn't – commit murder. He brushes the unworthy thought aside, suppresses that way of thinking. That's not what he's interested in. And he'll bet she didn't kill Alan directly, he surely hanged himself. Maybe Emily turned him down, maybe even none too gently. At least the police investigated the suicide thoroughly, he's sure they got that right. It's the stabbing which still bothers him. His own theory does have a few flaws he can't quite straighten out.

Was Alan attracted to Emily in the first place because they were both unstable? Is Emily so reticent about blaming Alan because she understands, because ...

The hunting knife. He sees Pop's hunting knife, bare, on the kitchen table.

... She knows what she was stabbed with – her own pruning knife? You bet. Valerie said the stabber must have picked it up in the garden, after Emily'd been summer pruning the espaliers and left it out there, by mistake.

Stabbed with her own knife, yes. No argument there. But how does Valerie explain that Alan knew it was there?

'Where did you get that knife, Dwight, honey?'

He sees the blade, moonlight makes if flicker in the dark. A little too convenient, or just unfortunate? And then Dwight remembers precisely what happened, what he's known all along and hasn't wanted to face.

'Thanks for everything. It was lovely.' Emily softly shuts the Bentley's door and he watches her in the rearview mirror, surprised that she walks, lightly and gracefully, across the lawn, not down, and into the shadows, by the espaliers. He remembers now, he sees her

219

lower her head, the gold glinting faintly, and thinks she's lingered by her favourite perch on the wall, by the beech hedge, for some woodland air before going into the cottage. He prised his eyes away and drove off, feeling he was prying into her private life.

Stoop.

It comes back to him now that he's seen the top of that crowning glory gilding down, even in the dark. Not just lowered. Emily bent down, perhaps to pick something up.

Remembers the knife, and gone to rescue it. Right?

So?

So it's then that Alan came towards her.

OK, Alan came up to her, jealous about her modelling, jealous about him for all he knows.

No running, no momentum. Obvious now. It's Emily who attacked Alan.

Dwight shudders as that possibility wells up. It becomes a clearer picture. Emily tried to use the knife on Alan. Just as she used it to decapitate saplings, and to slash rabbits. Except that Alan wasn't dead when she attacked him. Just weak – and vulnerable.

He was a loser, a lame duck, pestering her. Perhaps she simply held the knife up in defence, as he worked out before. And Alan, poor disturbed Alan, rushed at her.

He shivers as he works out that there wasn't the space to rush, she must already have been there.

'Are you cold, Dwight? D'you want me to light the fire?'

Clouds gather, thick and dark, and a chill wind blows in through the open window. But Dwight, though obviously shivering, isn't physically cold. The authorities were right. The case should never have been pursued. The stabbing wasn't a crime in the ordinary sense.

'Sorry, Valerie. Just someone walking over my grave.'

'Let's go out for a breather. I've got to deadhead the roses.'

So now he knows why Emily refused to give evidence against Alan, knows why she's so very quiet, knows why she's got worse and not better since that terrible night.

He wonders just how many ghastly things Valerie is covering up. Can she pretend indefinitely? Of course not, that's why she's bringing it up with him, however indirectly.

'The happenings in the woods haven't finished, you know,' he says on impulse.

Valerie trembles visibly; shivers. 'What can you mean?' Voice squeaky.

He tells her about finding the strung up Orpingtons.

'You're imagining it, Dwight.'

He pulls out the feathers, the fragments of tartan.

She looks at them, then at Dwight. 'You've known all along.'

'I worked out it was likely you who'd cut down the birds when we took Sheba there this evening,' he admits.

'We?'

'Jock and I. We've trained Sheba to track.'

'The matchbox.'

'She matched it up with bits of your tartan.'

'Of course.'

'I've always known that there's more to it than Alan, Valerie.'

'Always?'

'The very first day I met you, before I strayed into your garden, when Sheba brought that dead rabbit to me.'

'I did wonder, when you brought it up.' Valerie looks at Dwight critically. His cherubic looks fooled her, just as her little country bumpkin act fools most people. 'I didn't think you'd work it out, though.'

'One doesn't forget one's early childhood. And I had reason to remember better than most.'

'The owl?'

'That, and my father left us. I guess he couldn't take my mother's nagging, and my being an albino.'

'So that's why you've always understood just what I've been trying to do for Em. She can't help it, Dwight, it's an illness just like yours. But hers is in the brain, not an obvious physical defect. You're better off.'

'I guess.'

'Your mother protected you. And you know just how hard it can be, I take it.'

'You're doing too much, Valerie. She's a grown woman. Let her go.'

221

'Let her go? In her state?'

'You have to, Valerie, or she'll run. I know – I did it.'

'You did?'

'My mother tried to protect me from the world. I wanted to be part of it, albino or not. I escaped to New York. Some years I hardly bothered to visit with my mother at all.'

'You're a man.'

'Nothing to do with that, nothing to do with anything except that everyone has a right to live their own life the way they wish.' He looks to see if she can really take what he's about to tell her. 'Emily likes city life, Valerie. Sure, she doesn't want to hurt you, sure, she appreciates all you've done for her. But she wants the bright lights, and the glitz, and the razzmatazz. She's not you, friend. Let her go before she splits.'

'You know the sort of things she does, Dwight. I can't just turn my back on her.'

'There's someone waiting to take over.'

'You mean Matt? He's a dear boy, I know ...'

'Not Matt.'

'You're talking about Jock? I know he's been sweet on her for years, but he isn't right for her.'

The small cheap secateurs in her hand begin to attack the spent flowers on the rose bushes as she walks, agitatedly, almost frenziedly, around the little garden. Dwight follows as though on a lead.

'I'm not being snobbish, or anything like that. He's a delightful man, and he's got a good job, and he's really keen on the countryside. But Em won't hear of him.'

'Of course she won't. He's a countryman.'

'That's what she likes about him.'

'Only in an impersonal sort of way.'

'Well, I could go on, but obviously you've already decided who it is.' Suddenly she stops in her tracks and whirls round at him. 'Are you talking about you? Are you telling me she wants to marry you?'

Dwight laughs, a full-throated belly laugh. It's the best joke he's heard in months. 'It's not that I wouldn't be keen, you understand. But, no, it sure isn't me. But you're getting warmer.'

'I see.'

She returns to the deadheading, snipping incisively, viciously, cutting full blooms as well as the faded heads, swathing through the rose beds. Does she know? Is she putting it off?

'There's only one person you can be talking about.'

'I guess.'

'You apparently already know. I'm the one who's guessing, since I wouldn't have thought of him in a thousand years. We're talking about your friend Harry, aren't we?'

'That's so, Valerie. He's quite a lady killer, you know.'

'I think you mentioned that before. It never occurred to me as a possibility, Emily has so many handsome admirers. I can hardly believe she'd choose somebody like Harry. The only reason I even contemplated it is because Anne mentioned seeing Emily with him in Midhurst.'

'So you did recognise who she was talking about.'

'Not then, only when he drove up in that red car.'

'The Lambourghini.'

'Whatever it's called. Not something one can mistake for any other car, even when one doesn't know one from another. Looks like something from outer space.'

'No doubt it's meant to.'

'What you're really telling me is that Emily's been meeting this man in the woods, behind my back?'

'Meeting him, yes. In the woods, I wouldn't think very often. Mostly in Chichester. Or London.'

'Don't be ridiculous, how would she get there? What would she use for money?'

'I guess that's not a problem. She'd get the bus – or a taxi – to Petersfield and train from there.'

'Someone would have seen her and mentioned it.'

'They might not mention it.'

'And when she isn't seeing him ...'

'He runs a business in London; his time tends to be taken up.'

' ...she's stringing up birds and making altars.'

'The point is she only does it when he's not around.'

'Can't you stop it, Dwight? The whole thing's absurd. They'll be divorced in no time at all.'

'I guess. He's been married four times already. I wouldn't hold out on you.'

'He'll listen to you, he seems to think highly of you.'

'He won't listen to me.'

'You've already tried. I see.'

'The only thing I can say is he really is smitten with her. In so far as he understands what love means, he loves Emily. 'Beauty and the Beast', he calls their relationship. I guess he'll do the right thing by her.'

'I see,' she repeat, expressionless. 'As long as she has the beauty, of course.'

'And he can offer her anything and everything money can buy.'

'Money? What's the use of money?'

'It's handy,' Dwight says dryly. The insistence on the evils of money is getting on his nerves. 'In any case, Valerie, they're set on getting together. There's nothing to be gained by trying to stop them, you'll just antagonise the both of them. Settle for it, and you'll see something of her.'

'See something of her? He'll whisk her off to London if I'm lucky, New York if I'm unlucky.'

'I've thought about that. I'm going to offer to let them have The Woolhouse. Then you'll be neighbours.'

She's snipping at the rose-buds now.

'I think Harry's quite keen. He kinda fancies owning the place.'

'I think I need a drink, Dwight. A real one.'

'Of course I'd drive you, Valerie. But I walked over.'

'I keep some cooking sherry.'

He laughs out loud, he can't stop himself.

'What's so funny about that?'

'Drowning our sorrows in cooking sherry.'

'I thought she might like you, eventually.' Valerie looks at Dwight, tears moistening her eyes.

'I sure hoped so too, Valerie. But, be honest, would you want to saddle her with the possibility of albino children?'

'It wouldn't have worried me. You're a decent man Dwight, gentle, considerate.'

'Thank you kindly, ma'am.'

'I mean it. You, or Matthew, or even Jock. But Harry Solferino! He looks like a gangster.'

'He is a gangster.'

Her head snaps back sharply. 'You don't mean it?'

'A perfectly amiable gangster to his friends, but a gangster all the same. Don't mix with him, Valerie. He has no scruples.'

'And you expect me to allow Emily to marry him?'

'If it doesn't work out he'll settle a decent sum on her. I'll see to that bit.'

'Thanks for nothing.'

'Don't knock it. At least she'll be able to choose what to do with the rest of her life.' He sighs. 'And Harry's a regular kind of guy, at least when he gets his way.' He's cleared the cuttings up for Valerie and they walk towards the cottage. 'Most of that type marry and think the world of their families, you know. I guess so far Harry's been plumb unlucky.'

'You may be right,' she dismisses the subject almost carelessly. 'Why don't we take the dogs for a walk? I do believe the first woodland strawberries are ripening.'

Strawberries? She can think of strawberries at a time like this?

'Heel, Sheba.' The big black bitch comes bounding over, Raffy following as fast as his short legs allow.

'I think so, Dwight. Do look, the very first ones always ripen along my drive. Big red and luscious this year. A bumper crop.'

They walk down the little winding lane, their dogs in tow, picking ripe red berries from between the weeds.

CHAPTER 29

The scene of devastation which greets Dwight is awesome. All five ground floor windows facing the drive have been smashed, urns holding flowers on the terrace toppled, their contents strewn, the pots in smithereens, the plants dismembered, earth everywhere.

The front door stands wide open, the trail of destruction continuing into the hall. Is someone in the house?

Dwight advances cautiously. No sound. No pathway, either. The heavy tallboy is overturned, its contents scattered on Mrs Dean's polished hall tiles. The chandelier appears intact. He zigzags through into the living room, now almost in a daze, forgetting danger.

The French windows, facing into the back garden, are shattered. His velvet drapes, newly hung, wave soggily where the morning's deluge has wetted them. The beautiful Adam fireplace is hacked to pieces, the chippings scattered over the parquet and his latest Chinese rug. He can't...Sheba!

Mom's door wide open. He hurls himself into the house.
The phone still swinging, off the hook.

Dwight rushes outside, kicking debris out of his way, making for the kennel. Sheba! Where's his dog? His affection – his love – for the Labrador makes him dread almost at once that she's gone, the pain of loss stabbing through him. He curses himself for an idiot. It is, after all, only late Friday morning. Jock has almost certainly taken her with him and might not bring her round till afternoon, possibly early evening. He opens the wooden door. The empty kennel leers at him. He pauses, afraid to go nearer in spite of his reasoning.

Her eyes are fixed, unseeing, dead.

'Sheba!' he calls. 'Here, girl.' The sob in his voice urges him towards the kennel housing. There is no sound, no sign of life at all.

He imagines the body there, perhaps already stiffening. But when he goes in there's nothing tangible. Sheba's basket is out of place but still intact. Some scratch marks on the door, but those could have been there already. No body, no blood, no devastation. And no bitch. Jock: he prays Jock didn't leave her, or bring her back early by some unlucky chance.

Unlikely. It's only just noon; please God Jock still has her with him. He said he might bring her back late Friday, he had a lot do get through. Dwight fights down sickening images boring into his mind. Why does he find it so hard to believe the dog's fine?

He goes to phone the police. When they ask what time the incident happened he recalls that Jock most likely slept here last night. It must have happened after Jock left, between five and six in the morning.

Harry. He'll ring Harry, get him to come down earlier than planned, maybe tonight. Sleeping alone at The Woolhouse holds no appeal for Dwight at all. He'll ask Jock, if he can find him – but he'd prefer Harry. His brain, fuzzy from the shock, appalled at the thought of harm to Sheba, is clearing now.

This isn't likely to be Emily's doing, this looks more like the sort of damage a man would do. Several men, he decides, looking around.

A simple burglary? Well, not simple, certainly. Dwight hasn't checked as yet. But nothing, as far as he can judge, was taken. The hi-fi, though toppled, is still there, the CDs scattered. Someone fearsomely angry has smashed whatever he, or she, can lay axe on. The damage can only have been done with a heavy instrument. It doesn't fit the pattern of the woodland atrocities. This is vandalism of a different kind.

227

'Hi, there.' Harry's voice at the other end of the line. 'I thought we had a date tomorrow.'

'I've been robbed, Harry.'

'Honest, we said tomorrow around noon.'

'No, I don't mean that. Literally robbed.'

'In West Sussex?'

'The whole entrance and living room totalled.'

'You OK?'

'He – they – whatever had gone by the time I arrived.'

'And the dog?'

'I guess she isn't here yet.'

'OK, I'll be along tonight. You up to the mother?'

'I'll go over now.'

'She won't be so keen if she thinks that house of yours gets smashed up ...'

'It's the maniac. She'll allow for that.' He sounds surer than he feels. He doesn't believe this horror can be Emily, and neither will Valerie.

'We'll get on to that.'

'Meet you at the Fox and Hounds, Harry. Around seven.'

'Say hello to my girl for me.'

'Sure thing.'

Emily, Valerie told him, is off around eight every Friday morning to help Anne and Sophie in Chichester. She's not due back until later on, early evening. So, even if it fitted in with the motivations he's plotted out, it can't – well, is extraordinarily unlikely – to have been Emily who vandalised his house. Which means it quite likely wasn't Emily who committed the woodland atrocities in the first place. His theory is all wrong, and so is Valerie's. Lucky break he never mentioned his suspicions to Harry.

So who the hell is it? Jock after all? Doesn't make any sense; doesn't make any sense at all.

Pop's rifle is still smoking. He bags the kill in his left hand.

A sudden fury overwhelms Dwight. Maybe the vandals are the badger baiting trio he overheard? They spotted him and didn't let on? He draws a deep breath, stands erect. That's enough of whoever it is, right now. There has to be an end to it, once and for all. This nonsense simply has to stop because, if it doesn't, someone is actually going to get killed.

Alan is dead. Was he murdered? Is that a possibility?

Her throat is cut, wide open, slit.

Dwight busies himself reporting the burglary to the police, ringing a glazier, contacting Mrs Dean. Only Jock is inaccessible. So there's no way he can get hold of Sheba.

At last he sets off for Valerie's. It's already teatime. He's the messenger, the bearer of bad news, lots of it. What should he start with? The vandalism?

But when he arrives at Bramblings it looks deserted. The cottage stares at him, alone and silent, sitting snug, the lawns cut neat by old Jem's nephew, young arms neatening the little holding into somnolent submission.

He looks around, no sign of anyone. He knocks on the front door, no answer. He tries it. Open, as usual. Curious, he walks in, listening for returning barking. Nothing at all. The cuckooing of the clock, loud and penetrating, breaks the silence. Five o'clock. He sits down on the worn sofa, watching a lazy curl of ash spitting over the fender. A forlorn solitary air of emptiness fills the place in an eerie way.

'No one lives here,' he tells the realtor. 'My mother died.'

Has he imagined it all? Is he in some sort of dream, only to wake in Boston? He shakes himself out of self-hypnosis and pricks his ears at noises off. Valerie and Raffy coming back. He can hardly wait to greet them.

'Dwight! You are an early bird.'

'I took a chance.'

'I'll put the kettle on.'

'My house has been vandalised.'

She turns, eyes round. 'Burgled, you mean?'

'Smashed up. Nothing's been taken as far as I know. Just splintered furniture, pictures, even the fireplace ...'

'Smashed up?'

'With an axe, or a jemmy, or something of that kind.'

'How absolutely dreadful! Do you know when?'

'Today, I guess. Must have been early this morning. Jock's there most nights ...'

'Jock?'

'He often sleeps there when I'm in town. An arrangement we have.'

'And Sheba?'

'The kennel's shut, she isn't there. But then she's generally with Jock until late Friday.'

Valerie pulls out her cigarettes and lights one while waiting for the kettle to boil. 'One of these gangs, I suppose,' she volunteers.

'It's possible,' Dwight agrees.

The kitchen table is splattered, the dresser tipped up at an angle. Broken china litters the floor, glass splinters the upturned chairs, glistens the cooker.

Dwight isn't going to get into that. Just how is he to bring up the real reason he's here?

'Emkins is enjoying herself at last, helping Anne and Sophie with the boutique.'

'You told me. That's going well?'

'First rate. It's quite amazing how Anne has taken to it. Absolutely puts her finger on what to buy. The customers are flocking in.'

'And Emily and Sophie can't exactly be keeping them away.'

'It's the first time I've seen Em smile for weeks. I think we're there at last, I think we've won.'

'There could be another reason, Valerie.'

'Another reason?' She stops in mid drag. 'You've offered her another job and she's accepted? Abroad?'

'I've offered her any number of jobs, she's never accepted. No. Something quite different.'

She catches the nervousness in his voice. 'Well, spit it out then,

Dwight.'

'His clothes are gone, Dwight, honey. Your father's left.'

'I guess you know.'

She looks at him sharply. 'I don't. That's why I'm asking you.'

'Emily and Harry are engaged.'

'Harry?' She stares at him, apparently mystified.

'Harry Solferino.'

'They're actually going to get married?' She rattles the poker before she looks back at Dwight. 'So soon? It's all settled?'

'They asked me to tell you.'

'You mean they can't manage it themselves?'

'I guess Emily thought it would be a shock.'

'When?'

'Middle of August.'

'A late summer wedding.' She pours the tea. 'I see.'

'I've offered Harry The Woolhouse,' he says, hoping to ease her pain. 'He says living there will be real neat. That means Emily'll be quite near you.'

'Harry is going to take over The Woolhouse?' Valerie looks vague.

'Emily and Harry, Valerie. My wedding present to Emily,' Dwight says on impulse, smiling proudly. He realises he still longs to contribute to Emily's happiness.

'A wedding present.' Her cup shakes, clatters, spills tea into the saucer. 'Of course. They'll have wedding presents.'

'They'll live only a short walk across the woods.'

'Yes,' Valerie says, a sort of monotone. 'Just a short walk. Here, boy, here. Come to Mummy,' she suddenly says, over bright and over active. 'Look what I've got for you.'

She digs deep in the pocket of her dress and pulls out the sort of biscuit she fed Sheba when she and Dwight first stumbled across the Brookes and their cottage.

'It isn't as though you won't see them quite often.'

'You'll be telling me next how I'll be gaining a son, not losing a daughter.'

A car purrs to a stop and, getting up eagerly to see who it is,

231

Dwight notices Emily skipping across the lawn, waving the car goodbye as she dances, swinging a handbag, towards the cottage.

'It's Em,' he says, turning to Valerie.

'Are Sophie and Anne with her?'

'They've driven off.'

A transformed Emily comes into the little room, almost filling it in her eagerness to savour every cubic foot of air, of smoke, of anything she comes into contact with.

'Hello, Mummy,' she greets her, a happy smile over her face, her flowing hair around her, clasping the jumping Raffy to her breast. 'Hold on, my pet, this is my best blouse you're pawing.'

She sees Dwight and includes him in her radiance. 'Dwight. How nice to see you.'

'Hello, Emily. I understand congratulations are in order. I sure hope you'll be very happy.'

'Oh.' She looks slightly nonplussed, but not for long. 'Harry told you we've fixed the date, I suppose.' She looks at Dwight without a smile. 'And you've told Mummy. Well, thanks. I'm really happy.' She looks towards her mother who spreads out her arms.

'I'm so glad for you, darling,' Valerie says, tears in her eyes. 'I only want the best for you.'

'London isn't all that far away ...'

'Dwight told me about the house, darling. Isn't it incredible?'

'House?' The smile disappears behind a heavy frown. 'What house?'

Valerie looks expectantly at Dwight. 'Well, you tell her. It is your present, after all.'

Emily looks from Valerie to Dwight, her eyes steely.

'It seems so right for you, Emily. I think you and Harry should take over The Woolhouse...

'Live there, d'you mean?' The tone, suddenly flat and monotonous, turns hostile. 'Harry did say you'd offered to let him have it.'

'Sure thing...'

'And you've talked him into buying it right away?' Emily looks at Dwight full face. Her eyes glaze green, a stony green.

'Not buy, Emkins! He's giving it to you as a wedding present!' Valerie enthuses. 'So you won't be far away at all. Isn't that absolutely wonderful? You'll still be living in this part of the country.'

All the life seems to drain out of her. The vibrant dancing body, the sparkling eyes, the laughing voice – all gone. Emily is silent, intent on fondling Raffy's ears. 'How very thoughtful, Dwight. Does Harry know?'

'Not yet. I'm meeting him at the Fox and Hounds later.'

There's no response as Valerie thinks aloud about the wedding celebrations. Dwight feels he's intruding on the Brookes' privacy. He steals away and walks, his feelings mixed, towards the Fox and Hounds. Raffy follows him.

'Back you go, boy. Go on, home.'

The dog walks him to the top of the garden then returns, a small stubby figure alone on the wide lawn, trotting earnestly and briskly towards the cottage.

Dwight smiles as he dawdles dreamily along the drive, reaching towards the ripe alpine strawberries glistening like bloodstones among the weeds. Their succulent flesh melts into an acerbic tang which he's beginning to enjoy.

'The huckleberries are ripening now, Dwight, honey.'

He's too early for the meeting with Harry. Sauntering out of his way, peering at the overgrown woods, eyes and ears in communion with his surroundings, he wonders whether Valerie is right. A gang of local thugs, annoyed at a foreigner taking over one of their country houses, is trying to frighten him off, maybe. With a start he becomes aware of the sound of heavy footsteps, a rustling through undergrowth. Someone is walking a dog nearby. Jock and Sheba?

Coming towards him he distinguishes a tall blond-turning-grey middle-aged man, beige corduroys, a shooting jacket, a walking stick. He's flicking that at bracken shoots grown tough with hardening sap. The stick whistles like a knife, neatly decapitating them. Dwight is impressed at the ease with which he forges a passage for himself. A large silver-brown dog is slinking after him. A lurcher ... Where has he heard about lurchers in the area? He remembers now: badger baiting. And Emily's father, apparently, breeds them.

'Good afternoon.'

233

The figure stops momentarily and looks him over. Something oddly familiar about the nose, the eyes. That whiff which so often emanated from Emily, an odd mixture of stale cigar smoke and the acrid smell of kerosene. Reginald Brooke!

'Afternoon.' Abrupt and curt.

Where has he heard that baritone before? The badger baiter, that's the voice – and the odour. That's what Dwight now remembers. So that fleeting combination of smells he's so often caught on Emily stemmed partly from her father.

There is a steely disdain in the man's eyes, a contemptuous curl of thin lips. He looks patrician in the uniquely British way Dwight has come to recognise. The man lifts his head and strides off along the path Dwight just walked.

CHAPTER 30

Dwight walks on until he can hear the hubbub of voices from the Fox and Hounds. A friendly, familiar sound. Harry's Lambourghini isn't outside the local. Late, as usual.

Dwight sits down fretfully on a barstool, twirling his body, dividing his attention between Lily and looking towards the door. The barmaid displays a bottle of rye to him, ice cubes tinkling into the glass she reaches for deftly and quickly. Dwight drinks gratefully, watching, waiting. Harry is very late.

About to give up, Dwight takes a last sip just as Harry, the putative West Sussex resident, comes through the door and grins widely round.

'And one for me.' He laughs at Lily and watches her fill his order instantly.

'Bottoms up,' he announces. 'Right?'

'Where'd you finally spring from? I didn't even hear the car.'

'Round the back, old buddy.' Harry takes a long draught of rye and savours it. 'Too busy drinking to hear me, Dwight, old pal. Good to see you.'

'Let's have a go at the dart board.'

'That bad?'

'I don't feel good.'

'Did ya see how my little beauty looked today? Aint she the sweetest?'

'Sure buddy. She always looks great.'

'She says you broke the news to the old dragon. I owe you one.'

'You've seen her since?' So that's what kept him.

'Sneaked in a kiss in one of those leafy bowers you go on about. She says not to worry about the house for now. Wants me to take her on a trip around the world before we settle down.'

'No problem. I told Valerie it will be my wedding present to Emily,' he grins at Harry. 'She seemed pleased.'

'Gee, pal, Emily didn't mention that.'

There's something wrong. Dwight can't put his finger on it, precisely, but he's now sure that it wasn't a gang of local thugs who vandalised his house. Could Reginald Brooke be the vandal? Out of revenge, furious at Dwight for offering Emily work as a model? Perhaps even holding him responsible for Harry. The cigar butt — where is Sheba? 'Did you drive by the house?'

'Sure thing. I checked it out.'

'Is Sheba there?'

'Guys putting in glass, that's all I seen.'

'I'm worried about her.'

'C'mon, Dwight, you're suffering from shock.'

'There's something going on.'

'You bet.'

'I mean right now! I gotta go find her.'

'The dog?'

'I'm checking out the woods.'

'For chrissake, Dwight. It'll be getting dark.'

'You drive back to the house.'

Dwight strides out of the pub and up the lane without even a backward glance. Something is pulling him towards that sandy track, that winding sinuous deceptively beautiful track.

Her throat is cut, wide open, slit.

'Gimme a break, Dwight.'

Dwight is already out the door and off towards the woods.

'Hold your horses, for chrissake. I'm coming with you.' Harry puffs behind him.

They jog on until they come to the little overgrown pathway to

236

Bramblings. Dwight accelerates past, on to the clearing where he found that first altar. He uses his stick like a native to stop the groping tendrils of insidious brambles from tearing at his tweeds. The way seems more overgrown than ever, more like the thickets leading to *Sleeping Beauty* than he cares to admit.

The narrow clearing appears ahead of him. So bright, so sweet, so innocent – so breathtakingly beautiful. They walk past, quickly, silently, looking to left and right. Nothing unusual, no sounds, no animals.

'I keep telling you, asshole. You're just shovelling shit against the tide.'

'Up here.'

The overhanging arch of greenery, where Alan died not long ago, leads to a small field at the top.

'Jeez, Dwight. When are you going to stop jerking around?'

They heave and puff up to the ridge. The field lies ahead of them, the long shadows of evening stretching fingers of dark and pale along its length. A gleam of black at the far end, a sudden scud of clouds covering the sky which hide the mass at first, then shows the darkening shadows more distinctly when it clears.

'Lemme have those binoculars, Harry.'

Dwight trains the glasses to the far end of the field. He can see a mass of black, a large gleaming dark mass of jet.

'Over here, Harry.' Dwight is running now, panting and sobbing as he stumbles, lopes, staggers on. He stops in front of a crucifixion.

Glazed eyes stare at him.

Sheba is nailed to a makeshift cross, her massive head set down, hind legs crossed over, front legs spread out, cleft to make them splay. Her dead eyes stare ahead, open, wide, her mouth gapes teeth, fangs on either side of Valerie's tartan rammed down her throat.

He trembles, shakes, stumbles against her.
The body moves, the head lolls back, the widened gash pours blood.
He pukes, sinks to his knees.

Dwight gasps, then retches uncontrollably. Harry puts his arms around his shoulders.

'Dwight, baby.'

'I'll get her. If it's the last thing I do, I'll get that fucking witch.'

'This sure beats anything I seen before. Don't look, old pal. She's down the tube. There's nothing you can do for her.'

'I'm getting that bloody whore, that shitting fuckhead, that ...'

'Who?'

He sees Valerie, sitting on the little stone step outside the cottage, plucking a pheasant old Jem brought in for them.

Valerie!? Valerie. That's why Emily refuses to speak about the stabbing. It was Valerie who, thinking her daughter will leave her for a glamorous job away from Bramblings, used the pruning knife on her. Was Emily not stabbed in the garden at all, but in the house? Alan was there, just as Dwight worked out, but he only pleaded and tried to interest Emily, he didn't harm her in any way? Does that make any sense in this senseless scenario?

Who else could it have been? He sees the thin white smoke drifting slowly from the huge central chimney. Valerie has lit the fire. He remembers how she likes to sit in front of it, even in summer, smoking and poking in the embers. Raffy, her familiar, sitting by her side.

'I cook my spuds in it,' she said amiably only last week. 'And the fuel doesn't cost me a bean. I just pick up the fallen branches.'

Strong enough to bring them back by herself. Dwight, now furious, takes that on board. Quite able to build a cross with them.

'Gives me something to collect when I'm out walking Raffy.'

Always out and about in the neighbourhood.

'Sometimes we come up with something better, of course. When they've been shooting rabbits or woodpigeons, we often come across one the dogs have missed.'

She hasn't trained Raffy much, but his instincts are to pick up booty and bring it back to her. She trained him with sticks. A game, she calls it.

'Do you know, just the other day we bagged two geese? Flew into those awful wires between the pylons. They put them right near me, though I don't use their beastly electricity.'

'You mean they flew into the wires and were electrocuted?'

'Yes. Plummeted straight down. Raffy found them right away. Marvellous meat. Anne put the second one in her freezer for me.'

He finally knows. Valerie is the culprit, and blamed it all on Alan. She had the opportunity, the knowledge, the experience – and the motive.

'You think it's the mother?'

'There's no one else left.'

'Holy smoke, Dwight. Get your ass going. Emily's with her!'

He doesn't see it right away, even then. Harry grabs him by the arm and drags him back the way they came, down the steep slope, almost pushing him, then chivvying him along the track.

'Move it, man, move it. The girl's in danger!'

They veer, the rye in their blood, not young, not fit, puffing and panting, pressing on, their faces red and swelling. The fading light makes it difficult even for Dwight to distinguish path from the surrounding woodland.

'This way,' Dwight gasps, now at last scenting blood, and makes for the little path into the garden.

As they approach the wall where he first saw Emily, the white stone reflects light on to a curiously dishevelled figure looming up, apparently from nowhere, and lurching past them into the undergrowth.

'My God!'

Dwight turns momentarily, then blunders on. The figure could have been Jock, could have been anyone, but somehow the face is curiously familiar – and the smell. This is the man he met earlier on – Reginald Brooke.

He stabs his foot down hard to speed away.

He can't stop, Harry pushes him ahead and they pant on, the end in sight, taking in the door of Bramblings opened wide.

Heaving, trying to get their breath, their ears pounding with the strain, they stand against the doorposts, breathing heavily. A wailing noise, quite low at first and then crescendoing into sobs and howls of anguish, pulls them into the cottage.

Emily is kneeling on the floor, holding a figure in her arms, rocking and crying, weeping, wailing, sobbing in turns. There is blood everywhere.

Bright scarlet running down, a rush of red he tries in vain to stem.

The figure, apparently small and squat, is virtually unrecognisable. The face is hacked, the features destroyed, one eye gaped open, like a Picasso come to life. Mutilated Woman. What furniture there is is splintered to pieces. A piece of fur – Raffy, Dwight realises – is in the corner. Blood is spattered on the walls, the window, the fireplace. The poker lies, clearly as it has fallen, beside what looks like another piece of fur. Has the dog been cut in two? The fire tongs are set astride the sofa, its horsehair stuffing curling out at odd angles. Almost like Alan's hair. A bottle of elderberry wine has rolled, incongruously intact, beside the poker.

The girl is swaying back and forth, crooning and caressing the body in her arms, unaware of their presence.

'Jesus Christ.'

Harry picks up the phone. No sound. The line was pulled out and the phone hangs, the torn cord trailing, in his hand.

The phone still swinging, off the hook.

'OK, honey. Take it easy now, I'm here.' Harry takes the moaning weeping hysterical girl in his arms and sits, crooning to her. 'Get going, bub. Get to the nearest phone.'

Dwight looks about him, dazed. Something is worrying him.

Another heap of fur, another battered dog – that must be the lurcher. 'He could come back.'

'For chrissake, Dwight. Get cracking.'

'He might be out there.'

'Not now – not tonight, I guess. Gimme the poker.'

Dwight shambles out the door, up the trim lawn, rocks down the rutted drive and round the corner.

'Only a few minutes to Oak Court' he hears a laughing Valerie telling him. 'Why should we bother with a phone?'

There's no one beside him, no Raffy barking, no Sheba at heel.

Sagging, defeated, only just able to keep going by an enormous effort of will, he pushes himself up the steep drive to the Pontings' front door. He puts two fingers on the old metal bell pull and, leaning against the stone, allows gravity to drag the bell down without let up.

It takes time to get from the living room to the door in a big house without servants. He can hear Tatman barking a long way off, then pattering across the hall, racketing raucously on the inside of the letter box.

'Quiet, Tatman.'

The door opens slightly, the chain left on. Bright beaming light shines through.

'Who's there?'

He uncoils from the wall and looks at the eyes peering out at him.

'Dwight.' Sophie unhooks the chain and opens the door, then almost slams it back in his face in horror. 'You're covered in blood. What on earth's happened? Have you had an accident?'

She looks beyond him, expecting what? Sheba. He tries to dislodge his fingers from the metal. The effort required is prodigious and he feels light-headed with it. He takes a deep breath and once more forces himself to act.

'There's been a murder at Bramblings,' he says. 'Valerie,' he sobs now, 'Valerie is dead. And so are Raffy and Sheba.'

He watches himself slide down the stone porch wall, streaks of pink where his clothes were, and then oblivion.

CHAPTER 31

'We know these questions must be extremely upsetting for you, Miss Brooke – Emily. The court is aware of that and extends you every sympathy. But we need your co-operation. Please try to answer.'

Emily, head bowed, is sitting in the Coroner's court, a large black hat shading her face, black Dior silk enveloping her. Long slim fingers twist an enormous diamond on an engagement ring. It glints back and forth, a winking Cyclops, watchful, bright.

'Now, Emily. You say, in your statement to the police, that you came back from a walk to find your mother ...'

Bright scarlet streaming down, a rush of red he's trying in vain to stem.

Emily puts both hands up to her face and covers it.

'Take all the time you need, my dear.'

Dwight can tell that Gilbert Sunnington, in his capacity as coroner, is doing his best to make the ordeal as painless as possible for Emily. No doubt he fancies himself as the father figure now that Reginald Brooke is being held for observation in a psychiatric ward.

Dwight feels for her, the terrible memory of his own mother's violent death gripping him, the pangs of grief still too familiar. Emily has to cope with the horror, the pain, the grief of such trauma – and add to that her father's breakdown. Dwight aches for her, longs to be able to help her.

242

Emily's body, stooped with sorrow, trembles faintly. She draws herself up and looks towards her questioner.

'Was Reginald Brooke – your father – in the cottage when you came back?' Gilbert Sunnington asks now, his voice paternally caressing.

'I only saw my mother.'

'I'm sorry, Emily. I have to ask these questions.'

'I know,' she says, tears running down her face. 'I'll be all right.'

'We have to try to establish this.' Sunnington clears his throat. 'Do you know whether your mother was alive at this point?'

He trembles, shakes, stumbles against her.
The body moves, the head lolls back, the widened gash pours blood.

'Nhhh...' There is an uneasy hush as Emily gulps, then blows her nose. 'No,' she says, clearer now, still husky. 'Not really.'

'Could she have been?'

Her body flaccid, one limp hand dangling over the dresser top.

There is no answer. A shaking of the hat, waving grief.

'I'm so sorry to press you, we need to establish what we can.'

'I suppose so.' The words are barely perceptible.

'I'm sorry, Emily, what did you say?'

Another gulp, another blow. 'Yes.'

'Can you tell us why you formed this impression.'

Harry, sitting next to Dwight, leaps to his feet. Dwight realises he's about to interfere and grasps his arm, pulling him back.

'Please – no disturbances,' Sunnington says severely, his glasses catching the light and beaming it at Harry. 'Otherwise I shall be forced to have the courtroom cleared, and to hold this inquest in private.'

Emily looks up from under her hat and draws a deep breath. 'I saw the body twitch. I don't know whether that was simply a reaction after death, or whether she was still alive.' She sounds dry and brittle, now. And in control, her voice quite steady.

Her body twitches, slithers down, then bunches on the floor.

'You know about reactions after death?'

Another girding deep breath and Emily's voice rises high, virtually the sound of singing, loud and very clear. 'We live in the country. We keep chickens and use them for the pot.' A momentary huskiness as her voice lowers: 'I mean we used to keep them.' Her voice brightens again. 'I follow the hunt.'

'Points taken. Anything else which might suggest there was still hope?'

'Nothing. Her face was nonexistent.'

Lanky grey hair covers her back and shoulders, veiling her neck.

'What was your father doing at this point?'

'My father?' A vague, vacant look.

'Was your father in the cottage, in the room with you?'

Pop's rifle is still smoking.

Emily folds her hands into her lap and lowers her head, then lifts it. 'I don't know, I suppose so. I told the police ...'

'We have to establish what we can here,' Sunnington says gently. 'Try to remember.'

'I didn't see anyone. I didn't really notice anything except ...' Emily pauses for a moment. 'I noticed Raffy wasn't barking.'

'Raffy?'

'What's that you've got there, honey? Looks kinda dirty. Didn't I tell you not to bring garbage into the house?'

'Our Jack Russell terrier. He barks if something is wrong.'

'And he wasn't barking. So was the dog dead as well?'

'He wasn't moving,' Emily says almost dreamily. 'Not moving at all.' She smiles, some sort of reflex action Dwight presumes. 'So he must have been,' she finishes up, incongruously bright. 'Raffy would have defended my mother to the death.'

'Indeed. So what did you do next?'

'I rushed to my mother to see if I could save her.'

The tones are loud and clear now. Dwight marvels at the girl's strength.

He stares at the counter top, runnels of blood glisten the pale surface, trickling down.

'And?'
'I was sure it was too late.'
'What happened then?'
Emily sits bolt upright. 'I looked up.' Her eyes grow round and bright, her voice emphatic. 'My father was standing above me, the poker dangling in his hand, just staring round him. There was no sound of any kind. I didn't look, but even his own dog must have been dead.'

The carcass is curved round Pop's wide shoulders. He lurches towards the house.

'His own dog? He had a dog with him?'
'Fangs, his lurcher.' That smile again, fleeting but there. 'A beautiful animal.'
Dwight sees the surprise in Sunnington's eyes. Then he notices Harry, listening intently, looking at Emily. Harry turns to him and signals with his eyes, making a move to stand.
Dwight shakes his head and pulls him back urgently. 'They'll chuck you out, buddy,' he whispers. 'Sit tight, for chrissake.' Heads turn, Sunnington looks at them, but lets the matter pass.
'Your father's lurcher was dead? Is that what you are telling us?' The coroner seems oddly concerned about the dog.
Emily's eyes stop glowing and veil over. Dwight sees her revert to her bearing after the stabbing – alienated, shutting out the world.
'Fangs was dead as well.' The vibrancy has gone, the clear strong voice has sunk to grudging irritation. 'A mistake, I suppose. He must have poleaxed everything in sight.'
'Poleaxed?'
'Bashed, battered to death.' Her voice sounds exasperated.
'Can you be a little more specific, who is the 'he' you are referring to?'
She doesn't answer.

'Emily?'

'My father,' she brings out at last. 'My father was there. Reginald Brooke.' A sort of sing-song. 'He breeds lurchers.'

Again Sunnington looks surprised. 'But you didn't see him actually batter anything, and he didn't attempt to attack you?'

'I don't think he really saw me,' Emily breathes. 'He didn't seem to notice me.'

'How do you mean?'

'He stared and stared, right through me.' She's almost whispering, a loud husky whisper.

The eyes, still blue, pierce their dead stare through his.
Tears gather as he turns away, turns back, hand hovering above the eyelids.
Can't bring himself to touch her.

There is a short silence as the coroner bends over papers, shuffles them. He clears his throat. 'What happened next?'

'He dropped the poker.'

'He dropped it – he didn't try to use it on you?'

'No. He dragged himself out.'

'Dragged himself?'

'Held on to whatever solid surfaces he could find. He seemed to have no strength. There was blood everywhere, his hands were dripping with it. He sort of stumbled out of the room.'

'And then?'

'Then?'

'What happened next, Emily?'

'I don't remember ... I don't know!' she wails. 'What d'you want me to say?'

'Just take your time, my dear. Your father left, what happened next?'

'I think I just stayed with my mother.' A sob, a deep reverberating sob. 'What else could I do? She was covered in blood – I tried to clean it off!'

He pulls the oilcloth from the table, covering her.
He runs the faucet, spreads his hands under it. It takes forever to get them clean.

246

'Of course,' Sunnington purred. 'Of course. Don't distress yourself. That is all I am going to ask you. Thank you, Emily.'

'Can I leave now?' She rises to go. Dwight sees she's lost quite a lot of weight.

'I think Mr Watkins has some questions for you. He won't take long.'

Another man stands up. Dwight presumes he's Reginald Brooke's solicitor.

'I'm very sorry, Miss Brooke. One or two more questions.'

Emily sags down again.

'You say you were walking in the woods and came back to find this terrible tragedy.'

'Yes.'

'You were walking, but without your dog?'

'My mother's dog, yes.'

'Wouldn't you normally take him? Or was your mother afraid for some reason, keeping the dog at home to protect her?'

'No.'

'No, she wasn't afraid, or no, you wouldn't normally take the dog?'

'I was hoping to meet someone.'

Emily's answers to Watkins' questions are crisp and clear. Dwight marvels at her self control.

'In the woods?'

'In the lane leading to the woods.'

'May we know who that person is?'

'My fiancé.'

'And his name is?'

'Harry Solferino.'

'I see. You were with Mr Solferino all afternoon.'

'No, I was in Chichester.'

'And you returned to meet Mr Solferino.'

'No. I came straight home from Chichester at around six. My mother had a visitor.'

Mr Watkins looks up, surprised. 'Your father was already there, you mean?'

'My father? No, of course not. My father doesn't come to Bramblings.'

'Where's Pop, Mom?'

'So this was another visitor?'

'Dwight Delaney.' Emily hesitates slightly, looks towards Dwight and Harry, then continues. 'A neighbour and a friend of ours.'

'And then?'

'Dwight left. My mother had just been told of my engagement, we wanted to celebrate. I said I'd pick a few of those lovely strawberries which had just ...'

'The huckleberries are ripening now.' Mom smiles at him. 'Let's go pick some.'

A sob, an almost uncontrollable sob.

'Take your time, Miss Brooke.'

'They ripen at this time. We like to eat them with the new season's elderflower champagne.'

'Quite so. And then?'

'I was expecting Harry – my fiancé – to be in his car in the lane.'

'But you didn't come across him.'

'I did, yes. We spent a little time together, picked a few berries.' Emily looks up, her eyes vacant and empty. 'Harry told me he thought we ought to accept Dwight's offer to let us have The Woolhouse.' Again, a brittle stare, her eyes wide open. 'He likes the idea of settling here. He thinks it will be ideal, living near my mother.' A pause as Emily settles the hat firmly on her head. 'Then he drove off to meet Dwight at the Fox and Hounds.'

'He didn't go back with you to meet your mother, after you'd just got engaged? You returned alone?'

'Yes. Harry and Dwight were coming later.'

It's Dwight's turn to be surprised. That sure is news to him.

'Tell me, Miss Brooke, were you worried at all? When you were walking back, did everything seem normal?'

She pauses, steady now, one hand quiet in her lap, the other dabbing at her eyes with her handkerchief.

'At first it was. But not when I got nearer, not really.'

'Why not?'

248

'I thought I could hear voices.'

'Voices?'

'Telling me to hurry, telling me that if I didn't hurry it would be too late.'

'Too late for what?'

That smile again, so oddly inappropriate. 'I don't know. And then I heard Raffy barking from some way off. When I got nearer the barking seemed ...'

He hears her say his name, calling him, yet knows that is the past.

She looks up, the glorious eyes staring, unseeing.

'Seemed what, Miss Brooke?'

Emily shudders, clears her throat. 'Seemed almost frenzied, as though he'd gone berserk.' She cups her face in her hands.

'I'm sorry, Miss Brooke. Just take your time.'

'And then I heard what I can only describe as a scream.'

'No, son! No!'

'Your mother ...'

'I think it was the dog.' She smiles again. 'Dogs scream, you know. When they're being hurt, just like a human being.'

Watkins looks bemused, clears his throat. 'Do you know your father well, Miss Brooke?'

'I see something of him, yes.'

'And where is that? I understand he hasn't been to the cottage for nearly seventeen years.'

'He doesn't visit us, no. My parents agreed on that.'

'You meet him at your school where he's a governor?'

'That as well.'

'You meet him at other times?'

'In the woods.'

Taking the boat out with Pop. Fishing on the lake.

'Occasionally? Often?

'It depends.'

'Perhaps you can be a little more specific.'

'Sometimes as often as once or twice a month. When he happens to be doing business in the area.'

Emily met her father once or twice a month and Valerie had no idea.

'You're keen on meeting people in the woods.' Papers are shuffled.

'I think we are simply establishing location and identity, Mr Watkins. This is an inquest, not a trial.'

'Did you meet your father in the woods on that particular day?'

'No!' It's almost a shout, an odd incongruous sound. Then Emily's voice regains its former monotone. 'I told you. I was with my fiancé.'

'Quite so. You might, of course, have met him together,' Mr Watkins continues urbanely, probing, intent. 'Introduced your fiancé to him, perhaps,' he suggests amiably.

'We didn't see him.' Emily's eyes are truculent. 'He may have spotted us, of course.'

'Of course,' the solicitor agrees pleasantly. 'But apparently this isn't the first time there's been trouble with you and your father.'

The tones are succinct now. 'I can't remember who it was before.'

'Who did this to you, Dwight, honey?'

'But you do now.'

'Yes.'

'I can't hear that.'

'Yes, of course I do now!' Almost a shout.

'He attacked you with his knife.'

'Where did you get that knife, Dwight, honey?'

'No,' she says softly now, almost whispering. 'It was my knife.'

'I'm sorry, Miss Brooke ...'

'No!' she shouts out. 'It was an accident, I didn't – ' she stops. 'I mean he didn't mean to stab me! I just ...'

The coroner is looking at Emily attentively, and taking notes. He nods at Watkins to continue.

The night he brought Emily back from the Show comes back to Dwight. Stoop. She stooped down to pick up the knife. She'd simply left it there, forgotten it, after summer pruning the fruit trees. That's when Reginald Brooke came into the picture.

Reginald Brooke? Her father, by the cottage, at night?

He'd come to berate her for doing the modelling, Dwight finally works out, not Alan – Reginald!

The pieces are really falling in place. Reginald Brooke: it had simply not occurred to Dwight to give him serious consideration.

It should have done. He remembers now, the clues were all there. Right from the beginning. The smell of cigar smoke, mixed with that odd smell of kerosene. The will-o'-the-wisp! He'd known Emily was lying, known perfectly well that her father was with her. He can see the scene now, Emily and her father, a double cameo, coming towards him. Then Emily guilt tripping about the horse. The horse!

'Landrover's lame, Dwight,' he remembers Emily's pained accusation. 'I have to get him home.'

'Did I see you with a friend?' he'd asked her.

'There's no need to say anything to Mummy ... You do understand, don't you, Dwight?'

Emily, trained from early childhood to keep ambitions her mother disapproved of to herself, unable to confide in anyone, had taken what opportunities she could to meet her father surreptitiously.

Like he had his!

'Where are you off to, Dwight? It's late.'

A handsome man, carefree and jolly, her father must have seemed to Emily. Taking an interest in his daughter, carefully arranging to come across her as she went about her chores with dogs and horses, sometimes exercising the horses with her, all the time laughing and joking. How could she have thought of him as dangerous?

She almost certainly hadn't talked of boyfriends when she chattered to Reginald. Though not holding back she must have been aware that certain topics were taboo. Just as they'd been with her mother. But she did mention the Boat Show to her father, she'd told Harry, proud of the work she'd been offered. And she'd told him when she'd be coming back.

Emily must always have known, at some level, who had accosted her after the Boat Show that night, and that it was her own knife which was turned back on her, and that this was accidental. But she would not – could not! – identify Reginald. She'd just gone on repeating that it wasn't Alan.

Watkins begins to speak again, quite gently: 'But you do realise that if you had remembered who caused this 'accident' your mother might still be alive.'

'He was going for me!' Emily suddenly shouts. 'I had to stop him jumping at me ...'

'Your father?'

'Fangs!' she cries out, her hands twisting her ring, taking it off, digging the stone into her palm. 'The smell of blood! He must have been excited by the smell of blood.' She looks at Watkins, her eyes expressive. 'He's a lurcher, you know. The smell of blood excites them.'

'And he attacked you?'

'He was going for my throat! I had to ...'

'I repeat, Mr Watkins. This is an inquest, not a trial.' The coroner sounds severe. 'I do not think we need to pursue this point.'

'I'm sorry, Mr Sunnington.'

The phone still swinging, off the hook.
The blood now spurting from her neck.
The knife – his knife – still in his hand.

In his own hand. Dwight shudders as parts of the Boston scene come back to him. He hears nothing more of the inquest. Nothing until Harry takes his arm and edges him towards Emily after she's finished giving her evidence. Then Harry shepherds the both of them out of the courtroom.

CHAPTER 32

'We got a little time,' Harry says, stepping on the gas. 'Not much. Just enough, I guess.'

Emily is leaning back in the passenger seat of the Lambourghini. Dwight is squeezed in the back seat.

'You got a passport, sugar?'

'No. What will they do to me, Harry?'

'I guess we got time to get you to the continent, first thing.' He puts his hand on her knee. 'They won't do nothing. We'll get you to a good shrink. Any problems with the law, I get Moses on to it.'

'Moses?'

'Guy in New York, knows all the angles.'

'It's her father they're going to indict, Harry.' Dwight leans forward, unable to understand his friend. 'He's been detained for psychiatric assessment. They know he's had a breakdown.'

Pop slams the door as he runs out.

Harry ignores him. 'We need the best ...'

'No need to make a big production, Harry. They know Reginald Brooke did it,' Dwight persists, baffled by his friend's attitude. 'He hasn't denied it, he's just utterly silent and confused. They know he flipped, completely blew his stack.'

There's no response from Harry or Emily. Harry just concentrates on his driving, weaving through traffic, managing over ninety.

'Slow down, bud. There's a traffic cop on your tail.'

The car drops to seventy. Emily sits, wrapped in her own world, hunched into herself.

Dwight tries again. 'Must have spotted you guys together in the woods, and freaked out. He was there, I know that for a fact. Ran into him, and that hound, before I met up with you at the Fox and Hounds.'

'We'll get you sorted out good, sugar. I'll make it up to you.' The car swerves unnervingly as Harry places a hand on Emily's knee. 'What shall we go for? The world cruise?' The car is back on course, passing all other vehicles.

'Just get me out of here. I never want to see this damned bloody place again!'

'This is my home, Dwight, honey.'

Dwight feels utterly baffled. Is Emily saying she wants to be shot of West Sussex for ever? 'You mean Lodsworth? You don't want The Woolhouse?'

'No!' Emily turns right round and screams at him. 'No! I don't want the fucking Woolhouse! I never wanted it! I want to bloody get away – for good!' She tears the hat from her head, her hair tumbles down, dishevelled, her eyes blank orbs. 'I've had all I can stand. I never want to lay eyes on the place again,' she sobs. 'I *hate* it here!'

'She don't like the country, Dwight, old buddy.'

'You going to live in London?'

Harry puts a heavy foot on the accelerator. The big engine leaps faster to do his bidding. 'Who knows, buddy. We'll be on the move. South America, if we can get out before the law can get its act together. They got business going in South America, like any place else. I'll fly the doc over. We'll be fine.'

No one says anything more. Nothing but the purr of the motor speeding on the A3.

South America, Dwight turns over in his mind. Harry reckons Emily has to flee to South America?

Blurred images flitter through his brain. Is it because Emily killed the lurcher? Harry is worried about that?

'No, son! No!'

He remembers the physical sensation, the raising of the arm, the glint of light on steel... He remembers how Emily rattled the poker in the ashes, how she had strength enough to swing it, hard.

That's what Harry thinks. She used it first on Raffy, then on Valerie. The screams would have carried beyond the open door, to the woods, to Reginald prowling for a chance to meet his daughter.

He'd have rushed to Bramblings, arrived too late. Maybe he just stood, unable to move, too horror struck even to save Fangs. The girl's fury, attack, must have been unbelievable. Emily ... Emily bludgeoned her mother? And Raffy?

'She needs help, Harry.'

'Jeez, Dwight! What in hell d'you reckon I'm doin'?'

Dwight pictures the scene: Reginald wresting the poker from the girl's hand as her rage is spent ...

... he feels the quiver as he plunges the knife in, the lassitude ...

He and Harry must have arrived just as Reginald stumbled away, horrified, unable to help his daughter.

... the grief, the horror at his mother's death...

'You gonna stay on, Dwight?' Harry's voice seems to come out of time, out of space.

... the spurting blood, oozing on to his hands...

'At The Woolhouse?' Staying on? What the hell is he doing here in the first place?

'This how you found her, buddy?'
... he sees the knife in his own hand, glinting at him...

'I'm heading back home to the States,' Dwight surprises himself by telling them. 'I got unfinished business there.'

'Business? I thought you moved all that to the UK.'

'Treatment. I need some kinda care.'

Harry turns round, eyes concerned. 'Problems with your sight?'

'Sure, Harry. Real problems. I got to get a doc to help me see.'

Her throat is cut, wide open, slit.
The blood is spurting from her neck.
The knife – his knife – still in his hand.

The house in Needham comes back into view, crystal clear. He remembers all too well.

'Hi, stranger. I hardly ever see you, son.'
'I'm here, Mom.'
'You're all I have, Dwight, honey.'

He takes his knife – Pop's hunting knife – and plunges it, sinks it, into her neck.

And then he slits her throat from side to side. Three times.

Dissociative personality disorder

Dissociative personality disorder is a known psychiatric condition which may develop as an escape mechanism in some people. It can be a means of coping with unresolved trauma. The cause is unknown but some studies suggest a genetic disposition combined with early childhood exposure to sexual physical or emotional trauma.

People with this disorder are often unable to cope with emotional and professional stresses, and so escape into another personality to protect their quality of life.

Spellbinder is the story of two people afflicted by this disease. However, this novel is not in any way based on actual case histories. It is purely a product of the author's imagination.

About the Author

Tessa Lorant Warburg lives in England with her elder son, his Thai wife and their three lively children.

Originally a mathematician, Tessa began her working life as a computer programmer, then married an author who encouraged her to start writing. She wrote a series of unexpectedly popular books about her hobby of knitting under her maiden name, Tessa Lorant, and patented two knitting aids: *The Golden Gauge,* a device for isolating long knitting pattern lines, and *The Silver Gauge*, used for substituting yarns with others of the same thickness. She is featured as one of a handful of knitters in Richard Rutt's seminal *A History of Hand Knitting.*

After her husband died of cancer Tessa wrote, at his request, her first non-knitting book, *A Voice at Twilight.* This takes a look, not always solemn, at the experience of living – and dying – with the Big C. Tessa was awarded the *Oddfellows Social Concern Award* for this book, and the prize was presented at the House of Commons. As family members kept telling her how like her husband the book sounded she thought she might be able to use that skill to write fiction.

Tessa has now published six suspense novels and a family saga – a trilogy – set in North Germany and based on her mother's family.

And she's busy writing more books, both fiction and non-fiction.

ACKNOWLEDGMENTS

Many thanks to Evelyn Harris for reading the whole manuscript and making such very insightful comments. I would also like to thank the Blue Room Writing Group Members of 2011-2012 for commenting on various chapters read out to them.

I would particularly like to thank Mike Plumbley for his invaluable advice on designing book covers.

Any mistakes are, of course, my responsibility.

More novels by Tessa Lorant Warburg:
http:www.tessalorantwarburg.com

Thou Shalt not Kill

ISBN 978-0-906374-28-3

Guernsey, Channel Islands, 1991

Ruth Samuels is moving to Guernsey. She feels alive again for the first time since her husband's death.

Ruth recently met islander Matthew Frelé and knew right away that their attraction is mutual. He is enigmatic and exciting, but there's something odd about him. She senses secrets and a disturbing inner anger barely controlled.

Who is this man? What is he hiding? What is there in his past that holds him back from committing to a relationship? She guesses at horrors during his childhood under the German Occupation of the Channel Isles.

Having fled the horrors of Nazi Germany Ruth knows the terrible legacy of childhood trauma. When she presses Matthew for details of that time he refuses to discuss it. It's only when Nicol Rochet, a childhood friend, together with the one-time parish priest, the Abbé Saint Jude, bring pertinent facts to her attention that she's able to piece together the horrifying facts about Matthew's forbidden past.

The details are more dreadful than she could ever have imagined. The vile act of barbarism she unearths put even Hitler's henchmen to shame.

Can she save Matthew from those appalling memories? Or will they forever consume him, and destroy both him, and any hope of their future together?

The Girl from the Land of Smiles

ISBN 978-0-906374-30-6

Taiella Motubaki, originally from a remote Thai village on the border with Laos, meets Luke Narland, a London businessman. They fall deeply in love and plan to marry. Luke decides it is only proper to visit Taiella's parents so they can get to know him.

Luke has been on many business trips to Bangkok, but nothing has prepared him for this excursion into rural Thailand. When the village beauty is found raped and murdered Luke, a farang – a Western foreigner – is immediately accused of the crime. Entangled in a web of suspicion he finds nothing is as it seems.

Taiella, sure that Luke did not commit this atrocity, is desperate to free him. But she's in her twenties, unmarried, and with a farang boyfriend – and therefore a person of no account.

Who will help Luke prove his innocence? Will it be his Thai business manager, Teng Japhardee, his wealthy investor, Howard Spelter, Taiella's older sister, Pi Sayai, or perhaps it will be ladyboy Panjim Narcoso, Taiella's best friend in Bangkok? The story's resolution is both exciting and unexpected.

THE GIRL FROM THE LAND OF SMILES is not just a murder mystery, it is a fascinating journey through the real Thailand, hardly glimpsed by visitors to the Kingdom.

The Dohlen Inheritance Trilogy

The hand life deals you is a given; what counts is
how you play the game.
Emil Julius Dohlen

Book 1: *The Dohlen Inheritance*

Haunted by the legacy their German mother leaves them
the Dohlen orphans try to control their destiny by following
in their pioneering father's footsteps. They each create
fascinating and very different lives as their fortunes rise and
fall.

Prejudice and cruelty, greed and bigotry make their days
hell as the children fight to break away from the domination
of corrupt relatives, a bungling guardian - and each other.

Misunderstanding and tragedy overtake the young Dohlens
as fate pulls them back to Germany, where the threat of Adolf
Hitler's policies eventually leads them to an unexpected
realisation of their true inheritance.

Book 2: *Hobgoblin Gold*

Hobgoblin Gold spans the years 1932-1948. It tells the
extraordinary stories of siblings Gabby, Moppel and Doly as
they try desperately to escape the legacy of their traumatic
childhood and to build new lives for themselves.

Haunted by the past, quarrelling amongst themselves, they
squander the enormous fortune their father left them in
different and spectacular ways.

262

As Hitler comes to power the young Dohlens abandon their German heritage. The sisters spend WWII in the countryside south of London, struggling to survive without the wealth they took for granted in their childhood. Emil, meanwhile, succumbs to the siren calls of gangsters.

Can the young Dohlens now finally take full responsibility for themselves and emulate their father?

Book 3: *Ladybird Fly*

This final book of the trilogy spans the years 1948-1992. The Dohlen sisters, Gabby and Doly, are deprived of their husbands, property and income, so have to cope in a touch post-war world. Emil, meanwhile, has his own problems to solve.

Both sisters survive by using their wits and resorting to unique and entertaining solutions to their problems, but in entirely different ways. Gabby, a born operator, triumphs spectacularly while Doly enjoys a rural idyll, supported by friends but lacking cash. Emil finally learns how to try to become like his successful father.

The Dohlens breathtaking exploiits, often wickedly funny, reveal their true inheritance - The Dohlen Inheritance - which we can all aspire to.

THE THORN PRESS

BOOKS IN PRINT

The Dohlen Inheritance trilogy - Tessa Lorant Warburg
The Dohlen Inheritance
Paperback: ISBN 978-0-906374-06-1
Hardback: ISBN 978-0-906374-03-0
Hobgoblin Gold
Paperback: ISBN 978-0-906374-08-4
Ladybird Fly
Paperback: ISBN 978-0-906374-09-2

A Woman's World, 138-9 Chri Plus, Hilary Jerome
Paperback: ISBN 978-0-906374-00-9
e-book, October 2010

Snack Yourself Slim, Richard Warburg & Tessa Lorant
Paperback: ISBN 978-0-906374-05-4

Inktastic, Andrew P Jones
Paperback: ISBN 978-0-906374-04-7

The Master's Tale, A Titanic Ghost Story, Ann Victoria Roberts
Paperback: ISBN 978-0906374-21-4
e-book, July 2012

Wordfall, The 2010 Anthology from Southampton Writing Buddies
Editor Penny Legg
Paperback: ISBN 978-0-906374-26-9

Knitted Quilts & Flounces, Tessa Lorant
Paperback: ISBN 978-0-906374-29-0

Spellbinder, Tessa Lorant Warburg
Paperback: ISBN 978-0-906374-31-3
e-book, May 2012

Thou Shalt Not Kill, Tessa Lorant Warburg
Paperback: ISBN 978-0-906374-28-3
e-book, December 2012

The Girl From The Land of Smiles, Tessa Lorant Warburg
Proverbs translated by Praphaphorn Phonbuakai
Paperback: ISBN 978-0-906374-30-6
e-book, December 2012

All books are available from Amazon worldwide, and from good book shops

www.thethornpress.com